"With expert pacing and plotting, *Bone Thief* will keep you riveted until the surprising, satisfying end. Be warned, however—this one should be read in the light of day."

—Alafair Burke

"Bone Thief is that rare commodity in murder-mystery fiction which can actually give the reader nightmares. O'Callaghan twists imagination into unspeakable shapes."

—Alan Paul Curtis, www.who-dunnit.com

"A strong, sharply written debut—there's a fast-paced plot, intrigue, and a smart cop facing off against an evil-but-clever serial killer. O'Callaghan's writing style perfectly reflects the tense plot."

—Lisa Yanaky, www.bookbrothel.com

"Riveting, tightly written, an exceptional read. I thoroughly recommend it to anyone who loves an engrossing thrill ride."

—Sheila Leitzel, www.bookfetish.org

"But if you are a reader who likes chills running up and down their spine, this is a book for you."

—Anne K. Edwards, www.NewMysteryReader.com

"Bone Thief is one of the best debut novels I've read in this genre. If this suspense thriller does not scare the bejabbers out of you, nothing will." —L. A. Johnson

"This one will definitely give you the creeps . . . a thrill a minute. I didn't want to put it down."

—*Pilot* (Southern Pines, NC)

BY THOMAS O'CALLAGHAN

Bone Thief

The Screaming Room

THE
SCREAMING
ROOM

THOMAS
O'CALLAGHAN

PINNACLE BOOKS
Kensington Publishing Corp.
www.kensingtonbooks.com

PINNACLE BOOKS are published by

Kensington Publishing Corp.
850 Third Avenue
New York, NY 10022

All Kensington titles, imprints, and distributed lines are available at special quantity discounts for bulk purchases for sales promotions, premiums, fund-raising, educational, or institutional use. Special book excerpts or customized printings can be created to fit specific needs. For details, write or phone the office of the Kensington special sales manager: Kensington Publishing Corp., 850 Third Avenue, New York, NY 10022, attn: Special Sales Department; phone 1-800-221-2647.

This book is a work of fiction. Names, characters, businesses, organizations, places, events, and incidents either are the product of the author's imagination or are used fictitiously. Any resemblance to actual persons, living or dead, events, or locales is entirely coincidental.

ISBN-13: 978-0-7860-1812-3
ISBN-10: 0-7860-1812-7

First printing: May 2007

10 9 8 7 6 5 4 3 2 1

Printed in the United States of America

For Kelliann

ACKNOWLEDGMENTS

I owe a very special round of gratitude to:

Eileen O'Callaghan, my loving and supportive wife, who shares life in so many wonderful ways; Matt Bialer, a magician of an agent and trusted friend; Michaela Hamilton, a conscientious and extremely talented editor, who is a true delight to work with; Dick Marek, a man from whom I have learned much; Stephen Ohayon, PhD, a true gentleman who inspired me tirelessly from day one; Barry Richman, MD; Marla Feder; the Group; and, of course, Noreen Nolan, a gifted woman who shares her gift with me.

Lieutenant William F. Nevins, CDS, Commanding Officer of the Queens Homicide Squad (retired), for his expert technical advice and skillful guidance. He represents the New York Police Department at its finest.

My dear friend Priscilla Winkler, whose support through the years has been steadfast.

And to my loving granddaughter, Kristin, who calls me PaPa and watches me melt.

Prologue

The rain had stopped. The afternoon sun had resumed its assault on rotting corn shocks, casting distorted shadows across the abandoned farm. A pair of cicadas sounded, silencing the chirping of the nearby sparrows, sending them into flight.

In the middle of the field, a sturdy youth stood silently, eyes fixed on a mound of fresh clay.

A rush of cool air stirred wisps of his ripened wheat–colored hair. Bending down, he used a finger to inscribe the name Gus in the collected soil.

A second youth, a female, approached. "Can we go now?" she asked, wearily. "This is our tenth field and there's nothing left of him to bury."

"In a minute."

The girl looked around. "Someone could be watching, you know."

"Just need a minute."

"Well, you'd better make it a quick one."

The youth's eyes lingered on the newly formed grave. With a nod of satisfaction, he uprighted himself. As a smile lit his face, he used the heel of his boot to eradicate their victim's name. "Lovee," he said, "may the bastard rest in peace."

"You mean in pieces. Let's go."

Chapter 1

Cassie turned her head on the pillow as a sudden flash of light woke her.

"What the hell are ya doing?" she hollered. "It's two o'clock in the morning!"

Her brother, Angus, who was sitting up in bed next to her, grinned, his attention riveted to the gleam coming off the three-quarter-inch ball bearing he was holding between his thumb and index finger. The narrow beam of a pencil-thin flashlight had reflected off the ball's chromelike finish and shone directly onto her eyelid.

"I liked you better when you got off pulling wings off flies," she said, hiding her head under the pillow.

Angus, flashlight still directed at the ball bearing, brought his face to within inches of the tiny sphere, watching the reflection of his pupil get bigger and bigger, the closer he got. Hopelessly bored, and somewhat blind, he turned off the flashlight, slid his hand under the covers, and fondled his sister's rump.

"Not tonight, we ain't," she said through clenched teeth. "We got lots to do tomorrow. Get some sleep!"

Angus slid out of bed, slipped into a pair of boxers, and

ambled toward the door, opening it. A blast of warm air caressed his body. The sensation aroused him. He glanced over his shoulder. His sister was snoring. He pushed open the screen door, sat on the top step, and glanced upward. It was a cloudless night. The moon, just shy of full, cast shadows on the weeds and tall grass that surrounded home sweet home; a fitting salute, perhaps to what would begin at dawn. The thought of finally executing what they had planned brought on a surge of adrenaline. He wouldn't sleep. Unlike his sister, he'd stay up and wait out the darkness.

A slug, slithering toward him on the surface of the step, caught his attention.

"I can kill ya, little fella. But I won't."

He had the urge to pet the small mollusk but decided instead to dabble his finger in the slime that trailed behind it. He brought it to his lips, applying it as a woman would lipstick.

Women. They fascinated Angus. Every curve. Every smell. Every everything. In his next life, he planned on returning as one. He could feel what they feel. Think as they think. God! Even screw as they screw!

He heard a rustling. It was not the willow tree, which was as limp as he was. No, something was pushing through the grass. A deer perhaps. He hoped so. He liked the sound they made just before dying, after he stalked them and twisted their neck, snapping their cervical vertebrae.

There it was again!

The rustling.

Following the example of the snail, he slithered down the rickety steps and began his pursuit, certain his sister wouldn't start their big day without him.

Chapter 2

The Greyhound's Michelins groaned over the roadway scarred with jagged potholes. But Angus and Cassie didn't let it interfere with their game. Despite the jostling, the plastic markers held firm, their bottoms magnetized to the shimmering surface of the game board. But the cards were a different story. Using an index finger, Angus pressed down on the Time of Your Life deck while Cassie did the same to the Pay the Piper pile, containing the cards tenaciously inside their holding trays.

Angus picked up the dice.

"C'mon ten," he whispered, releasing the cubes, which rolled across the board and settled as a six and a three.

"Close enough!" he said, counting off nine squares on his trek along the path that meandered around and about the game's playing field: a map of the city of New York, featuring its landmarks.

"That puts me on topa the town at the Empire Freakin' State Building!" He slammed down his blue marker on the prized square.

His action activated a tiny speaker embedded under the

skyscraper's icon, and music sounded, replete with vocals: Frank Sinatra's rendition of "New York, New York."

He reached for a Time of Your Life card.

"Well, lookee here. I've just been awarded a three-hour shopping spree at Paragon Sports. And it entitles me to disregard the next Pay the Piper Card." He reached in his pocket and ran a finger across the blade.

Touching the weapon aroused him.

Cassie sneered. She palmed the dice and blew into her fist.

"Mama needs a new paira shoes," she said, letting loose the dice, which skittered across the board and settled as a one and a two. "Shit! I gotta pay the piper!"

Cassie counted off the three squares. Angus handed her the Pay the Piper card.

"Read it and weep," he said.

Cassie's lower lip jutted forward.

> *You've been caught shoplifting at Macy*s.*
> *Lose a turn.*

"Hellhole of a city," she muttered.

"Lemme show ya how it's done." Angus reached for the dice for the first of his next two turns, his and the one she had lost.

The cubes clattered across the board. A five and a six.

He eyed the board and counted off eleven squares.

"I'm halfway through their beloved Kings County! C'mon twelve!" He rattled the cubes in his hand.

Cassie groaned as a double six rolled to a stop.

"Yes!" he cheered, reaching for his marker.

"Hold it!" she said, gesturing at the Greyhound's rain-slicked window. The bus had entered the terminal and was coming to a stop. "Remember what we said. Once the bus arrives, we set it all in motion at the tourist traps closest to our pieces."

Angus eyed the board and grinned.

"Well, then, Coney Island's my next stop."

"And me?" said Cassie. "I get to start settling the score at the American Museum of Natural History."

Chapter 3

The sun cast slivers of light through the glass cupola of the American Museum of Natural History. Below the rotunda, Jurassic skeletons welcomed the sunrise.

A chime alerted the night watchman that his shift was over. It also prompted the electric illumination of all halls and galleries throughout the vast labyrinth. Light from halogen lamps flooded the museum, revealing the "Star of India", the world's largest blue sapphire; the fossilized skeleton of the "Turkana Boy," a one-point-six-million-year-old specimen of *Homo erectus,* along with countless other natural and cultural treasures.

At 10:00 A.M., a second chime sounded and the watchman unlocked the massive entrance door. Within minutes, a swarm of seven-year-olds, chaperoned by the field-trip coordinator, Harriet Robbins, poured into the marble-floored lobby, shattering the repository's silent solemnity with giggles and laughter.

"Boys and girls, first we are going to visit Triassic Hall. Who can tell me what marked the Triassic period?" asked Miss Robbins.

"Me! Me! Me!" echoed a chorus of young voices.

"Okay, Elizabeth, tell the class."

"It comes before the Jurassic period. It's when the first dinosaurs were born."

"Very good," said Miss Robbins. She led the pack inside the enormous exhibit hall.

The children, with wide-open eyes, approached a pair of teratosaurus skeletons.

"Our first meat eaters," Miss Robbins said.

Matthew, the know-it-all, strayed from the group, hoping to find a critter he had not yet encountered on his dinosaur CD-ROM. He drew near a towering assemblage of bones he knew to be the plateosaurus, but what he saw between its legs didn't fit. Maybe Miss Robbins could explain. He rejoined his classmates and tugged on the teacher's skirt.

"Matthew, do you need to go to the boys' room?"

"No, Miss Robbins."

"Then what is it?"

"Isn't the plateosaurus a plant eater?"

"Of course it is."

The boy pointed his finger at the assemblage of bones.

"Then how come that one's got a dead lady coming out of its butt?"

Chapter 4

For Marian Dougherty, Wednesday, June 4, was a special day. Not only was it her fifteenth birthday but also it was the day she had promised she would try the hot new street drug with her main squeeze, Manuel Ortiz, the leader of a gang known as the Tiburones.

It was ten o'clock in the morning. Marian and her two friends, Donna and Carmelita, were standing on Coney Island's boardwalk, clustered outside the Wonder Wheel's ticket booth waiting for the ride to open. It appeared that Manny was a no-show. Could it be he was all talk and no go?

"Marian, you got dissed," said Carmelita, hands on hips.

"Dissed . . . dissed . . . dissed," Donna echoed.

"No, I didn't," the birthday girl gloated as she watched her young Romeo in Nike T-shirt and Hilfiger jeans climb the steps of the boardwalk and strut toward them.

Marian shuddered in anticipation, having looked forward to this monumental step just as much as she feared it. But all her friends had already done the drug and she didn't want to feel like a wimp.

"Yo! I'm a walkin' birthday present," Manuel boasted, sidling up next to the girls.

"Your little honey's afraida heights, Manuel. You gonna cure her?"

"She's in for a double dose of magic, Carmelita. She's with the head of the Tiburones."

The teens watched as the machinist opened the gates, allowing entrance to the giant Ferris wheel.

"We're in the red one!" Marian hollered, rushing toward the empty cage, hoping her excitement didn't make her look like a kid.

"Yo, man! Today she learns how to fly," said Manuel to the ride's engineer. "This here's a twenty. That should cover us all. And here's an extra ten-spot, just for you. Make sure that red cage stays on top for a while."

"You got it," the handler said, sliding the cash into his jeans.

"Marian, we'll be right behind you. If you freeze and you wanna spit it out, don't let him see ya do it." Carmelita smiled and mouthed a "Happy Birthday" before joining Donna inside their own painted cage.

"Yo! Let's get this thing off the ground!" hollered Manuel, climbing in next to his darling.

Gears engaged and metal whined as the giant Ferris wheel lifted the fun-seekers into the air.

"So? You ready or what?" asked Manuel.

Marian looked around. Her friends were in the cage behind them. "Ready!" she said.

"Here it comes with a gift," said Manuel.

"Wow!" she said, putting on the earrings.

"They ain't no real diamonds. But they're real crystal. Just like this." He produced the packet of meth capsules.

"Bein' way up top's gonna add to the rush."

Marian clenched the mini-ziplock in her fist.

"Being on top with you is rush enough."

Howling like a wolf, Manuel wrapped his arm around his birthday girl and stared skyward.

"Ready or not, here we come!" Marian hollered, then

wished she hadn't. I'm not a kid! Not no more! I'm gonna fly! I'm gonna fly! she heard an unconvincing internal voice cry out.

The cage stopped, having reached its zenith. No one had come for the view.

Marian turned her head. Panic seized her. "Let's go back down," she whimpered

"Why? We just got here!"

"There's someone looking at us in the next cage!"

"Whaddya—take somethin' before we got on? That's Carmelita and Donna!" pointing to the two wide-eyed teens in the cage behind them.

"No!" Marian shouted. "The *next* car!"

In the cage behind their friends a man sat like a propped-up marionette. There was a large gash on the side of his ashen face and red stains on his T-shirt.

"Hey, you! Get us down!" screamed Manuel.

"What's he doing?" stammered Marian, her eyes fixed on the unexpected visitor.

"He ain't doin' nothin'. I think he's dead."

Chapter 5

The weatherman on CNN had predicted a late spring shower the afternoon of June 4, 2006. But his prediction had not intimidated New York City Police Lieutenant John W. Driscoll, Detective Cedric Thomlinson, Sergeant Margaret Aligante, and the brass of One Police Plaza. They had gathered under threatening skies and were listening to Monsignor Norris's final oration at the burial site of Driscoll's wife, Colette, at Pinelawn Cemetery in New York's Nassau County.

The late Mrs. Driscoll had been comatose for six years, but the Lieutenant, nevertheless, had dreaded the reality that one day the electronic monitors would signal her death. The end came at 6:07 A.M. on Saturday, May 31, when for the first time in a long time, Colette experienced tranquility. She expired without fear or rattle, surrendering the spirit that had governed her body for the past forty-four years.

Her parting brought a sense of finality to Driscoll, who had stayed married and loyal to his wife throughout the six long years of her unconsciousness. But her passing left an enormous void. And the unsought freedom riddled him with guilt and shame.

A hand grabbed hold of Driscoll's arm as the coffin was lowered into its freshly dug grave, where it would find its resting place alongside the couple's predeceased daughter, Nicole. The hand was that of Detective Thomlinson, Driscoll's long-term friend and confidant.

"She's finally at peace," he said.

As Colette's coffin settled on moist clay, a gust of wind ravaged the funerary wreaths, scattering lilies and gentians across the finely trimmed lawn of the cemetery. Above the burial site, angry clouds continued their threat. A second gust accosted Monsignor Norris's cassock, shuffling the pages of his leather-bound Bible. Within seconds, the sky ruptured, pelting the graveyard with wind-driven rain.

"John . . . it's time to go," Thomlinson urged, nudging the Lieutenant.

"Gimme a minute," said Driscoll.

Thomlinson nodded and hurried for the cover of his waiting automobile, leaving Driscoll behind.

Alone, before the flooding grave, Driscoll stared down at the mahogany coffin that sealed his past.

"Au revoir, ma cherie," he whispered, his tears mixing with the rain. "I will miss you dearly."

As he turned and headed toward the line of gleaming automobiles, he thought he heard a whisper amid the clatter of rain pelting the monumental maples that surrounded the grave site:

"Adieu."

Chapter 6

Outside Porgie's Place, a New Orleans–style jazz band welcomed the caravan of mourners with a fanfare of brass and conga drums.

Inside, a sumptuous buffet offered specialties of the islands, while an adjoining table flaunted a variety of rums from the four corners of the Caribbean Sea.

It was Trinidadian-born Thomlinson's idea of a funerary feast. The only thing missing was a bevy of dancers in straw skirts. John Driscoll, an Irishman, was more accustomed to the somber reflection that followed the grim and mournful wakes he had attended during time spent as an altar server at Saint Saviour's Roman Catholic Church in Park Slope, Brooklyn. He felt the gathering was irreverent but didn't wish to offend his benefactor.

"John, you gotta check this out," Thomlinson said, approaching Driscoll, crystal tumbler in hand.

"What is it?"

"The cognac of rums. Bermudez! From the Dominican Republic. One taste of this and you'll think you're royalty."

Driscoll gave Thomlinson a sympathetic smile, for he knew his friend, a recovering alcoholic, would like very much to indulge. The Lieutenant took the glass, lifted it, and took a sip. The rum was suave, rich, and silky on his palate.

"Damn! That's good stuff!" he said.

John Driscoll was the commanding officer of the NYPD's Manhattan homicide squad. He carried his six-foot-two stature formidably, often intimidating adversaries without so much as a word. There was a swagger to his walk, not unlike Gary Cooper's stride in *High Noon*. Precinct women found him irresistible, especially when they gazed into his enigmatic eyes. Colette, though, had found the key that unlocked their mystery. But after the automobile accident that sent her into a six-year coma, all agreed his eyes had become gray and lifeless.

The other notable feature of Driscoll's face were his lips, which were expressive, even when he was silent. In them, Colette discovered Driscoll's tenderness. They did not belong to his Celtic jawline. They were more Mediterranean, almost Middle Eastern, and responded to his emotional states: expanding when contented, contracting under stress, and vibrating when anxious. Colette had learned to read his heart and transcribe his thoughts by observing the tremors.

The Lieutenant was a snazzy dresser, often clad in a well-tailored jacket by Hickey Freeman or Hart Schaffner & Marx, with a pair of slacks by Joseph Abboud, a tie by Richell, and shoes by either Johnston and Murphy or Kenneth Cole. Halston 14, his wife's favorite fragrance for men, had become his favorite as well. His fondness for upscale cologne and fine English tailoring had earned him the moniker Dapper John.

And with Dapper John before him now, Thomlinson said, "It's time to get it on with the cuisine of Jamaica, Lieutenant. This here is roti. It's goat meat cooked with potatoes in a sauce of turmeric, coriander, allspice, and saffron. It really hits the spot! Here, try some." Thomlinson handed Driscoll a bowl and filled it.

Driscoll took a taste of the meal, inhaling its aroma. His

friend was right. It was delicious. He felt a gentle tap on his shoulder. When he turned, his eyes widened.

"Mary!"

"I'm sorry, John."

He embraced the woman. "You've got nothing to apologize for. Not today. Not tomorrow. Not ever."

"I decided this morning. This nonsense has got to stop. I'm your sister, for God's sake!"

"Ssshh. Ssshh," Driscoll whispered. He hadn't let go. He continued to hold her, stroking her hair. "Ssshh. Ssshh."

When Mary Driscoll-Humphreys pulled back, her gentle round face was slathered with tears. She tried to speak. Although her mouth opened, she couldn't produce a sound.

"Come. Let's sit."

Driscoll escorted his sister to a corner, where a gentleman in a suit was seated. He immediately stood and extended his hand. "You must be Mary. Your brother and I have been friends since the academy. I've heard so much about you. It's nice to finally meet you. I'm so sorry for your loss."

Driscoll placed a supportive hand on his sister's back. "This is Leonard DeCovney, Mary. He kept me in line through training."

"It's nice to meet you, too," she replied. She had regained her voice and unfortunately continued to use it. "John, I need to go now. I'll call you when school lets out."

The woman disappeared as silently as she had arrived, blowing her brother a kiss before the siblings lost sight of each other in the crowd.

"How's she doing?" DeCovney asked.

"I don't know," said Driscoll.

"She still taking . . ."

Driscoll answered the incomplete question. "That's what scares the hell out of me. I know she picks up her medication and that she refills it according to schedule because her pharmacist calls me. But does she take it? I honestly don't know. Why don't I know? Because, according to her therapist, she needs to be on her own as much as possible through what she describes as a phase. Nothing more. A phase. You wanna take a crack at what that means? I don't." Driscoll's eyes narrowed. "I pray she knows what she's doing."

"The therapist."

Driscoll nodded. "Mary changed the lock again. Added a couple more. I'm running up a tab at Ace Hardware having keys made. I should be the one on the medication."

"I don't know about that. For a man who buried his wife today, you look like you've got a handle on things."

"I've had help. I think Colette's been prepping me for Mary, who, inside her head, is finding it increasingly more difficult existing in the present. It tends to keep my feet firmly planted. It saddens me to think my sister will never feel a sense of prolonged attachment to anything."

"On that, my friend, I'd say you're wrong."

"Why?"

"Because she has you."

"But between the two of us, I'm the only one who knows it. By the time she gets home, she won't remember she was here."

"That may be so. But she knows how to find you. Which translates to—she has you."

Driscoll was deeply touched and somewhat relieved.

"Come on, John. I'm buying." Deputy Commissioner DeCovney led Driscoll over his bridge back to life and into a circle of friends.

"Thank you, sir."

"My door's always open."

"I know."

When Driscoll rejoined Thomlinson, his anxiety was in check.

Brooklyn's borough commander, James Hanrahan, approached the two men with distraction in his eyes.

"You gotta try this," Hanrahan said, handing Driscoll a fork with a chunk of meat on it.

"What is it?"

"Jerk pork. It's Jamaican."

Driscoll bit into the morsel.

"Wow! That's a three-alarm fire," he sputtered, waving his hand in front of his mouth.

"Give it a minute," Hanrahan warned. "It's got a helluva back draft."

"This is no brisket," Driscoll managed, his mouth ablaze.

A man in a dark suit walked up to the borough commander and handed Hanrahan a cell phone. "Chief, you'd better take this call," he said.

Hanrahan took the cell phone, his eyes narrowing as he listened to the caller. He then spoke directly and quietly into the phone. His communication complete, he turned to face Driscoll.

"Looks like someone's got it in for tourists."

"How so?" Driscoll asked.

"Some kid spotted a dead Chinaman riding the Wonder Wheel in Coney Island while a second grader uncovered a second corpse at a dinosaur exhibit at the American Museum of Natural History. The body at the museum was set up to look like dinosaur dung. Her ID says she was from Berlin. Crime Scene thinks they may be linked because the cause of death appears to be blunt force trauma for both and their bodies were posed. And get this. Both vics were scalped."

"Scalped? That's a new one," said Driscoll, still fighting the fire inside his mouth.

"Tell me about it."

"Who caught the murders?"

"Elizabeth Delgado. Brooklyn South Homicide. And Frank Reynolds from Manhattan North."

"Frank I know. Never heard of Delgado. She new?"

"Transfer from Robbery."

"A homicide rookie. Glad I'm not on this one."

"What's that you're drinking?" Hanrahan asked.

"Rum," Driscoll answered, confused by Hanrahan's sudden interest in his beverage.

"I'd have another one, if I were you," said the borough commander.

"One'll do fine," said Driscoll, detecting an uncomfortable look on Hanrahan's face. "Is there something you want to tell me, Jim? Who was that on the phone?"

"We're not about to discuss police business at your wife's wake, for Chrissake!"

"Police business is all I have right now. My wife's at peace and I'm not about to sit home and stare at the walls. I'm gonna need distraction. Big time! And work will be just the ticket."

"You sure?"

"Very."

"You've been assigned to the tourist homicides."

"Says who?"

"Mayor Reirdon. That was him on the phone."

Chapter 7

Angus sat on the cold slab of slate that encircled the top of the well. They had done it. Finally done it. Yet, he didn't feel satiated like he thought he would. Thoughts ran rampant inside his head. That was the norm. His eyes were distracted, though, lost to the efforts of the orb-weaving spider that was crawling surreptitiously across its web. A nocturnal feeder, the spider. Angus appreciated that, for he, too, despite all that had happened, preferred the night and its often undetected happenings.

He was born at night. Or so he had been told. A harsh night, bitter cold and unwelcome, was how his father had described it. "As unwelcome as you," he'd scoff. His cruelest derision coming when he was drunk, which was nightly.

Angus's eyes were still fixed on the spider, but the timbre of Father's voice bellowed in the recesses of his mind, unleashing uninvited memories.

"Angus! You little bastard. Get in here!"

"With another can of beer" was left unsaid, but I knew better than to rile the guy, and remembered, robotically, to stop at the fridge before entering the smoke-filled room*

*where Father sat, eyes fixed on the black-and-white screen of
the Emerson TV.*

*"We're not finished yet," he reminded me with a sneer,
causing me to tremble and often wet my pants. "And that sister of yours? I've got something real special in store for
her!"*

*Most nights the Budweiser worked to my advantage, act-
ing as a soporific godsend. But only for the night. Another
day would follow, giving way to another night. One more
spell of darkness I'd need to live through, saddled with
dread. And when the beer didn't work its magic I'd be hauled
into the godforsaken room behind the furnace, forced to
strip, and climb atop a cold porcelain enamel-topped table.*

"Lay still, Angus. Don't make me have to say it again."

*Father would then reach for the rubbing alcohol and san-
itize a portion of my skin. With the cold tabletop pressing
hard against the side of my face, I eyed the row of shot
glasses that held the assortment of inks. I cringed, feeling
the touch of Father's rough fingers as he applied the Vase-
line. Next came the feel of the small stencil being placed on
my body, accompanied by the whirring sound the electric
machine made when it was turned on.*

*It was then that I closed my eyes and forced my thoughts
to carry me to that faraway place where I wouldn't feel the
sting of the needles perforating my flesh.*

Chapter 8

Three days had passed since Driscoll appealed to his boss, Captain Eddie Barrows, that he be allowed to tie up some loose ends on a prior case. Something didn't feel right. He couldn't stay focused until he resolved it. Besides, the latest murders were being investigated by capable homicide detectives, and it was Driscoll's feeling that they should stay there. It would give the rookie a chance to sharpen her teeth. So what if the victims were tourists? New York was full of them. His curiosity was piqued, though, by the scalping. What was that all about? He also wondered what the Mayor's reaction would be to his resistance, but that thought would have to stay on hold. Right now, there were more pressing matters at hand. The Mayflower Moving Company had just completed packing all of Driscoll's furnishings and personal belongings aboard their truck. It was time now to pay his last respects to the house that had served as his sanctuary for the past twelve years.

He whistled the first few lines of "Time after Time," turned his back on the moving truck, and climbed the three wooden steps to his porch. Sinatra's rendition of Jule Stein's love ballad had been his and Colette's wedding song. Driscoll hummed or whistled the opening lines often.

As he pushed open the front door to the Toliver's Point bungalow, the sharpness of Betadine antiseptic and the sterile smell of bleached linen still hung in the air. What had once served as a makeshift intensive care unit for his comatose wife was now a barren room, reminding him of the hollowness of his own life. The hospital bed and the cluster of life support equipment were gone. It had been no small feat to convince an anxious hospital staff to agree to such an unorthodox arrangement as home care for a comatose patient. But that's where Driscoll had wanted his wife. Home. Surrounded by her treasured paintings. And, after his acquisition of some pretty costly medical equipment, funded in part by Driscoll's health insurance and supplemented by a sizable advance against his pension fund, Saint Matthew's hospital had granted his wish.

But now that chapter of his life had ended.

Colette. It was she who had discovered Toliver's Point. While she was a landscape painter at the New York Art Student's League, a friend had invited her to spend a day at the beach. She found the Point's natural setting in an urban environment enchanting. She returned often to sit at the water's edge and paint. She fell in love with the locale to such a degree that five years later she put a down payment on her first piece of waterfront property: a summer bungalow in Toliver's Point.

The first night Sergeant John Driscoll was invited to the bayside community, he thought he had been transported to some distant island. After he and Colette married, the summer bungalow was renovated, winterized, and transformed into a comfortable residence they were proud to call home.

Trying to keep feelings of abandonment in check, he cast one last glance at the walls of the bungalow, emptied now of their aquarelles and serigraphs, bolted shut the door, and headed for his parked cruiser, where he sprang the lock on the trunk and retrieved the for-sale sign, which he planted in the lawn. It was then he heard the sound of tires creeping on asphalt. Two shiny black Chryslers, bookending a Lincoln stretch limousine, pulled in at the curb. Driscoll watched as the limousine's tinted window slid down.

"If Mohammad doesn't come to the mountain, well . . . then, the Mayor of New York must pay a visit to his top cop," the Honorable William "Sully" Reirdon said as he stepped from his automobile.

It annoyed the hell out of police brass, but the newly elected Reirdon prided himself on being a hands-on Mayor. Bypassing the police commissioner, borough commanders, and bureau chiefs was commonplace for the man. Hell, he once had a one on one with a beat cop because some alarmed Bronx resident complained of strangers in her neighborhood when she called his weekly *Concerned Citizens* radio forum. And here he was now, in Toliver's Point.

"You're trespassing, Mr. Mayor. This is Democrat country."

"Well, will you look at that? You've got a million-dollar view of my city," said the Mayor, casting his stare across the bay.

"You could buy the place, Mr. Mayor. Keep a close eye on your city."

Sully Reirdon smiled at the suggestion.

"But something tells me you didn't travel out here to discuss beachfront real estate."

"You know why I'm here, John."

It was Driscoll's turn to stare across the bay. "I'll sure miss the view, but the efficiency I'll be buying in Brooklyn Heights will cut my commute time in half," he said.

"John, I am very sorry about your wife. I know I should've been at the funeral, but I was in Albany arm-wrestling with the governor. He knows we need more cops, but he won't release the sixty-three million he promised the city when he was elected."

"How about assigning some of those cops to a drunk-driving detail?"

"I'll give it every consideration," the Mayor said with a nod, aware of the automobile accident that had robbed Driscoll of his wife and daughter. "John, despite what Katie Couric says, I'm not an insensitive man."

Driscoll stared at the politician.

"I appreciate your not wanting to sign off on a case without crossing all the T's. In fact, it's admirable. I'll make certain a competent commander does just that. Right now my city needs you. There's a guy killing tourists, for Chrissake! And that makes him the department's priority one. Do you know how much money visitors dropped in the Big Apple last year?"

Driscoll obliged the Mayor with a shrug.

"Twelve point six billion! I want you to focus on the here and now. There'll be no time to waste on yesterday's cases. Nobody gets to hold New York hostage on my watch. I want this tourist-scalping killer stopped dead in his tracks. And I want it done now!"

"I wouldn't be able to fully focus, Mr. Mayor. I'd be the wrong man for the job." As soon as he heard himself say it, he knew he had pushed the envelope too far. But there was no way of retrieving what'd been said. "Besides, the fact that these two victims were tourists could be a coincidence. The twelve-plus billion speaks for itself. There's a whole lotta tourists in New York."

"Coincidences don't happen in my city."

Driscoll raised an eyebrow.

"You know, John, you're beginning to piss me off!" Reirdon stormed to his limousine and ducked inside. "As long as I run this town and you're on my payroll, you'll do as I say. Peter, get me outta here!"

The Lincoln's tires charred the asphalt. With the two security autos in tow, the Mayor's limo disappeared along Point Breeze Boulevard.

John Driscoll sat on the steps of his porch. Despite his obstinacy, he knew the assignment was unavoidable. It would become his job to formulate a strategy to catch this villain.

Why make waves? You're not the only cop in town, John. Reirdon said he'd have a competent person nail the case shut. It's not like its outcome rests on the type of hammer he uses.

Unpocketing his cell phone, he rang the Mayor on his car phone. Driscoll detected arrogance as Sully Reirdon's voice echoed in his ear.

"So, you've decided to come around, have you?"

"Do I have a choice?"

"This city doesn't need a bout of mass hysteria, John."

"If these murders lead to a rash of killings, I'll need to establish a task force. And it would be a big help if the FBI is kept at bay."

"You'll wrap this up before it causes an international stir?"

"God willing."

"What else will you need?"

"Please. No female detectives assigned to this one."

"I'd have never guessed you were a chauvinist."

"I support affirmative action and the advancement of all working women. But I just buried my wife. Call it superstition. Nothing more."

"You have my promise. No women."

"Thank you."

"Oh, and John, there's one thing more."

"What's that?"

"You'd better lighten up or you'll never unload that house."

Driscoll could detect Reirdon's smirk right through the phone line.

"Then I'll just bulldoze the place down to the sea," he said.

"You do that and I'll nail you for pollution of the Atlantic shoreline. What are you asking for the place, anyway?"

"It's out of your price range, Mr. Mayor."

"Oh, I don't know, I could get an insider's deal on, say, a thirty-year mortgage."

"Better shop for a five. You may not be in office that long."

Chapter 9

"No, the Atlantic Ocean isn't gonna wash the house away. It's been sitting three hundred yards from the water for the past forty years, for Chrissake!" Driscoll bellowed into the phone to his realtor. "Tell you what. I'll throw in a couple of life vests just in case." Driscoll wasn't having a good day. "Maybe these folks would prefer the USS *Nautilus*! Hell, if they're left wing, I could get them a good deal on a moth-balled Russian sub. Whiskey class!" Driscoll slammed down the receiver, jarring Socrates, his electronic cockatiel, who, faithful to his programming, squawked. The battery-operated bird had been a gift from members of a former command. Though he'd like to, Driscoll felt it would be ill-mannered to dispose of it.

"Lock 'em up! Aawkk! Aawkk!"

The door to Driscoll's office opened. Detective Thomlinson poked his head inside.

"Lieutenant, there's a sergeant here to see you."

"Throw away the key! Aawkk! Aawkk!"

"Turn that damn bird off, will you?"

Thomlinson walked over to the bird and clicked off its miniature toggle switch.

"A sergeant? What's he want?" Driscoll asked.

"Something about the Mayor keeping his promise," Thomlinson answered with a shrug of his shoulders. But the look on Thomlinson's face said to Driscoll that something was up.

"Well, then, show him in," Driscoll said, warily.

With the hint of a smile, Thomlinson reached for the door and invited Driscoll's newly assigned assistant to enter.

The Lieutenant's eyes widened. Standing before him was Sergeant Margaret Marie Aligante. A dazzler. At five-foot-seven she had a figure that would rival any of Veronese's models. Her anthracite hair was long and cascaded onto her shoulders like a mane. Her dark eyes sparkled. Her nose was regal, and her jaw delicate. They created a face that was riveting and inviting. Too inviting for Lieutenant John W. Driscoll. There was history between the pair. They had recently worked together on a major homicide and during that investigation had realized they had feelings for each other and had expressed those feelings. Despite the fact his wife was in a permanent coma, Driscoll considered himself a married man and had spent many a sleepless night feeling guilty about his attraction to Margaret. But the attraction, a mutual one, was unmistakably there and so they had started seeing each other socially. At what most considered the close of the case, she and Driscoll agreed it wouldn't be a good idea for the two of them to work together. Margaret willingly took a transfer to another homicide squad and they continued dating. When Driscoll's wife died, the emotionally distraught Lieutenant asked for a time out, a request that Margaret granted.

"Margaret, what gives?" It appeared to Driscoll that Margaret was trembling.

"I come bearing a message. Believe me, it wasn't my idea."

"Message? What message?"

"Reirdon told me to tell you, and I quote: 'I'm best suited for the job because no team delivers closure faster than we do. And as far as City Hall is concerned, police officers come

in only one color. Blue. And as to gender. They surrender that
each and every time they pin on their shield.'"

Was this the man's idea of a joke? Reirdon had promised
not to send a female assistant. And of all people, Margaret!
Goddamn him! Goddamn that son of a bitch!

Margaret sat down in a swivel chair. She looked dazed. "I
swear, John. I had Lieutenant Troy try to convince Reirdon
to leave me be. No such luck. The Mayor was hell-bent on
having me work with you."

Driscoll shook his head. That bastard! And look at me.
I'm the fool who placed his trust in the word of a politician.
He caught Margaret's doleful gaze. She must feel terrible for
her unwilling role in this deceitful maneuver. He softened. "I
was glad to see you at the funeral," he said. "That meant a lot
to me. But I guess you know that."

"How's Mary?"

"She's hanging in there. Thanks for asking."

Margaret smiled.

"Well," said Driscoll begrudgingly, "I guess if we're going to work together again, now would be a good time to
bring you up to speed." He stuck his head out the door to his
office and gestured for Thomlinson to come inside. Once the
three were settled, he began. "We have two bodies, and the
medical examiner coincides their approximate time of death.
That gives us a four-hour window. We know the vics weren't
killed where they were found. Crime Scene reports two massive head wounds but no hair, brain matter, or blood splatter
where the bodies were discovered. And since the media has
been all over it, I'm sure you know both victims were
scalped. We could be looking at two perps, but we can't rule
out the possibility of one guy doing both murders."

"The American Museum of Natural History and Coney
Island are less than an hour apart. One guy coulda easily
done the two," said Thomlinson.

"I think it's best to consider this the work of one person

until the evidence tells us otherwise," Driscoll continued. "We've got the perp posing the bodies at both sites and concurrent causes of death. And, judging from what the autopsies revealed . . ." His voice trailed off, his mind wandering to the cold and sterile environs of the medical examiner's mortuary he had visited earlier in the day. He envisioned himself marching down the long corridor toward the double-glass doors marked "City Morgue."

Behind those doors Driscoll came upon a spacious room with white tiled walls and a high ceiling. High-wattage halogen bulbs illuminated an array of cadavers positioned atop stainless steel gurneys. Those corpses, their chests and abdominal sections gaping, were attended by three coroner's assistants, who were dissecting and weighing lifeless organs.

On one such gurney, near the center of the room, one of the two tourists was being examined by Larry Pearsol, the city's chief medical examiner, and Jasper Eliot, his assistant.

"Item D214B67. Arrival Date, June 4, 2006." Pearsol's voice boomed into the Uher recorder. "Deceased is Helga Swenson, tentatively identified by International Passport. Remains are that of a well-developed, well-nourished female. Weight sixty-eight-point-six kilos. Height one-hundred-sixty-seven-point-six centimeters. No remarkable scars, moles, or tattoos noted. Initial examination of decedent's fingernails reveals no evidentiary properties. Inspection of genitalia reveals no indication of rape or assault. There is no semen present. Examination of the cephalic region reveals sharp force trauma resulting in a massive head wound, measuring seven-point-six-two centimeters to right parietal, causing fracture to the skull and bone splinters to penetrate the brain. Twelve-point-seven-centimeter linear penetration to the skin of the forehead noted. Irregular tearing of scalp—"

Pearsol hit the OFF button on the recorder to tell Driscoll that the same cranial wound pattern and evidence of scalping appeared on tourist number two, Yen Chan.

"Lieutenant, whaddya make of the head wound?" It was Sergeant Aligante's voice. The question rocketed Driscoll back to the present.

"Maybe an ax," Thomlinson suggested as Driscoll reexamined the eight-by-ten glossies in the open file on his desk.

"More likely a tomahawk. Our boy's into scalping." Driscoll was becoming more comfortable with Margaret's presence.

"Someone piss off the Navaho and we don't know about it?" Thomlinson ran a finger across his forehead and grabbed hold of his hair.

"The posing says the guy's into showcasing his work," said Margaret. "New York might be his new exhibition hall."

"Say it ain't so," groaned Thomlinson,

"I agree with Margaret." Driscoll smiled at her. "This guy likes to show off his work. Right now he's probably fantasizing over his kills. But after awhile his recollection of the murders will fade. And so will the power those fantasies have had in keeping him satiated. Once that happens, he'll need to kill again. He's like anyone with a compulsion. He gets high on the first kill, but in order to keep the high going, he'll need to do it again. I'd say our guy'll want to expand. Artists have a whale of an ego. He's gonna want a bigger and bigger audience, a standing ovation from eight million, nine hundred thousand New Yorkers. These two murders may just be the warm-up."

Thomlinson had a puzzled look on his face.

"Whaddya thinking, Cedric?"

"How the hell does he know his targets are tourists?"

"He's gotta get close enough to hear them speak. That'd be my guess," said Margaret. "I say he stalks them, waits until they're alone, whacks them, and then drags them off to hide them in some burrow for the night until morning, when it's showtime."

"Coney Island and a museum. We're talking crowded

crime scenes. How come no one saw anything?" asked Driscoll. "And the posing? No one sees that goin' on?"

"The guy's gotta be one strong son of a bitch," said Thomlinson. "He carried a two-hundred-pound man up the side of the Wonder Wheel, for Chrissake."

"How's this?" said Margaret. "He selects a number of random targets that he thinks talk funny. Strikes up a conversation with one or more of them, where he learns who's from out of town. Then he lurks in the shadows waiting for one of the poor suckers to stroll into his lair. And, whack! And you're gonna love this. A public toilet! That could be the lair. One of the stalls would serve as a safe place to hide his victim until closing time."

"And nobody notices the vic's missing?"

"The guy goes after loners."

"Possible," said Thomlinson. "But that says two doers. One guy can't spend all that time setting up his targets, kill one of them, wait 'til the middle of the night to showcase his work, and be able to do it in two places at the same time. Remember, the ME coincides their approximate time of death."

"Okay," said Driscoll. "We may be looking for a pair of killers. Cedric, get on the horn to the press and the media. We want to hear from anyone, and I mean anyone, at either location who may have been approached by a stranger. Margaret, call the Bureau of Indian Affairs. See if they've got any take on this. Then get a hold of Crime Scene. I want every toilet, every storage area, and any other stand-alone structure at the museum and on the boardwalk swept. They're to look for blood and any other trace evidence that may be related to the crimes. But, Cedric, you have a point. How does our boy drag a two-hundred-pounder up the side of a Ferris wheel?"

"We're lookin' for one helluva bench-presser. Maybe two."

Chapter 10

HEUREUX QUI COMME ULYSSE A CONQUI LA TOISON

That was the inscription etched on the stainless-steel back of Driscoll's pocket watch. Colette had presented Driscoll with the watch on their wedding night.

"Happy, he, who like Ulysses, had conquered the Golden Fleece," was the translation. She had chosen the verse from Dubellay, the Renaissance poet.

And hadn't John Driscoll discovered in Colette the magical Golden Fleece, the object of his heart's desire? Hadn't he been an urban Ulysses, seeking that other, the woman he would love forever? And hadn't their love produced a kind-hearted child, Nicole? Sadly, though, he had gained the fleece only to see it wrenched from him by a driver plastered on Cuervo Gold.

Driscoll was alone in his new residence, the Brooklyn Heights co-op. He was feeling morose, contemplating the inscription on the back of the watch, running his thumb along the etching like someone reading Braille.

He sat at the dinner table, set for one, and filled his glass with De la Morandiere Chardonnay, her favorite wine.

She was afraid of thunderstorms! The thought raced to his consciousness. He recalled seeing a PBS special on the life of Abraham Lincoln. Mary Todd Lincoln, the first lady, suffered from the same dread of thunder. The president, it is said, was known to leave the affairs of state and hurry home at the first sighting of a storm so he could comfort his wife. Driscoll smiled, remembering cutting short his own shifts and hurrying to Colette's side when the heat of the day met the cool of the night, producing ferocious late-summer downpours.

"John, they frighten me so," she would murmur.

It became his unspoken vow. To keep her safe from the storm . . . safe from the darkness . . . and safe from the perils of life itself.

Driscoll took another sip of Chardonnay, placed the glass on the table, and headed for the stove, where he would prepare the evening meal: roasted chicken breast with Gruyère and mushrooms. Without warning, a bolt of lightning electrified the sky over Brooklyn Heights, illuminating the small kitchenette in which Driscoll stood, igniting yet another remembrance.

Colette and he had been strolling the Toliver's Point shoreline when the first rumblings of a summer thunderstorm intruded on their reverie. Colette clutched Driscoll's hands and dragged him from the beach as luminous clouds began to billow. They headed for home. As soon as they reached the bungalow, Colette rushed to the bedroom, where she sought shelter under a comforter.

After the squall passed, she opened her eyes and found herself wrapped in Driscoll's arms.

"Tell me," she whispered.

"What?"

"Just tell me."

"You already know."

An impish smile crept across Colette's face.

"What?" he frowned.

"It's time for some sweetness."

Driscoll rummaged through his pockets and produced a roll of butterscotch Life Savers.

"Silly man," she said.

"Some gals are never happy."

"Just tell me."

"Je t'aime," he whispered. "Are you happy now?"

" *'Je t'aime à la folie,'* you're supposed to say. That means you love me madly."

"That's right. I do love you madly."

"And I . . . you," she said.

"Then we'd better do something about it."

"Let's get married," she gushed, her face looking like that of a schoolgirl.

"But we're already married."

"Let's do it again! We can have a second honeymoon!"

"Okay. Where would you like to go?"

"You pick."

"I have a place in mind," he said. "You'll love it."

"Tahiti?"

"Arles."

"Why there?"

"Wouldn't you like to see what Van Gogh saw?"

"What a fabulous idea! I can pack up my easel and off we'll go. When are we going?"

"You pick the date."

"How about . . . my birthday?"

"Perfect."

"Is this for real?"

"Sure it is."

All talk ceased. Eyes danced. Hands intertwined. Driscoll leaned in and placed a soft kiss on her neck.

"What say we start the honeymoon now?" she murmured.

"Splendid idea," he whispered.

Chapter 11

Margaret Aligante had put her calls in to Crime Scene and the Bureau of Indian Affairs. She was sure the forensic boys would do their part but had gotten a "not in our neck of the woods" response from a John Nashota at the BIA. She was fatigued. She had spent the better part of the past twelve hours trying to locate Phyllis Newburger. If truth be known, she hadn't spent much time in the labyrinth that was the NYPD database. This Italian American cop was superstitious, and looking for her childhood psychotherapist in the official archives made her feel as though she'd be inviting someone to take a peek over her shoulder. Margaret, the resourceful woman that she was, chose to cloak herself in the anonymity of the Internet.

Anxiety lay behind her search. And for this tough cop, anxiety took on but one form: men. More precisely, the prospect of a romantic relationship with one. Sure she carried a gun, was proficient in the martial arts of aikido and tae kwon do, and took nonsense from no one. Still, none of these attributes protected her from the pure dread she felt at the mere notion of getting serious with a man. And despite her ever glowing internal red light, Margaret knew she was headed for such a relationship with John Driscoll, once again her boss. They were sure to pick up where they had left off. But now the man was single. Jesus H. Christ! Single! Panic attacks, which she thought she had outgrown, were burgeoning. She knew her only remedy was to seek professional help. But the only psychotherapeutic help she had ever received was provided to her as an adolescent by Phyllis Newburger, who helped her face her childhood demons and withstand their threat. Margaret knew some of those same demons had been awakened, prompting her current feeling of angst. She needed to see the Newburger woman. In her mind, at least, there was no one else to turn to.

Using Google, she happened upon Newburger's name in affiliation with a Saint Finbar's Foundling, in New Rochelle. The Web site indicated that she was the director of placement services, but the article, which extolled and praised the foundling's humanitarian efforts, was eight years old. And so, when she called Saint Finbar's, she was disappointed but not surprised to hear that Newburger had moved on. Where, they didn't know or weren't saying. She thanked the staff member for her kindness and continued her Web search, seeking out associations that might have an address for the woman.

One such organization was the New York chapter of the National Association of Social Workers. A local number was featured, but when she called, a clerk explained that she had gotten a no-hit when searching for any Phyllis Newburger in their database. Good God! thought Margaret. It had been over twenty years. Could the woman be dead?

Margaret ventured on. Her search at Anywho.com produced a long list of Phyllis and P. Newburgers, with both local and long-distance phone numbers. She printed a copy of the listings and put it aside. She would cold-call only as a last resort.

As daylight faded in her small study, the translucent surface of her desktop's monitor grew brighter and soon became the only light in the room. Margaret pushed her roll-away chair back from the desk and rubbed her eyes. It was then, in the twilight, always in the twilight, that her past caught up with her.

Dusk was imminent. Time to get out of sight; make herself disappear. Go to that place. That place of safe harbor, if only in her mind. But as twelve-year-old Margaret rolled herself into a ball and squeezed herself into the narrow cubbyhole, she could still hear the footfalls outside her bedroom door. She prayed to Saint Rita he'd pass.

Some nights he did. Some nights he didn't.

And on those nights. On those Godforsaken nights, when the Lord was asleep and the saints were at play, the door would creak open and in he'd walk.

"Margaret?"

His tone was always the same. One of expectancy.

The ritual that followed was played out in darkness.

"You'll do it to show how much you love me," he'd say. "C'mon, a little faster. Hold it a little tighter. That's it! Just like I showed you."

Margaret followed his instructions carefully. The goal was not to upset the man. God forbid that happened. It only made him drink more and Margaret knew what that meant. The alcohol would dull his senses and interfere with his concentration. Even so young, Margaret realized, perhaps not on a conscious level, but realized nonetheless, that sex was, indeed, ninety percent mental. And if he drank enough, fast enough, she'd have to do it all over again. But this time with her mouth.

"You're Daddy's little girl, aren't you?" he'd stammer. "You love your Daddy, don't you? Now, slow it down. Just use your palm on the tip. That's it! Oh, yeah! Slower, now. A little slower. That's it! Ohhh . . ."

The sound of the phone ringing shattered the nightmare.

"Hello," she managed.

The voice was familiar but she couldn't place it; part of her was still under the influence of the terrifying memory

"This is Claire. Claire Bartlett. From the foundling? You called our office. Left this number?"

"Oh? Oh, yeah. Thank you. Have you come up with something?" Margaret's heart began to race.

"Yes, we have. One of our resident therapists knows what became of Miss Newburger."

"That's good news. Tell me."

"I'm afraid she's dead, Miss Aligante. She died close to three years ago. At an assisted-living facility in Nanuet."

Margaret tried to respond but couldn't.

"I'm sorry," said the caller and after a moment of silence hung up.

As Margaret placed the receiver on its cradle, she was certain she heard the sound of footfalls making their way toward her door.

Chapter 12

Once again that billion-dollar New York City skyline made Kyle Ramsey awaken minutes before dawn, climb atop his Bontrager ten-speed racer, and make a swift dash across the bicycle path of the Brooklyn Bridge. Greeted by a saffron sky, Kyle came upon the runway that led him to the upper stretch of the historic overpass. Filling his lungs with Brooklyn air, he lifted his body to gain increased thrust from his gluteus maximus muscles, and the bike rocketed up the incline; the Edward Jones financial wizard upshifting in rapid succession. As he was circumventing the first stanchion of architectural pylons, Kyle noticed a body slumped against the massive brick column. It was a dozing wino still clutched fast to his empty pint. Indifferent, Kyle increased his speed and continued across the bridge's medial span. By the time he reached the second set of pylons, his spandex biking gear was drenched with sweat. He checked his wrist chronometer: 48.6 seconds. Good. But not good enough. Yesterday, he covered the same stretch in 42.9. Last evening's second martini proved costly.

Someone or something darted out in front of him. Kyle swerved to avoid contact, but collided headlong with the shadowy figure, who let out a groan before running off. Kyle tumbled and crashed into the span's wooden decking. The bike careened against the second brick column of the bridge. The errant pedestrian was now a vanishing speck in the distance.

"You son of a bitch!" Kyle screamed, painfully scrambling to his feet. "You're dead meat when I get ahold of you!"

He righted the ten-speed and mounted it. The front wheel, bent from the impact with the brick column, locked in his grip. The frame looked like an accordion.

"That bike cost me two thousand dollars, you bastard!"

Something else caught his attention. A figure was strewn near the base of the second column. Was that a camera and tripod lying at his feet? Curiosity drew him closer. He bent down and picked up the camera. A Leica.

"That sucker costs nineteen hundred dollars!" he mumbled, fingering the casing, tempted to make it his. Loot for the taking. No? He examined the camera closely. Sure, it came fully loaded with a Summilux-M f/2/50 mm lens! "Wow!" he said, discovering its 0.85x viewfinder. He clutched the camera to his chest and eyed the probable owner sprawled before him. *What's wrong with him,* he wondered?

That's when he spotted the rivulet of blood.

This guy's hurt. And pretty bad, at that.

Kyle lifted the man's head. "Good God, what happened to your hair?" Blood flowed heavily from a massive wound, just behind the right ear.

"Jesus! I think this guy's dead!"

He didn't know what to make of it. If this was a mugging, how could the thief miss the camera? *Maybe,* Kyle thought, *he had interrupted a crime in progress.* His mind wandered to the fleeing pedestrian. Pressing his ear to the victim's chest, he thought he heard the man's heart still pumping but then realized the sound was emanating from the vibrations caused by the pre–rush hour traffic below. His original suspicion was confirmed. The guy was deader than dead. What were needed now were a cop and a coroner. Retrieving his cell phone from his saddlebag, he powered on and punched in 911.

As he ended the call, his focus fell, once again, on the camera.

Chapter 13

The sound of the alarm clock jarred Driscoll from an uneasy sleep. It was 6:30 A.M. Police sirens echoed in the distance. Their wailing was growing increasingly closer. He checked on his kid sister by opening his cell phone. There were no messages. He walked to the window and took a peek outside. Two hundred yards away, the Brooklyn Bridge glowed in the dull morning mist. At the entrance to the bridge were two parked police cruisers, their array of emergency lights flashing. A police helicopter hovered above, its searchlight bracketing the span's northwest pylon. An ambulance sped east on Tillary Street, the bridge's Brooklyn foothold.

I guess the Thirty-ninth Airborne is on its way, he mused, closing the shutters and heading into the kitchenette, where he hit the switch on the Braun espresso machine. The whine of another police siren tore through the dawn.

He found his Bushnell field glasses in the hall closet, behind several boxes of shoes. Ambling back to the window, he took a closer look. There were three more police cruisers parked at the foot of the bridge, lights ablaze. He watched two ambulance attendants cart off a body. There was a man bending over, examining a bicycle. The man righted himself.

That's Jimmy Capelli, Brooklyn South's top dog!

Driscoll found his cell phone atop the kitchen counter, next to his keys. He rushed back to the window and punched in a number.

He watched in amusement as Capelli patted down each pocket in search of his phone. Finding it, the top cop flipped it open.

"Capelli, here."

"Who dressed you this morning?" said Driscoll.

"Who the hell is this?"

"You look like Robin Hood! Who in their right mind wears a bright red tie with an olive-green suit?"

"Who *is* this?"

"It's Driscoll. And have I got my eye on you."

"Driscoll! Where the hell are you?"

"I lay out an extra three hundred a month to have a view of the Brooklyn Bridge, and this morning I gotta see your ugly mug?"

"Funny man you are, John. Your landlord must have thrown in a pair of binoculars."

"That's why you're a detective. Whaddya got?"

"A DOA. He took one hard to the head. You're sure to get a call. This one's been scalped."

Driscoll's eyes narrowed. "What else ya got?"

"There's some pretty expensive camera equipment lying around. There's even a professional tripod. We're figuring the DOA for the photographer. What brings a guy out onto a bridge at six in the morning?"

"Any witnesses?"

"All we got is an anonymous call to 911. Otherwise, zip."

"You ID the DOA yet?"

"Guenther Rubeleit. He's carrying a German driver's license. You know Reirdon's not gonna be happy with that."

"Tell me more about the head wound."

"It's ugly. Just behind the right ear."

"I see a bike there. Looks all bent up."

"Yeah. Looks like it hit something. I'm figuring maybe it belonged to the DOA."

"Doubt it."

"Why's that?"

"Tourists don't get around on bikes. Especially one carrying a tripod. It's gotta belong to somebody else. Make sure the lab boys are all over it." Driscoll heard a beeping sound on the line and rolled his eyes skyward. "Gotta go, Jimmy. I got another caller and I'm sure I know who it is."

Chapter 14

Cassie couldn't sleep. That was unusual. Was the killing spree she and Angus had begun weighing on her conscience? Her brother warned her that might happen. She still had a portion of her soul left, was how Angus had put it. She glanced next to her. Angus's eyebrows were twitching, an indication he was dreaming. Where did his nocturnal escapades take him? Did he, like she, still dream of Mother in the hope that she'd return and somehow put an end to the madness? Or was what Angus said the truth? That the only thing she was good at was leaving us behind.

Cassie gathered the covers around her as uninvited memories swirled.

"One little, two little, three little Indians . . ." Father's voice sounded, as he pressed his pockmarked face into mine. "Circle the wagons! The injuns are comin'!"

Grabbing hold of my arm, he yanked me from my bed. "Time to get ready, little darlin'."

After dragging me down the stairs, he steered me into the small room behind the furnace, where I was forced to climb atop a table and lie down.

"*One little, two little . . . lie still little darlin'. Daddy needs to get this just right.*"

Using angular brushes, Father dabbed at the acrylic paint and applied a colorful array of markings to my face.

"*This is just for practice, mind you, little darlin'. When I get the war paint just the way I want it, we'll make it permanent. Four little, five little, six little Indians . . .*"

Chapter 15

"Examination of the cephalic region reveals sharp force trauma resulting in a massive head wound, measuring seven-point-six-six centimeters to right parietal, causing fracture to the skull and bone splinters to penetrate the brain. Thirteen-point-eight-centimeter linear penetration to the skin of the forehead noted. Irregular tearing of scalp . . ."

Larry Pearsol's words echoed in Driscoll's ear as he and Thomlinson, seated in the Chevy cruiser, blended with the flow of traffic on Second Avenue. It marked the third time the medical examiner had used those words in as many weeks. And it officially tied the crime on the bridge to the other homicides, making it part of Driscoll's investigation. New York had another serial killer on its hands and, thanks to the press, the city's populace was reminded of it with every newscast and in every headline. The *Daily News* went with DEADLY TOLL ON A NO TOLL BRIDGE while the *Post* opted for NUMBER 3 SCALPED!

Driscoll had spent the better part of his morning listening to the ranting of Joseph Santangelo, the chief of detectives. How the man had risen from inspector to chief was a mystery. There had been other more qualified candidates for the job. The belief was that he had some politician or cash-cow benefactor in his pocket. Chief Santangelo, derisively called "The World's Greatest Detective" by his squad commanders, was his usual cantankerous self, telling Driscoll he'd be directing traffic down on Canal Street if he didn't turn up a lead in the case soon. But after his posturing, he gave Driscoll the green light to set up a task force. A contingent of thirty detectives and three sergeants, from throughout the borough, would be handpicked by Driscoll. The support team at TARU, or Technical Assistance Response Unit, would be ordered to stand at the ready. And Fleet Services would supply ten additional cars and two surveillance vans. A Tip Line, a phone number established by the department at which the general public was encouraged to report any pertinent information, would be established and manned twenty-four-seven by a police investigator. The line had proven to be a valuable aid in many previous investigations. Thomlinson would be Driscoll's broom, his right-hand man. He would oversee the Tip Line activity and other administrative duties. Any directives that came from him were to be interpreted as coming from the Lieutenant.

Crime Scene had reported their findings to Driscoll immediately after the barrage of mortar fire from Santangelo. Helga Swenson's blood had been found in the third stall of a second-floor ladies' lavatory in the east wing of the museum. The blood of victim number two, Yen Chan, was found in one of those industrial green Port-a-Potties near the entrance to Cleary's Boardwalk Fun House, just steps away from the site where his body had been found. Now came the hard part. Crime Scene would have to process two public facilities where hundreds, if not thousands, of fingerprints and other forensic evidence would be found. This wasn't television's *CSI*. The NYPD Crime Lab was understaffed and lacked the high-tech gadgetry of the highly equipped labs featured on TV. But they got the job done, just not within the sixty minutes it took their TV counterparts. But, as Driscoll was fond of pointing out, the NYPD did it without those annoying commercials.

All precincts throughout the five boroughs had been ordered to beef up their presence at all tourist attractions throughout the city. This presence was to be provided around the clock. Thomlinson had made some of the forensic team's findings known to the news media, asking that they include the information about the holding sites in their reporting. The general public was urged to call the task force's Tip Line with information about any suspicious activity they may have encountered in and around the restrooms, the attractions, or on the bridge. Trace evidence of three other blood donors was also discovered at the museum. Test results showed all three to be menstrual blood. Driscoll figured as much. After all, it was a ladies' room. Considering that the crime scenes themselves had been violated by being trampled upon by the general public, Driscoll wasn't banking on much, if any, pertinent evidence. But the preliminary forensic reports did prove Sergeant Aligante's theory to be correct about where the victims were held. And her assertion that the killer had a conversation with the deceased before rendering the fatal blow was also likely. The autopsies of all three victims revealed no defensive wounds. And all three were indeed tourists. The sad part was that none of them saw it coming. Support for Margaret's speculation was encouraging news. Score one for the good guys. And a slam dunk for Margaret!

Fifteen minutes later, Driscoll pulled the cruiser into a restricted parking space in front of Thirty-two East Houston Street, NYPD's Crime Lab, where he tossed the Police Department Vehicle Identification card onto the dash.

Once inside the building, he and Thomlinson were greeted by Ernie Haverstraw, the lab's top criminalist, who reminded Driscoll of the ubiquitous hefty man you'd inevitably run across in the meat department of every Gristede's grocery store in the city.

The three men crowded around the Bontrager ten-speed bicycle that had been recovered from the Brooklyn Bridge. It was still coated with blotches of white powder, the residue of the technician's search for fingerprints.

"That exerciser-on-wheels retails for about twenty-one hundred dollars plus," said Haverstraw. "But now it's fit for the junkyard. Not only was the front wheel damaged but also the frame was bent in the collision. Whoever left it behind knew it was a total."

"What'd it hit?"

"Something made of brick. My guess would be one of the columns on the bridge."

"Come up with any prints?" asked Thomlinson.

"A few. But none that matched any in our databases."

"Figures," said Driscoll.

"Found something, though." The technician held up a clear plastic envelope about the size of a pack of cigarettes. Driscoll squinted to see what was trapped inside. "We found it wedged into the brake assembly on the bike's handlebars. We know it doesn't belong to your victim."

Driscoll brought the bag to within inches of his nose. He was able to identify the find: the jagged edge of a bloodstained fingernail. He handed the pouch to Thomlinson.

"Now if we could only get hold of the guy that belongs to this nail . . ." Thomlinson said.

"That won't be easy," said Haverstraw. "We tested the blood. Another no-hit. We're still waiting for the chromosomal scanning results on the blood's white cells. That'll give us the likely race and gender."

"Tell me more about the bike," said Driscoll.

"It's imported from Italy by Stranier and Sons. You'll find it available in only three stores in the Northeast. One's in Darien, Connecticut. Another in Manhattan. And one more in Southampton. But you see that emblem? *That* bike ran the

Tour de France. And your rider is a professional who bought it right here in Manhattan."

"I'll be damned," said Thomlinson. "All that from a bike?"

"Well, the serial number helped." Haverstraw grinned like the Cheshire cat.

"So we've got a name," said Driscoll.

"That we do. The bike's owner is one Kyle Ramsey. He lives at Two-Thirty-one Pineapple Street. Downtown Brooklyn. That makes him a Brooklyn Heights resident, Lieutenant. Right in your own backyard."

Chapter 16

The club was called the Wet Spot, and it was ladies' night. k. d. lang's sultry voice flooded the dance floor as a crowd of drag queen revelers responded rapturously to the balladeer. Sweat glistened. Tongues explored. Limbs intertwined. Flesh clung.

At the bar, a ponytailed lass dipped her pinkie in her mimosa and tickled the cherry. Her pristine white blouse, her parochial-school jumper, and her bleached cotton knee-highs made her look like a Catholic schoolgirl.

"I could drink Veuve Clicquot all night," her bar companion singsonged as she ran a teasing finger under the small of the schoolgirl's foot. "They call me Gretchen," she added with a wry little smile that accented a Betty Boop face.

"Dance! Dance! Dance to the music! Grind! Grind! Grind to the beat!" The DJ's rhythmic incantations exhorted the excitement seekers to heightened realms of rapture spurred now by Janet's Jackson's "Nasty."

Circumnavigating the bar, waiters, costumed as mermaids, scurried in stiletto heels to deliver drinks.

"I just love ladies' night. Don't you?" Gretchen crooned.

"That I do," said the schoolgirl. "But I'm inhaling enough noxious perfume to hatch a pulmonary tumor."

"Oooooo, pulmonary! Sounds raunchy. Sure like the sound of that. You a nurse or an obstetrician?"

"Silly," the girl giggled.

"Why don't you lead me to your examination table? I just love stirrups."

"All right, then. Hi-ho, Silver!"

Gretchen signaled the bar's mermaid for the check.

The Catholic schoolgirl rummaged through her over-stuffed bra and produced a crisp $50 bill.

"The libations are on me," she said, grabbing hold of Gretchen's hand, before heading for the exit.

"You Kyle Ramsey?" The voice cropped up out of nowhere. It stopped the Catholic schoolgirl dead in her tracks. When she turned around, the glow of a woman's face stared back at her.

"Sorry, honey. The name's Celeste. And who might I ask are you?"

"We've got your bike," Sergeant Aligante said flatly, producing her shield.

Gretchen quickly disappeared, swallowed up by the throng of gyrating dancers.

"Do I look like I'd be riding a bike in this getup, darling?"

"Your bike. The Brooklyn Bridge. Am I ringing any bells?"

The etchings of fear began to form on Ramsey's face. He climbed back onto his barstool and invited Margaret to join him.

"It was just supposed to be an early-morning jaunt. That's all. The guy's dead. Right?"

"What guy is that?"

"The guy whose head was bleeding."

"The man's dead, all right. What can you tell me about him?"

"What's to tell? He was lying there when I found him. I'm the one who called 911."

"Been to Coney Island recently, Mr. Ramsey? Or to the Museum of Natural History?"

A look of panic seized Kyle Ramsey.

"Wait a minute. Does this have something to do with those two tourists who were killed?"

"This'll go a lot easier if I ask the questions."

"I'm sorry. But that's gotta be it. Why else would you be here asking questions?"

"Which you haven't answered."

"I've never been to Coney Island. It's a dreadful place. And the last time I was to a museum I was six years old. Honest!"

It appeared to Margaret that the man was about to cry.

"We think there may have been someone else on that bridge, Mr. Ramsey."

"You're damn right there was. There was this guy. At least I think it was a guy. Anyway, he darted out in front of me. I swerved the bike to avoid him and hit the goddamn bridge." Ramsey leaned in conspiratorially. "I think I may have hit the bastard."

"We do too."

Margaret eyed the man dressed in Catholic schoolgirl attire. Could she have found her serial killer hiding behind lipstick, mascara, and a padded bra? Every instinct said no. His story too closely paralleled the evidence. And why would a killer leave a traceable ten-speed racer at the scene of a murder?

"Let me buy you a drink," said Margaret. "What'll it be?"

"I'll have another mimosa."

"Make that two," said Margaret to the bar's mermaid.

"You look more like the Cosmopolitan type, if you don't mind me saying," said Ramsey. "And don't you feel just a tad out of place in this meat emporium?"

"What? You don't like my Versace blouse?"

"On the contrary, I like it too much."

Whoa! Was this guy a switch-hitter? Margaret couldn't remember ever being hit on by a man dressed in drag. Oddly enough, she found it amusing. Life's just full of surprises, she thought.

"Kyle, tell me about the guy you think you hit."

"From the top?"

"From the top."

"Okay. I'm racing across the bridge. I do it every morning. That particular morning I was trying to better my time from the day before. As I'm closing in on the second piling, I check my stopwatch. I'm doing okay. Then out of nowhere this guy . . . or girl. Whatever! Let's call him a guy. This guy pops out in front of me. Smack! I hit him. At least I think I did. It all happened so fast. Anyway, the guy does a cartwheel and I hit the floorboards. Man, did that hurt! When I get to my feet the guy is bolting and my bike looks like an accordion. That's when I spotted the man with the head wound. I checked for a heartbeat. There didn't appear to be any. So I called 911."

"Why didn't you identify yourself?"

"I should have. I know. The whole thing was just too scary. I just wanted to get the hell out of there."

"Why'd you leave the bike behind?"

"It was beyond repair. It wasn't until I reached home that I remembered the bike's serial number and that it might be traceable. I was gonna head back to retrieve it, but by that time the bridge was filled with police cars. I made a mistake in leaving it, huh?"

"Let's get back to the guy you hit. Wha'd he look like?"

"I never saw his face."

"He was a foot in front of you!"

"It all happened in a flash. I think he had a hood on. Maybe a baseball cap under that. But I didn't see his face. That's all I can tell ya. Honest."

Margaret glanced around the crowded club. The music

was still blaring and the crowd was still jostling to the beat. An odd smile creased her face. She turned her attention back to Kyle Ramsey.

"All guys, huh?"

Ramsey returned her gaze. "Like a little piece of heaven. Wouldn't you say?"

Chapter 17

Driscoll pulled the rain-battered Chevy to a complete stop as the Long Island Railroad's red and white crossing gates descended up ahead. He narrowed his eyes, focusing them on the rearview mirror, hoping to sidestep a haunting recollection from his past. But the thunderous sound of the passing commuter train catapulted the nightmarish memory to consciousness. On a sunny morning in August, when Driscoll was eight years old, he had been standing curbside, watching his mother climb the steps of the LIRR's Jamaica station. Ten minutes later, as the Manhattan-bound 10:39 came rumbling in, the woman launched herself into its path, ending her life and indelibly scarring John Driscoll. He never forgave his mother for her selfish act and never forgave himself for that notion.

His heart was still racing when a car horn sounded. The train had passed, the gates were up, and a motorist behind him was politely asking Driscoll to proceed. Guilt ridden, he put the cruiser in drive and stepped on the gas.

Thirty minutes later, with the rain still playing havoc with the cruiser's windshield wipers, Driscoll guided the Chevy past the limestone pillars that marked the entrance to Saint

Charles Cemetery. Although his mother was interred there, it wasn't her grave he had come to visit. After giving the security guard a nod, he followed the curves in the road until he came to within fifty feet of the section where his wife and daughter were buried. Pulling the Chevy to the curb, he turned off the engine and sat motionless, lost to reflection. Lightning filled the luminous sky, followed by a slow rumble of thunder that echoed through the graveyard. Driscoll thought it sounded like the drumroll that preceded an execution.

Silence filled the cruiser's cabin as the rain subsided. Driscoll opened the car door and was engulfed by cold and damp air. Heading for the gravesite, he noticed green moss had begun to obscure the headstone's carved lettering. He used his handkerchief to scrape away the uninvited decay.

"*Bonjour, ma cherie,*" he whispered to his bride, standing somberly before the mute stone. "Nicole, Daddy is here," he added.

Was it merely the wind that rustled the nearby willow or was his salutation being answered?

He marveled at the sweeping motion of the tree, smiled, and returned his focus on the grave.

"I miss you," he said. "Both of you." He leaned over and placed his hand on the damp granite stone as serendipitous thoughts whirled into a kaleidoscope of memories. He saw himself and Colette lounging on the open porch outside their Toliver's Point bungalow; a wooden glider providing a view of an ocean varnished in moonlight. The liquid sounds of Debussy serenaded them, as notes from Nicole's flute wafted through an open window.

Without warning, the intrusive peal of a cell phone interrupted his reverie. He reached inside his breast pocket and turned the unit off. But it was too late. His daughter's concert had ended and the vision had ceased.

"Gotta go," he grumbled.

Forcing a smile, he climbed behind the steering wheel of

the Chevy and guided it along the winding road that led to the cemetery's exit, taking note of the tombstones that stood like sentinels on either side. Too many lives lost, he thought, reaching the limestone pillars, where the security guard gave him his customary salute. Odd, even the dead need guarding, he said to himself as he veered the cruiser onto Saint Philip's Drive.

On the entrance ramp to the Meadowbrook Parkway, he remembered he had turned off his cell phone. He reached in his pocket and turned it back on. It rang almost immediately. He flipped it open.

"Driscoll."

"Lieutenant, I've been trying to reach you. Something wrong with your phone?" It was Thomlinson. He sounded anxious.

"I was elsewhere. Whaddya got?"

"The DNA results are in on the nail."

"It's about time. Meet me in my office in forty-five minutes."

"Will do."

When Driscoll arrived at his desk, he found Thomlinson seated beside it. Driscoll slid into his seat and unpocketed a pack of Lucky Strikes and lit one up.

"Thought you were off those things."

"I am," he said, shooting Thomlinson a glare. "Let's see what Forensics has to offer, shall we?"

He reached for the secured file, broke its seal, and leafed through a score of typed pages.

. . . Complete search of the national DNA database produced no match.

. . . subject unidentified. "Now, that's a surprise," he quipped and read on.

. . . In conclusion, chromosomal scanning, utilizing standard Bayesian interpretation, suggests the subject to be

Caucasian . . . Polymerase chain reaction-short tandem repeat methodology, reveals the subject to be male.

"Male?" He lowered his brows and shot Thomlinson a puzzled look. "Why would he have used a ladies' room at the museum? A place where he'd run the risk of being seen?" Driscoll stared long and hard at the italicized printing as if expecting it to change gender. When it didn't, he used an index finger to circle the word. "Cedric, could we be we looking for some sort of cross-dresser?"

"It worked for Hadden Clark." Thomlinson was referring to a notorious cross-dressing serial killer who had a penchant for wearing ladies' clothing while perpetrating his madness.

"Well, my friend, we either have a crafty one on our hands, or our two-killers-acting-in-tandem theory is looking better."

Chapter 18

Detective Cedric Thomlinson was running late. Traffic had come to a complete standstill on Brooklyn's Belt Parkway. Flashing lights in the distance and the trickling of cars in the opposing lanes indicated an accident up ahead. There was nothing he could do but wait out the efforts of the EMS and other emergency personnel. It wouldn't be long before uniforms from Highway Patrol 2 would reopen the three-lane thoroughfare.

After fifteen minutes, Thomlinson was rolling again. He hastened over the Gil Hodges Memorial Bridge, hugged Beach Channel Drive as it curved left, and made it to his destination: Saint Rose of Lima's Church on Beach Eighty-fourth Street in Rockaway Beach. He squeezed his Dodge Intrepid into a tight parking space, got out of the car, and headed toward the heavy oak door that led to the parish community room.

Father Liam O'Connor's eyes narrowed as he watched Thomlinson enter the room and take his assigned seat. O'Connor, a titan of a man, was a Jesuit priest with a strip of white hair surrounded by gray. As a certified alcohol and substance abuse counselor, he had run the NYPD's Confidential Alcohol and Drug Abuse Program for the last thirty-one years. Most of the inductees who filled the room had been ordered into the program by their commanding officer. For Thomlinson, this was his second go-round. A rarity for the department, but not a precedent. He had Driscoll to thank for the exception. The Lieutenant, who had become a good friend, was a master at calling in favors.

The crowd that surrounded Thomlinson tonight was a mix of men and women, all of them police personnel, and all with the same purpose: to gather the strength to keep from drinking. Thomlinson scanned the room, where faces displayed hope or despair. Most in the crowd were young rookie cops ensnared by the lure of local bars that neighbored their precinct, where they could revel the night away with other cops. Always with other cops.

Some of Father O'Connor's fledglings recovered, regained their lives, and went on to become productive police officers. Some didn't. For them, often fighting off the inclination to put the barrel of their service revolver in their mouth and pull the trigger, another career awaited. Thomlinson, at age forty-three, with twenty years under his belt, felt he leaned more toward the whiskey-faced veterans who made up the rest of the crowd, many of whom were barely holding on until retirement.

"Hello, Cedric. Glad you could make it." O'Connor placed a warm hand on Thomlinson's shoulder before making his way toward the front of room. A young officer, with a wife and two kids, had just finished speaking about the struggle he was having with alcohol. A struggle that threatened both his marriage and his career.

"Would anyone else like to speak?" Father O'Connor asked.

Thomlinson cast his eyes to the floor. He had plenty to say but chose to keep it to himself. He knew he was not well respected by his fellow officers, present company included. The resentment stemmed from an incident that occurred while he and his partner, Harold Young, were undercover working Narcotics. A controlled buy was all that was to go down that afternoon. Nothing more.

It began with a drug dealer stepping out of the shadows of a darkened hallway and asking Thomlinson if everything was cool.

"Yeah, mon. Everything's cool," Thomlinson had assured him. But that wasn't the case. Thomlinson had spent the night before tossing back shots of tequila at Cassidy's Hideaway and was hungover. So when a gun materialized in the dealer's hand, followed by shots, the ill-prepared Thomlinson caught one above the right shoulder blade and was knocked to the floor. In the cross fire that followed, undercover police officer Harold Young was killed.

As Thomlinson was lying on a rescue vehicle's stretcher, he caught the look of astonishment on the face of the sergeant who had helped him climb in. He was staring at Thomlinson's gun. A gun that was still in its holster.

In the official report it was indicated that Thomlinson was situated behind Detective Young and could not fire without the risk of hitting his partner. But Cedric Thomlinson knew his drinking was a major factor that helped deliver the officer to an early grave. That reality would follow him for life.

The NYPD is like a small town where news travels at lightning speed. Thomlinson soon became known as the cop who didn't pull his gun in a shootout. Not a good handle to be saddled with. The resultant ostracism brought on more guilt, which led to heavier drinking. The heavier drinking spawned depression and with it, thoughts of suicide.

A compassionate borough commander, Todd Emerson, now retired, had a sense of what was going on. He arranged for Thomlinson to be transferred from Narcotics to Homicide. New surroundings would do him good, Emerson reasoned. There, Thomlinson would report to Lieutenant John Driscoll, a man with a reputation for fairness. But Driscoll was a keen observer as well. It wasn't long before the Lieutenant recognized Thomlinson for what he was. A drunk. He tried reasoning with Thomlinson but couldn't promote change in a man unwilling to own up to his addiction. Driscoll was faced with a dilemma: What to do with this newly assigned detective, a liability to both the job and to himself? Thomlinson was heading for a serious breakdown, the consequences of which could directly affect not only the new homicide detective but the Homicide squad itself.

Driscoll was forced to make a move that might have ruined Thomlinson's career but that may have saved his life. He placed a call to the representative at the Detectives Union and had the detective "farmed." Thomlinson was stripped of his gun and shield and spent the next six weeks in a recovery program at a retreat house in the secluded woods of Delaware County—"The Farm." Thomlinson had little choice. If he refused to complete the program conducted by a group of certified alcohol and substance abuse counselors, he'd be fired.

Thomlinson acquiesced and was eventually returned to active duty.

Yet, here he was, back in the program. Again.

Father O'Connor took a seat next to Thomlinson. "You stayin' out of trouble?" he asked.

Thomlinson nodded.

"How's she doing?"

The priest was asking about a teenager, the reason the detective was back.

"She's a fighter," said Thomlinson.

"You're a fighter, too," said the priest. "It takes stamina to keep the sleeping tiger at bay."

In the course of a prior investigation, the detective had been ordered to drive to the young lady's house, pick her up, and bring her to Driscoll's office, where she was to provide a helpful statement. It was a routine assignment. On his way, though, he stopped to buy a Lotto ticket. While he was standing in line, waiting to purchase what he hoped would be a ticket back to the islands, the young girl was abducted.

In an attempt to silence the voices of condemnation that riddled his brain, Thomlinson turned, again, to alcohol.

In this man's police department, very few get a second chance. He had Driscoll to thank for that, and he silently voiced his appreciation during the communal Lord's Prayer that ended the meeting. After that, Thomlinson walked out into the brisk night air, made his way to his cruiser, slipped in behind the steering wheel, and repeated the prayer. This was, after all, his second go-round.

Chapter 19

Another hot and steamy Sunday morning in July greeted the first visitors to the Intrepid Sea, Air, and Space Museum. Among them was a wiry-haired man with his six-year-old son.

"Permission for me and my son to come aboard, sir?" The man was addressing the sailor who was guarding the gangway to the museum's main attraction: the *Intrepid*'s flight deck.

"Permission granted," the sailor replied, firing a rigid salute to the little freckled-faced boy flaunting a white ensign's cap inscribed USS IOWA.

"Let's go, Daddy!" the boy said.

Scurrying up the steel-studded steps, they reached the carrier's upper deck. It was immense. Gutted warplanes stood silent under a blistering sun. A semicircle of onlookers had formed around the exhibit's newest acquisition: a Russian MiG-21.

The boy's attention was diverted to a loud commotion erupting behind an F-14 Tomcat. Filled with curiosity, he bolted behind the aircraft. A bare-chested youth, his wrists in handcuffs, was yelling at his girlfriend. Provoked, the girl lunged forward, striking her restrained Romeo on the side of his head with the heel of her shoe.

"See that? See that? Why ain't ya handcuffing her?" the youth screamed. "Ain't that assault with a deadly weapon?"

"Any more out of you, young lady, and you'll be riding in the wagon, too," the military guard warned. He barked orders into his handheld radio. "Reilly, here! We got ourselves a situation on the flight deck. Get a transport ready."

"What exactly we lookin' at?" the dispatcher's voice crackled back.

"A domestic quarrel . . . with injuries. I cuffed the agitator after he slapped his girlfriend in the face. While I had him immobilized, she hauls off and tattoos him on the side of the head with her shoe."

The guard positioned himself between the two combatants to block another blow from the irate girlfriend.

"Look, Jack! Over there! That's a Fighting Falcon! Let's get a closer look," the father urged, hoping to distract his son from the fracas.

"D-a-a-a-d. This is getting g-o-o-d."

"We came to see the planes, remember?"

"But, D-a-a-a-d."

The father steered his son to the steps that led to the exhibits featured below.

"Why was that lady hitting that man?" the boy asked, descending the steps ahead of his father.

"I don't know, son. The man must have done something bad."

"Was the policeman gonna take him to jail?"

"Sure looked that way to me."

As the boy and his father were nearing the bottom of the steps, a prerecorded voice sounded from a loudspeaker: "Ladies and gentlemen, the USS *Intrepid* was used by NASA as the primary recovery vessel for the Mercury and

Gemini space programs. Just imagine yourself returning to Earth and the first people you see are the sailors aboard this floating airport . . ."

Reaching the hangar deck, the man led his son to the exhibit marked "Aircrafts of the Pacific." He pointed at the Grumman F6F Hellcat, which was painted in the navy's tricolor camouflage: sea blue, intermediate blue, and insignia white. He then read aloud from the aircraft's polished plaque: "The Hellcat's most successful day in combat came on June 19, 1944, during operations in the Mariana Islands. During this air battle, which became known as 'The Great Marianas Turkey Shoot,' the Japanese lost over three hundred seventy-five planes. Eighty were lost by the United States. . . . Wow! Pretty impressive, eh, Jack?"

"Sure is," the wide-eyed youth said, stroking the underside of the plane's sleek fuselage. "Look! Over there! What's that one?"

A larger aircraft had caught the boy's attention.

"Let's go have a look," said his dad.

They headed toward the next exhibit. The father depressed its red button, activating its tape.

A prerecorded voice began its narration: "The three-seat TBM 3-E Avenger, with a wingspan of over fifty-four feet and an overall length of forty feet, was the country's primary torpedo bomber during World War II. Loaded with two thousand pounds of bombs and armed with three manually aimed fifty-caliber machine guns, the Avenger had a maximum speed of two hundred seventy-six miles per hour and could climb over one thousand feet per minute."

"Wow! That's almost as fast as Mommy when she's out shopping, eh, Jack? . . . Jack? . . . *Jack*?"

"I'm under here, Dad." The boy had made his way below the fuselage of the plane. "Looks like this one sprung a leak," said the boy pointing to a puddle that had formed under the belly of the plane.

"That's odd!" said the father. "These models have no engines . . . and that looks too dark to be fuel." Bending down, he palpated the goo between his fingers, then brought the smear to his nose.

As his father stood in confusion, Jack climbed the steel staircase to the plane's cockpit.

"What the hell is going on?" the man exclaimed, suddenly realizing what it was his son had found. "This plane is bleeding!"

"Daddy!" the boy cried out. "This one's got a pilot!"

Chapter 20

Larry Pearsol completed the postmortem on Tatsuya Inagaki, the tourist from Tokyo whose lifeless form had been removed from the cockpit of the American fighter plane.

"Examination of the cephalic region reveals sharp force trauma resulting in a massive head wound, measuring seven-point-six-four centimeters to right parietal, causing fracture to the skull and bone splinters to penetrate the brain. Thirteen-point-two-centimeter linear penetration to the skin of the forehead noted. Irregular tearing of scalp . . ." said the ME, removing his surgical gloves. "Sure looks like the same handiwork that felled the last three victims, Lieutenant. But how would the killer pull it off with a twenty-four-hour police presence?"

"That's the sixty-four-thousand-dollar question."

Bill Heisek, Manhattan's borough commander, had been hauled into the Mayor's office along with Police Commissioner Brandon to explain why the officers of Midtown North looked upon these killings as a "Task Force thing." One universal shortcoming of the department was that almost everyone was territorial. Where the hell were they while the killer struck and posed his victim? the Mayor wanted to know. Heisek was at a loss for an answer, much to the chagrin of Sully Reirdon and the commissioner. He could only assure both men that it would never happen again. It was a sure bet he'd make good on that promise, for if he didn't, he'd be demoted to the rank of duty captain.

The Mayor was particularly perturbed because the press had trampled all over the police department. The *Daily News* headline read: NYPD CAUGHT NAPPING, while the *Post* ran with COPS BLIND TO LATEST SLAYING.

Driscoll, standing next to the corpse of victim number four, reflected on Pearsol's findings. What am I missing? he pondered. And what's with the scalping?

"I do have some good news," said the ME. "I found some scrapings under the vic's fingernails. Looks like maybe some skin with traces of blood. Could belong to your suspect. I'll have the lab boys run the DNA and blood profiles right away."

Driscoll nodded. The skin tracings and the blood meant this victim had a chance to fight back. With any luck, the next one might survive.

"Larry, what kind of psycho straps a Japanese tourist into the cockpit of an American fighter plane?" asked Driscoll, eyes fixed on Jasper Eliot's eight-by-ten glossy displaying the newly found cadaver.

"Could it have something to do with Pearl Harbor? Maybe your perp lost a loved one and is seeking revenge?"

"But the other three appear to be random."

The two men exchanged a puzzled look.

"Let's see what we've got so far," said Driscoll. "First, the hit on the German woman at the museum. Then Yen Chan, a Chinese male at Coney Island. Number three is Guenther Rubeleit, also from Germany. And now our Japanese friend here. One woman and three men. He, she, or they have crossed gender. That's something your textbook serial killer doesn't do. They usually target one or the other."

"Your whacko is killing tourists and tourism at the same time."

"Tell me about it."

"Three of the four victims were discovered by children, weren't they?"

"Aligante picked up on that. Although his murder sites are places where you're likely to find kids, we haven't ruled out there being some sort of correlation. Right now we're thankful children aren't his victims."

"I'll bet Reirdon's thankful. I'm sure, sincerely. But the media would go ballistic if a child were killed. Every parent in the city, too."

The Lieutenant groaned, reaching for his cell phone that was sounding in his pocket. "Driscoll, here."

A booming voice echoed through the unit's tiny earphone, causing Driscoll to nod at Pearsol. "Him," he silently mouthed.

"That's number four, John. I'm running out of patience."

"Mr. Mayor, we're doing all we can."

"I just got off the phone with the Japanese embassy. They're screaming bloody murder. According to them, the New York City Police Department has its head up its ass. And the family of the latest victim is suing the city for three hundred million dollars! They've been disgraced. The guy's grandfather survived the Battle of Midway, for chrissake! Now he's ready to commit hari-kari on his futon! He says it is the greatest dishonor of his life to have his grandson dumped in the cockpit of an American fighter plane. That was the plane that sunk three Japanese aircraft carriers in the South Pacific! And there's more! Germany's ambassador called me last night. He wants to know why New York is such an unruly town and why I haven't caught the killer. You got an answer for him?"

"Mr. Mayor, I'm staring into the chalky white face of that Japanese grandson right now. The thought of his life being snuffed out by some crazed killer sickens me. We will put an end to these murders." Driscoll lifted the cadaver's right hand and examined the underside of the nails, where the skin scrapings had been collected. "I believe our perp is getting sloppy, Mr. Mayor. Mistakes usually spell end of story."

"Soon, John. Make it soon. Like I said, I'm running out of patience."

Chapter 21

Cassie and Angus were seated across from one another in the makeshift breakfast nook; Angus rearranged the letters in his Alpha-Bits, while his sister read about their murderous exploits heralded in the *Post*.

"You think they're on to somethin', calling us savages? Savages, Indians, Indians, Savages," said Cassie.

A sly smile crept across her brother's face. "Could be," he said, an eyebrow raised.

Cassie rifled through the pages of the paper, stopping when she came to the editorials. "I'm thinkin' of maybe writin' to the editor. Tellin' him and his goddamn writers our side of the story. Savages? Screw him!"

"It does piss you off, doesn't it?" Angus leaned in, amused by his sister's reaction.

"What?"

"Them callin' us savages."

"They should only know," said Cassie.

"If they did, they'd be thanking us for riddin' the world of scum. Take a look on Page Six."

"What am I lookin' for?" Her eyes scoured the page.

"The blonde cutie with the pouty lips."

Cassie zeroed in on a two-by-four snapshot of Debra LaFave. "Who's she?"

"Babe City!" Angus grabbed the paper from his sister's hands. "Too bad it's in black and white. She's got blue eyes ya could swim in."

Men!

Angus cleared his throat and read from the article as though he were auditioning for a play.

"Debra Beasley Lafave, a former readin' teacher at a Florida middle school, once charged with several counts of havin' sex with a fourteen-year-old . . ." Angus shot his sister a grin. "And you thought female offenders were a rarity."

"I never said they were rare. Just unusual."

"Why couldn't our pigeons look like that?" Angus's eyes bored into those of the femme fatale.

"It's a good thing they don't. The tomahawk wouldn't be the only bulge in your pocket." Cassie swatted him on the side of the head and tore the paper from his hands. "Stay focused!"

"All work and no play . . ."

"To hell with play! Who's next?"

"A Pakistani called. Very bad connection." Angus put his thumb to his ear, finger to his mouth, and mimicked the caller. " 'Hello, Mr. Gus. My name is Abdur Rahim. I'm from Islamabad. I like your Web site. I'm in New York and have U.S. dollars.' " Angus held up a Post-it note displaying the caller's number. The disposable cell phone rang. "Mmm . . . another lamb," he said, answering it. After a series of "uh-huhs," Angus jotted down a number, depressed the END button, and grinned at his sister. "That was Abigail from the good ole' US of A. In town on business from California and said she could use some entertainment. Sounded more like she needed a fix. Maybe we oughta switch things round a little. Give the men in blue some domestic fieldwork. Whaddya think?"

Cassie looked like she was mulling it over.

"Wanna hear the Pakistani again?"

"Screw the Pakistani. They're always in a rush."

Chapter 22

Blue skies prevailed over the city as Driscoll stood at the end of the dock in Toliver's Point. The wooden landing, some three hundred feet long, jutted out into Jamaica Bay. It was commonly referred to by the locals as Sullivan's Pier, named after the tavern that sat at its entrance. It had been five days since the attack on the last tourist and Driscoll was growing restless. He'd often come back to the Point to escape his demons, and today he found diversion by watching the playful antics of a handful of teens.

The mixed gang, two boys and three girls, clad in bathing suits, were horsing around in the water. Driscoll watched as the tallest boy squatted down near the dock's edge and clasped his hands together to form what appeared to be the launching pad. The three girls, their faces ripe with laughter, were lined up behind him. The girl they were calling Sally, stuffed into a skimpy one-piece, sashayed forward and placed her foot and trust into the hands of the squatting teen who swiftly catapulted the corpulent plum off the dock and into the air. She soon crashed into the water with a loud splash.

Larry, as everyone was calling him, now got into the game, posing as the announcer.

"Ladies and gentlemen, the judges give that sad excuse for a dive a three-point-nine."

His makeshift microphone was a can of Diet Pepsi. Driscoll thought Larry sounded very much like W. C. Fields.

"Sally, your boobs hit the water before you did," Larry hollered. "Next time keep 'em in your top."

The embarrassed teen's face turned beet red. She grabbed hold of her twisted bathing suit and disappeared under the water.

"Way to go!" cheered the catapulter, giving Larry a high five. "Okay, Peggy. Your turn."

"No funny stuff, Billy," the freckle-faced teen warned, slipping her foot into the teen's grip and closing her eyes.

"Up we go!" Billy roared, launching Peggy into the air.

The girl tumbled head over heels before neatly slicing the surface of the water.

"Ladies and gentlemen, the goose has touched down," Larry whined, still in W. C. Fields mode.

Driscoll reached into his linen jacket for a pack of all-organic additive-free American Spirit cigarettes. He lit one up and inhaled deeply. A Lucky Strike it wasn't. It was a relief, though, to have his throat stroked by a feather rather than singed by a torch. He took another drag and glanced across the bay at the Manhattan skyline in the distance.

Such a contrast, he thought. Here, high-spirited teenagers were at play, while only five miles away a murderous spree was holding the city in a vise of fear.

He snuffed out the cigarette's butt on the dock's railing and watched dusk slowly blanket the metropolis. The neon sign of Sullivan's tavern came to life in fluorescent blue, beckoning him. It was time for a drink. Maybe two.

He walked toward the portal and ducked inside. The familiar scent of draught beer and oak flooring welcomed him.

"Hey, John. Good to see ya," a bright-eyed waitress said, scurrying toward the dining room, balancing a large tray of oysters on the half shell high above her head.

"Likewise, Kathy," Driscoll replied, heading for the bar.

The walls of the barroom were made up of glass sliding doors. They offered a panoramic view of the bay and of the city that hugged its opposing shoreline. The bar itself was U-shaped and crowded. Casually dressed couples, awaiting tables in the dining room, sipped from their glasses of Chardonnay and absorbed the ambiance, while the bar's regulars nursed Bass ale from frosty mugs, their eyes glued to the TV screen, where Mike Mussina of the New York Yankees was pitching a no-hitter against the division-leading Boston Red Sox.

Driscoll spotted an opening at the top of the U, next to the service bar, and made his way toward it, sidestepping another waitress on the run.

"Your girls should be on Rollerblades," Driscoll said to Kevin Conlon, the tavern's proprietor, at the bar.

"Now there's a novel idea. Meals on wheels!" Kevin smiled broadly at the suggestion. "What'll it be? Your usual?"

"That oughta do it."

Kevin gestured to Chris, the bartender.

"A Harp for the Lieutenant."

Kevin Conlon, with his grizzly white beard and gravelly voice, seemed more suited for a Gabby Hayes Western than as a restaurant owner here in suburban New York. A well-bred Irishman and true wine aficionado, he prided himself on offering gourmet meals and gracious service at an affordable price.

"The bad guys still one step ahead of the posse?" Conlon asked, offering Driscoll a Macanudo.

"And then some," Driscoll frowned, stuffing the cigar in his shirt pocket.

"Any truth to the rumor?"

"Which one?"

"That the police have made a breakthrough in the case."

"Ah, that Matt Lauer report. He should stick to the Thanks-giving Day parade."

The bartender returned with a frosty mug of Irish brew and placed it on the bar in front of the Lieutenant. "Why can't Monica Lewinsky make it as a surgeon?" he asked with a sardonic grin.

"I'll bite," said Driscoll.

"Because she sucked as an intern," came the reply.

A whisper of a smile creased Driscoll's face.

"You'll have to excuse our staff's highbrow sense of humor," said Conlon. "It comes from cutting too many classes at Bar-tending 101."

Their conversation was interrupted by the sound of Driscoll's cell phone purring inside his breast pocket. The Lieutenant answered it.

Criminalist Ernie Haverstraw's voice echoed in his ear. "The DNA is back on the traces of skin and blood we found under the last victim's fingernails."

"And?"

"Are you sitting down?"

"That I am. At Sullivan's."

"You finished your drink?"

"Yeah, why?"

"You'd better order another. Make it a double."

"Why? You don't like me sober?"

"Okay. Have it your way. The DNA is a perfect match to the male's blood on the torn fingernail we found entangled in the brake assembly of the bike."

"Yeah. Yeah. Our male serial killer. Tell me something I don't know."

"Like I said, Lieutenant, it's a perfect match to the male's blood. Only thing is, this DNA is female."

Chapter 23

"Whaddya mean the DNA is female?" Driscoll asked as he stormed into Haverstraw's lab.

"Tests don't lie, Lieutenant." The criminalist pointed to a collection of illuminated data on the monitor of a desktop computer.

"Break it down for me, will ya? Using layman's terms."

"The geneticists ran the usual chromosomal scanning, utilizing the Polymerase chain reaction-short tandem repeat methodology," said Haverstraw.

Driscoll shot him a glare. "Layman's terms," he repeated.

Haverstraw shrugged and continued.

"They got an exact match to the DNA sample on file in the database."

"You mean the blood on the fingernail of our male suspect."

"That'd be the one."

"But you're telling me this specimen is female. That would be impossible."

"Oh, it's possible. Let's have a cup of coffee and I'll explain."

Haverstraw sauntered over to an aluminum table that supported a Bunn double-burner coffee server, some Styrofoam cups, and a half-eaten Entenmann's Danish ring.

"Still take yours black, Lieutenant?"

Driscoll nodded.

"Want some cake?"

"I'll pass."

The two men took a seat opposite each other at a wooden workbench next to a full-sized rolling blackboard. A chalk-scrawled formula for who-knows-what was strewn across the hardwood-encased slate. Haverstraw took a sip of his coffee and stared fixedly at Driscoll.

"Lieutenant, there is no mistake in the DNA. The killers you're looking for are a set of twins."

"Twins?"

"Identical twins."

"Male and female twins?"

"There are three types of twins," said Haverstraw. "Identical, fraternal, and conjoined. I'm not the street sleuth, but I think we can rule out conjoined. Fraternal twins wouldn't match genetically. And these two match."

"An exact match?"

"We snip off the tail from the letter *e* in 'exact.' Voilà! We got a match."

Driscoll envisioned a circumcision. Had no clue as to why. His expression said: What?

Haverstraw wondered why he felt obligated to explain his sense of humor to everyone. "For where it'll lead you, they match."

"I thought all boy-girl twins were fraternal," said Driscoll.

"They usually are. Identical twins come from the same egg. Follow me on this one. The twinning begins when it separates after fertilization. It's possible for one twin to have the full complement of forty-six chromosomes, including the XY sex chromosomes of a male, while the other twin has only forty-five chromosomes. Either the Y or one of the X chromosomes is missing. If it's the Y that's missing, the twin is left with a single X chromosome. Bingo! Dad gets his little girl. But not without a cost. Although the partner twin, having the X and the Y chromosome, becomes a healthy baby boy, the female is born with Turner syndrome. It's a rarity of nature."

"How rare?"

"Very! With a capital *V.* Take the United States for example. You're likely to have one such birth every twelve to fifteen years."

"In the entire country? That is rare. What else should I know about this syndrome?"

"There are some medical indicators. They only apply to the female. She's likely to be short in stature, an average height being four-foot-seven. She may have webbing of the neck. Additional folds of skin cascading onto her shoulders. Her eyelids may droop. Her ears may be oddly shaped and sit lower than normal on the side of her head. Sometimes a low hairline is present at the base of the skull. The arms may turn out at the elbow. She may have an unusual number of moles. Might also be infertile. She could develop high blood pressure and diabetes and be at extra risk of ear infections and cataracts. Heart, kidney, or thyroid problems can also develop. She may be flat-chested, her nipples widely spaced. If she has breasts, they're likely to appear undeveloped. Her chest might also appear shieldlike. Obesity is another possibility. Or, Lieutenant, she may have no apparent physical abnormalities at all. Unless she's diagnosed by a doctor, she might not even be aware of her condition."

"Great! She might have a target on her, and she might not." Driscoll groaned.

Haverstraw shook his head sympathetically. "Well, at least you know what her accomplice will look like."

"I don't even know what she looks like!"

"Consider this. You may know more about her than she does."

"What I need to know is who she is, not what she is."

Haverstraw gulped down the remains of his coffee.

"Do you think there'd be records of such rare twins?" asked Driscoll.

"Depends," said Haverstraw.

"On?"

"On whether they were ever tested. Oh. And there's one more thing. Although Dr. Henry Turner first described the condition in 1938, it wasn't until karyotyping was discovered in 1959 that the medical practitioners had a way to detect it."

"Karyotyping?"

"A chromosome analysis. A blood test."

Driscoll stood and smiled at the criminalist. "Ernie, you've been a big help. I now have a place to start." On leaving, the Lieutenant's eyes drifted to the desktop's LCD screen. Its scientific hieroglyphics stared back. He pointed to them and cast a quizzical look at Haverstraw.

"Like two peas in a pod," said the criminalist, leaning back in his chair.

Chapter 24

Cedric Thomlinson was always thrilled when an investigation required him to visit CyberCentral, the tiny wood-paneled technical support room on the fourth floor of Twenty-six Federal Plaza. Was it the humming sound emanating from the room's sophisticated computer equipment that hypnotized him, quelling his impulses, inviting the most pleasant euphoria? Was he, perhaps, overwhelmed by technological advances that allowed the pooling of infinitesimal and very personal information on the average citizen culled from every government agency, foreign and domestic? Or was he simply a willing victim to a flight of fancy at the mere glimpse of Leticia Hollander, the vivacious, soft-spoken Caribbean woman who was the center's enticing technician?

"Cedric, what brings you into my den of data?" Leticia cooed, eyes fixed on a computer monitor.

"Duty calls and I am a slave to my job."

"Slavery was abolished. No?"

"Not at the New York City Police Department. We're just not shackled anymore."

Leticia allowed her eyes to drift upward to the meet the detective's gaze.

"So, what'll it be today?"

"I'm looking for twins, where the pair is listed as identical yet of opposite sex."

"You mean fraternal."

"That'd be too easy. We'll stick with identical twins of opposite sex."

"Never knew they existed. But you're the boss. There'd likely be medical records. I don't suppose you've got a judge's order to authorize such a search."

"I'd need fifty. We'll be checking from Maine to California."

They both knew the U.S. Health Insurance Portability and Accountability Act of 1996, commonly referred to as HIPPA, and a long list of state regulations forbid unauthorized access to an individual's medical record. They knew of no exceptions.

"Any leeway under the Patriot Act?" Leticia asked.

"We're not after terrorists. At least, I hope we're not." Thomlinson gave Leticia a sympathetic smile.

"Damn! I know that look. You want me to do another news article search."

"'Fraid so. Can't jeopardize the investigation with an unlawful inquiry." Thomlinson hoped that someone, the twin's parents, a local support group, a camp counselor, a teacher, or the twins themselves, before embarking on a life of crime, might have brought their uniqueness to the attention of the press. Rarity attracts the curious. The curious buy newspapers. The publisher of *Guinness Book of World Records*, who has raked in millions on such exclusivity for decades, proves that. Privacy guidelines being what they were, it was his only hope.

"Damn!" Leticia hated searching newspaper archives. There was no fixed database. It meant hunt and peck through a string of Web sites featuring hieroglyphic-like listings from thousands of papers across the country. From the *Oshkosh Gazette* to the *New York Times,* the stories spanned the early 1900s through the present day. What made the task tedious was that the keywords entered came back hidden, though highlighted, in gibberish.

To dramatize the point, Leticia tapped her fingers across the keyboard, producing this:

- THE DAILY ESQUIRE, Ross   tfes   dskk   ..,, /;' uu % 16, 1973
  Page un

- Barrelll ill, Rfesmen set Tagge's inry
- gge ir **Twins** two wins not synergy
- Lutb;lltl e's feeet and tvevvvvh 13th complete gamp an
- & :::: andell's wfwfwfees choice vvcdonsin jjids used single
- a9werfifth wdffaaslam home | four-hitter thiqdnadmjijd seven loaded
  the bases in Surdaj's tallies in the second and iith aa
- run ofawfffffaju75tgdgdrst \ strikeoutssareeagbw eJohn fourth inning
  andwrrw stanzas toegdn the Satgrday GRrrf B^Y, rvrj (gPdf—cafgff
  fiff sasresgrorhh4h hbrgr55t5t 7hgert4rrefr34rr tthju
- ferewff fwer fgrgre333fvfefdfdde deeefddetrhtyyhuegt
  ssd fee reeee333 rerefett4rrsrre rereref
- 3fr5g Raptts, lo\\grtew **Twins** seven games behinffggfee e
  wwfr3co grfrr r and ler rn't seri rrw wurt grme were Uewiue
  iwweir huhi ew#%YYY &$$#EI >>>> UGGY
  YTTGYuyguhhuh huii
- Jujjsjssjsdsd qw w wwwwwww hh loss to Floridae first half
- Hsaa jjjj kqqeqhqiw edwo wkkl **Twins** ??iUUtle 111dfeenda ree
  walks and a ssssed bsll) bael m two of the hrcc 4c44!@#inced T
  gtbdj ewwe wwewee233 rff feererwere8884 rirjjijjij%$##Hdefweir-
  rjwkefwe
- **Twins** b erf e ww 44 2 the top of the inning&&& uihjiuhuwef
  wwww errfet5y ttrtyyeast gonee jjjj because jdfj kfwjejfmm
- »ir , , ,.. ^ Lr4$$ u dd0033 uu 3^^^nuj 88%43 uuu>>>>> - - - - - - - - - u
  - - - - - - - - 7 77ggyg 3@@4g
- Galsolie rr   Ethl ge
- Jjjyh yt &….. .jhgu''PP btt   ?///? ujhhjuiuiuiu

She grabbed Thomlinson's index finger and used it to poke at the four highlighted **Twins** she had unearthed. "You see them? You think we're gonna have better luck when we type in 'Turner'?" What came next was placing the cursor on each **Twins** and depressing both the CTRL and ESC keys, bringing them to mostly remote news articles referencing twins. It appeared that most were about the playing prowess of the Minnesota Twins. "You, Cedric Franz Thomlinson, are goin' nowhere till this is done! You got that?"

Yes! cheered Thomlinson. "I won't budge," is what he told her.

Leticia stared at the screen and shook her head. "How far back do you wanna go?" she asked, surrendering to fate.

Thomlinson grinned and awarded her a vial of Visine.

"Cute."

"Keep it within the United States. For now. And give the *Guinness Book of World Records* a sweep while we're at it. Disregard anyone who would now be over sixty or under twelve."

Leticia started counting on her fingers. "A math whiz, I'm not," she said, catching Thomlinson's grin

"Since there's no way to detect newborns as being identical, I'm hoping for an entry later in life. It's a long shot, but under the circumstances, our only shot."

Manicured fingertips danced across the keyboard, turning the computer's screen into a kaleidoscope of newsprint.

After five hours and forty-six minutes of squinting, moving on, and squinting again, their zigzagging cross-country cyberjaunt produced four possibilities. Onetime residents of Ohio, Arkansas, Georgia, and West Virginia would now become the focus of Thomlinson's investigation.

Leticia clicked PRINT, and the pair watched as their nearly six hours of arduous labor filled one sheet.

The Gem City Chronicle
Dayton, Ohio: February 4, 1967

Proud parents, Helene and Paul Matthews of St. Finbar's parish applaud vigorously as unique identical twins, John and Kathleen, take a curtain call after their school's performance of *A Midsummer Night's Dream*.

Southern District Gazette
DeWitt, Arkansas: June 29, 1964
Dwayne and Ernestine Parkins mourn the loss of their two-year-old daughter, Connie May. She is also survived by grandparents, Sonia and Sunny-Bob Peters, Claire and Leroy Parkins, and identical twin brother James. In lieu of flowers the family asks that donations be made in Connie's name to the March of Dimes.

The Bibb County News
Macon, Georgia: January 4, 1987
Education: *Twins* magazine reporters expected to arrive at Central High on Thursday to interview Tulia and Earnest Gibbons, our fine state's unique set of identical twins.

The Pendleton Press
Franklin, West Virginia: November 1, 1996
Seeing double on Halloween? At St. Elizabeth's annual jack o'-lantern fund-raiser, the best costume award went to five-year-olds Angus and Cassie Claxonn of Oak Flat, who came as themselves. The youngsters are a rare breed. A set of opposite-sex identical twins. Foster mom, Raven's Breath, isn't telling us how that happened. Trick or treat? We're in the dark on that one.

"Raven's Breath? What kinda name is that?" said Leticia.

Thomlinson wasn't sure. "Is there any way of telling where these twins are now?"

"I'll give it my best shot."

Leticia cross-referenced the names through every possible entry these twins might have made through life. A kaleidoscope of records was considered. They included twin networking groups and armed forces records, as well as death records. When all was complete, Thomlinson had what appeared to be promising addresses for the Matthews and Gibbons twins. Since Connie May Parkins was dead, James Parkins was in the clear. There was no record of any address for the Claxonn twins. Not even in Oak Flat, West Virginia.

Leticia loaded the collected data on the three sets of viable twins back into the computer. There was one remaining search to consider. Again, her fingers danced across the keys. She was looking to see if any of the six had ever been arrested for a crime. Both she and Thomlinson were left staring at a blank screen.

As far as CyberCentral was concerned, the six were as clean as the winds of winter.

Chapter 25

Angus was in the shed. The game board, originally designed for Monopoly, now had a New York City tourist map affixed to it, with a cellophane grid of squares overlaying it. One of the sound chips embedded under the surface of the map wasn't working. The chip, designed for use inside talking or musical greeting cards, and activated when the card was opened, resembled a shiny new dime. Angus studied it closely under the magnifying glass. He'd have to go online, order a new one, download the singing voice of Old Blue Eyes, and slip it back into its sleeve under the Statue of Liberty National Monument. Of course, he'd lay out the extra bucks for an overnight delivery. What good was the game if it didn't sing?

"Angus!"

His sister was a screamer. It usually meant she saw a spider.

"What is it this time?" he hollered back.

"It's got a zillion legs! Come quick."

He put down the chip and headed inside to deal with the skittering demon. En route, he remembered the last time he heard those lungs in high-pitch mode. It wasn't that long ago.

* * *

"Angus!" It sounded more like the shriek of a wounded hawk than a human scream, and it awakened him. It was nearing four in the morning, and the small house was otherwise quiet. Where was his sister? And, more important, where was Father?

"Angus!"

He followed the anguish-filled scream to the cellar, finding his sister, stripped naked and bound to the porcelain enamel-topped table in the room behind the furnace. Father lay sprawled in the corner, his arms and face covered in sweat; his pants at his knees; a honing blade at his side. He was breathing heavily and reeking of alcohol. Had he succumbed to its anesthetizing effects? Angus hoped so. He shook him. Father made no sound or movement.

He approached Cassie. Tears trickled down her face, where eruptions of exposed tissue oozed blood.

"He raped me after butchering my face," she whimpered.

"Why didn't you call out before . . . ?"

"He said he'd kill me if I made any noise. I waited until I figured he'd passed out."

"Shsss. It's okay. I'm here."

"Please. Help me."

Angus unfastened leather straps, took Cassie into his arms, and carried her up to their cramped sleeping quarters, his eyes coming to rest on the corner of the glass face of a Pachinko machine that they had ceased to play with. It served now as a catchall for soiled clothing. Shoving the laundry aside, he used his fist to shatter the glass and collected the ball bearings contained inside. Running to his dresser, he retrieved a sock and poured in the half-inch spheres. Thus armed, he returned to the room and beat his father to death.

Chapter 26

Thomlinson, Aligante, and Driscoll were seated around the Lieutenant's desk in what had become a war room. A detailed map of the city was displayed on an upright particleboard behind them, red thumb tacks denoting where the bodies had been found. Driscoll was discouraged. To date, there had been no calls to the Tip Line from anyone seeing anything suspicious in the two restrooms, on the bridge, or onboard the USS *Intrepid*. These sons of bitches were good, he thought.

He glanced over to the corner of his desk where the two-inch letters of the *New York Post*'s headline stared back at him: DOUBLE ☺ ☺ TROUBLE!! He had alerted the media that the string of killings may have been committed by a set of male and female identical twins. The populace at large was urged to report any sightings of such look-alikes.

Thomlinson was already in the loop, so the Lieutenant took the time to explain the significance of Turner syndrome in twin births to Margaret.

When he had completed his X and Y summation, it was Thomlinson's turn to speak.

"Our search produced four sets of twins that fit the profile. The oldest pair is in their early fifties, the youngest is sixteen."

"Four sets from all that newsprint? Some rare condition," said Margaret.

"Turner syndrome itself isn't so rare," Driscoll said. "It hits one in two thousand females. It's when you factor in the possibility of it affecting identical twins that the numbers get infinitesimal. In any case, it's their DNA that'll be their downfall, rare or not."

Thomlinson continued with his report.

"I kept the initial search inside the United States. Leticia is checking on similar articles abroad. She'll let me know what she comes up with so we can prepare our protocol for Interpol and any other foreign agencies. Back to the land of the free. I placed a call to Ohio . . . to the Dayton Police, there. I filled them in on the details of our investigation. They accommodated me by paying a visit to a local address I had come up with for John Matthews, the first twin on the list. Turns out he lives in a camper just outside of town. Neighbors report he spends most of his time hoisting bottles of Rolling Rock and yelling at the TV. And while our last tourist was being murdered here in the Big Apple, Matthews was drinking himself into a stupor at one of Dayton's bars. This according to Dayton PD, who were able to substantiate his alibi. On to his twin sister, Kathleen. The woman succumbed to Alzheimer's at an early age. Six months before the killing spree began in New York she had wandered off the grounds of her Florida nursing home and was hit and killed by a rented Jeep driven by two college preppies on spring break."

"Puts the Matthewses off the list," said Margaret.

"Fate had other plans for the Gibbons twins," Thomlinson continued. "I located a discreet Web site for Tulia Gibbons who, three years ago, opened 'The Best Little Whore House in Savannah, Georgia.' She has no criminal record. Probably because Elijah McCormack, a state senator, was a frequent visitor. So the tabloids report. Somehow, I couldn't see a madam who makes a living offa tourism leave her emporium to knock off tourists in New York. Besides, our little entrepreneur was busy setting up Tulia's Too, a second den of iniquity, while the city was under siege."

"What became of her brother?"

"Ah, government records tell all. The guy's a nuclear engineer working for the navy. He's currently stationed at a submarine base in New London, Connecticut."

"That puts him pretty close to the crime scene. No?" said Margaret.

"According to his commanding officer, he's working on a nondiscretionary project to update the computer technology onboard the USS *John Marshall* and the USS *Triton.* His work record is clean. And his log provides a perfect alibi."

"What about the teen twins?"

"On them I've got something interesting. About where they were born."

"Oak Flat?" said Driscoll.

"Mining country," said Thomlinson. "In Pendleton County, West Virginia. At the base of the Allegheny Mountains. Almost uninhabited. But here's the good part. Closest cluster of residents would be on an Indian reservation, three miles outside of town, and according to the news article a Raven's Breath was listed as the twins' foster mom."

"You thinking what I'm thinking?" said Margaret making a scalping motion with her hand.

"We could be getting lucky," said Driscoll with a grin.

Chapter 27

The late afternoon skies were overcast above the lush flora of the Bronx Zoo. Earlier, a sudden summer thunderstorm had sent the zoo's visitors and most of its predators in search of shelter. With the pavement still wet, one of the zoo's hot dog vendors pushed his aluminum cart to its customary spot on the path that led to the Ethiopian Baboon Reserve. It would be a few minutes before the crowds ventured outside again to resume their gawking.

Adjusting the flames on the gas canisters beneath tubs of simmering frankfurters, the vendor hadn't noticed he had customers. A high-pitched voice startled him.

"Say, ma man, how much you charge for yo hot dogs?" It was the voice of a gruff-looking wiry-haired youth. Another slovenly teen crowded his cart.

"Two dollars," the Pakistani merchant stammered.

"Man, that be highway robbery," said the youth, flashing a sardonic grin. "Freddie, don't you think ma man here is dissin' us?"

"I don't set the prices. I just sell the stuff," said the vendor.

The tormentor's smile, conveying its veiled threat, froze.

The youth's switchblade was pressing hard against the vendor's waist.

"Please, please. I want no trouble," pleaded the vendor.

"Yo, ma man," the second youth taunted. "Leroy here is a mean mother and there'd be no stoppin' him if he gets pissed. Tell ya what we're gonna do. I'll tell Leroy to lose the blade while you hand over yo cash. You catchin' my drift?"

With unsteady hands, the Pakistani rummaged through his pockets and produced a handful of singles.

"That's all you got?" squawked Leroy, grabbing hold of the loot.

"My shift just started."

"You shittin' me?"

"I am a truthful man. My shift just started. Those singles are mine."

"Not any more," said Leroy, jamming the fistful of dollars into the pocket of his oversized trousers.

"Yo, Leroy. It be time to split," said the second culprit, his ears detecting the distinctive sound of an approaching moped.

As the pair of petty thieves strutted away from the shaken merchant, the hot dog vendor flagged down the scooter-mounted security guard.

"I've been held up!" he cried, pointing his finger in the direction of the fleeing thieves.

The guard revved up his scooter and took off after the pair. When the two robbers caught sight of their pursuer, they sprinted up a grassy knoll that was bordered by a ten-foot-high steel fence.

"C'mon, Freddie, we gotta get outta the park," hollered Leroy, climbing to the top of the fence and hurling himself over, dropping twenty-five feet on the other side, where the fence was supported by fifteen feet of standing concrete.

"Wait for me," Freddie shouted, hurrying up behind him.

Midway up the fence, Freddie glanced over his shoulder. The security guard had parked his scooter at the bottom of the knoll and was marching up the hill, nightstick in hand.

Eyeballing the guard, the fleeing thief climbed higher. He froze when he reached the top. On the expanse below, he saw four black baboons baring saber teeth and advancing toward Leroy, who had hit the ground hard and was now scrambling on all fours. As Freddie watched in horror, the largest primate pounced on his doomed friend. The animal's canines tore into Leroy's flesh, lacerating both tendon and bone. Leroy let out a bloodcurdling scream as fluid from his punctured lungs filled his trachea. In the seconds that followed, the baboons tore Leroy's body to shreds.

It took nearly an hour for three animal handlers, armed with stun guns, to corral the baboons and force them back into their cave.

By now, a handful of uniformed policemen, EMTs, and a plainclothes detective had arrived. They joined three coroner's assistants who were busy scooping up Leroy's remains and stuffing them into a body bag. The curious baboons watched the activity through a thick metal grid that sealed the mouth of their sanctuary.

Detective Luis Raios, dispatched from the Fifty-second Precinct, had never entered a wild animal's den before. He felt jittery at the sight of the four baboons, their faces pressed hard against the steel grid, examining his every move. He knew he was an intruder, trespassing on their limited kingdom. He walked toward a cluster of boulders in the center of the expanse, aware of the anxious primate eyes of the baboons. In that instant, Detective Raios felt what he had never felt before in his metropolitan life. Like prey. He saw in those sets of sienna brown eyes the impulse to kill, and he knew he was the target of that impulse.

"And what do we have here?" he muttered, slipping on a latex glove before reaching in, behind the boulders.

He had come upon an odd item for the baboons' lair: a ladies' brown high-heel shoe. Rotating the shoe in his hand, he deciphered remnants of letters on its inner side: G cc. S ze 6 ½ . Gucci? Size 6 ½? He examined a dark stain on the shoe's heel. Baboon shit . . . or human blood? he wondered.

And where was the other shoe? He scanned the immediate area. Nothing. Cautiously, he approached a second cluster of rocks that adjoined the baboons' quarters. A putrid stench assailed him.

"Don't they ever hose out that cave?" he yelled to the trio of animal handlers.

"A crew goes in there once a month," said one, moseying on over to where the detective was standing.

"Don't you smell that?" Raios winced, popping a handful of tic tacs into his mouth.

"Whoa!" the handler gasped.

"I'd better check out that cave," said Raios. "Any chance of moving those overgrown monkeys and raising the gate?"

"But we just got them in there!"

"Then I suggest you get them out."

The overlook, west of the grassy knoll, was now congested with spectators. When the immediate area was cleared, the animal handler approached a small metal box embedded in a concrete wall near the baboons' cave. Using a brass key, he unlocked the box and depressed a button inside. The gate on the mouth of the cave went up.

"Detective, you may want to stand behind me," the handler suggested.

"You got that right," said Raios.

Though the gate had been lifted, the baboons remained inside.

"They waiting for some sort of invitation?"

"C'mon, Whiskers . . . c'mon, Plato . . . come on out, Joe . . . Figaro, c'mon. It's time to play," coaxed the handler.

"Are they always this shy?"

"Never."

"Keep tryin'."

"Hey guys, the rain's over. C'mon now, I got a handful of Good 'n' Plenty. They're your favorite." He shook his hand, rattling the sugar-coated candies. "Come and get them."

The baboons stood defiantly inside.

"Maybe they lost their sweet tooth," said Raios.

The handler approached their hollow and sprinkled the pink and white confections on the ground just outside the mouth of the cave.

Nothing happened.

"They're not goin' for it," said Raios.

"These things always work. There's something really wrong here." The handler stepped back. "Okay, have it your way, guys."

With Raios in tow, the handler sauntered over to the metal box and depressed a red button.

"I'm setting off an ultrasonic sound inside their cave. It's a frequency we won't hear. But it's like fingernails on a blackboard to them. It'll get 'em outta there in a hurry!"

"In what kind of mood?" Raios grumbled as the pack of baboons let out a ferocious growl. "That howling doesn't make me feel too comfortable."

The four primates lumbered out of the cave and scrambled for the Good 'n' Plenty.

"These the same guys that ripped apart that kid an hour ago?" Raios asked, eyes fixed on the docile foursome.

"The very same."

"Then I'm glad I'm in here with you."

The two other handlers netted the baboons.

"Detective, the cave's all yours," the lead handler announced.

"I hope ya got some of those candies left. That smell is only gonna get worse inside and I'm fresh outa tic tacs."

The handler tossed Raios the near-empty box.

Armed with a Parks Department flashlight, a mouthful of licorice, and a hunch, Raios approached the cave. Was it merely the stench of the baboons' habitat that assaulted his sinuses, restricted his breathing, and filled him with nausea? Or was it something else?

He crouched down and ventured inside the cave, his eardrums reverberating with the throbbing of his heart. Ten feet in, he heard a buzzing sound. Following it, he found a frenzy of flies disturbed by his flashlight.

Beyond the flies, the beam of light exposed a rib cage. It appeared to be human. And still fastened to the end of one elongated fleshy bone Raios found what he was looking for: the matching Gucci shoe.

Chapter 28

The voice of the TV spokesman for Hair Weave International startled Driscoll out of his sleep. What happened to Robert Taylor and Lana Turner? he wondered, taking in his surroundings. The last thing he remembered was Lana Turner turning down the overtures of Mr. Taylor in a black-and-white film on American Movie Classics.

"Call me now and I'll throw in a year's supply of conditioner at no extra cost!" the adman barked.

"No! I don't need a hair weave. And you can keep your damn conditioner!" Driscoll growled, pulling himself out of the recliner. "Where the hell's that remote?"

The TV spokesman was dialing the number that appeared at the bottom of the screen. Driscoll heard the sound of a phone ringing.

"Yeah, right!"

He leaned forward and depressed the TV's power button and watched Mr. Hair Weave fade to black. Silence prevailed. Momentarily.

Again, he heard the sound of a ringing phone.

Mary?

Following the sound into the kitchen, he spotted his cell

phone next to the plate that had held his ham-and-cheese sandwich and answered it.

"Sorry if I woke you." It was Margaret. She sounded anxious. "The ME just called. We may have ourselves another one."

"Where'd they strike this time?"

"The Bronx Zoo."

"The ten o'clock news did a piece about the guy who jumped into the baboons' compound and got ripped to shreds. You're not talking about him, are you?"

"If it wasn't for him, we may have never found the other body."

"What other body?"

"A precinct detective found the half-eaten body of a young woman in their den. Pearsol's finding it hard to come up with an exact cause of death, with the condition of the remains and all, but she does have sharp force trauma to the right parietal. How she ended up as a Happy Meal for the baboons is anybody's guess."

"Got an ID on her?"

"I'll say. Try Abigail Shewster. *The* Abigail Shewster."

"Holy shit!"

"We sent out for dental records just to confirm, but her California driver's license was found at the scene. It makes sense. She arrived in town last Thursday for this week's grand opening of the Zoo's Old World Primate Pavilion. The one the Shewster Pharmaceutical Corporation had so liberally funded."

"California. That makes her a domestic tourist."

"Wouldn't be the first time a perp changed the rules."

"Hold on. I got another call coming in. And I think I know who it is."

Chapter 29

The Mayor's call was to inform Driscoll that Malcolm Shewster would be at Gracie Mansion at six o'clock sharp. It was safe to say that the pharmaceutical mogul would not be in a cheerful mood. Driscoll, too, had been "invited" to attend. That gave him a little more than five hours to get a rundown on the investigation and come up with an answer as to why the New York City Police Department failed to protect the daughter of one of the richest and most influential men in the state of California.

The Lieutenant knew the mayoral residence well. He had been a guest of many of its former illustrious tenants. David Dinkins boasted a powerful backhand and often preferred to discuss important police matters on the tennis court. Ed Koch was a gourmet, and Driscoll remembered some memorable entrees. Abe Beame was a gracious host, boastful of the grandeur of the estate. But, with the mansion's present inhabitant, it was strictly business. And business his way.

A member of the Mayor's security detail ushered Driscoll into a Georgian-styled reception area, where a second officer escorted him into the Blue Room. Sitting in a plush divan, a wiry-haired man with eyes the color of Caribbean waters was arguing vehemently with the Mayor.

"John," the Mayor said without rising, "Mr. Shewster."

Shewster, clad in a charcoal gray three-piece Armani suit, resembled George C. Scott in some of his memorable roles. Driscoll eyed the handsome silver-haired man with his head tilted forward, his stern mouth above a tightly fitted tie, with eyes simmering, and a look of contempt filling an angry face. He acknowledged Driscoll with a nod.

"The city is responsible for the grief of a father who has lost his daughter because of our ineptitude," the Mayor pronounced.

"Mr. Shewster, I know what it's like to lose a daughter," Driscoll said, offering his hand. "My heart goes out to you. We did everything . . ."

"We didn't do enough!" Reirdon barked.

Shewster, deaf to their exchange, stared at the Mayor. "This killer is laughing at you. The both of you. It's his show, isn't it, Mr. Mayor?"

Reirdon saw the accentuation as a jab.

"Like hell it is!" he growled. "This city is my town."

"My daughter's body was ripped apart by zoo animals. Save your proclamations for your next campaign."

Driscoll studied Shewster's face. It was filled with pain.

"Tell me why a twenty-two-year-old woman who comes to your city for a ribbon-cutting ceremony ends up as dinner for caged beasts."

The Mayor's eyes caught Driscoll's. There was no answer in their exchange.

"A year ago, research and development at Shewster Pharmaceuticals, my company, introduced a miracle drug. After two weeks on it, your arteries are swept clean. Its chemical compound had been designed to Roto-Rooter those arteries like Drano through clogged pipes. Imagine that! An end to heart surgery."

Neither the Mayor nor Driscoll knew where he was going.

Shewster reached in his vest pocket, produced a Cohiba Crystal Corona, and lit it.

"Word reached me that someone in our department had leaked the formula for this compound to Merck. Now, mind you, our miraculous drug was going through its preliminary testing. We were not yet ready to go before the FDA with our breakthrough. We didn't want to cure the heart this year only to kill the kidney the next. But that doesn't matter," he grumbled, watching a spiral of cigar smoke loft skyward. "What does matter was that our secret had been funneled to the other side by someone on my payroll. As CEO, what was I to do?" Shewster's eyes narrowed. "I fired the entire department! Four hundred and sixty-three pink slips. Problem solved. Leak sealed."

"You can't be suggesting I fire my entire police force?" said Reirdon.

"Drastic developments require drastic measures."

"Mr. Shewster, I'm an elected official. I'm not the CEO of some West Coast medical company. I can't fire the entire police force!"

"Then what is it an elected official can do?"

"Not that we live in two different worlds. But corporate maneuvering has no hold on city affairs."

"Well, while your city-paid sentinels are standing watch, your killer is knocking off ducks in a pond. And to top it off, nobody sees a goddamn thing until the carcass floats to the top."

Driscoll was too familiar with the feelings of loss that preyed on Shewster. And of how bitterness spawned rage.

"Why is the body count still climbing?"

"It's just not that simple," Reirdon replied.

"Let me tell you what is simple. I'm prepared to offer a large sum of money to the man who delivers the psychopath that killed my daughter, an only daughter, found ravaged inside a goddamn cave, three thousand miles from home, in some zoo."

Tears welled up in Shewster's eyes.

Hmm. Human after all, thought Driscoll.

The grieving father produced a small vial of pills and popped two into his mouth.

"This drug grossed fifty-two million dollars in first-quarter sales this year alone. I never thought that one day I'd be popping them myself. Here. Be my guest." Shewster tossed the vial to Reirdon.

"A good Merlot does it for me," the Mayor replied, catching the plastic bottle in midair and handing it to Driscoll.

"Phenaladin 500 mg. Warning: May cause drowsiness. Avoid consumption of alcohol," Driscoll read. "They wouldn't like that at Sullivan's. I'd better stick to my Harp."

"These are the best hostility eradicators and anxiety relievers money can buy," Shewster boasted. "Okay, enough informality. Let's talk about your inquiry. Tell me what you've got so far."

"Mr. Shewster, our investigations are confidential," said Driscoll.

"Lieutenant, I'm not 'Mr. Joe Public.' My corporation hasn't donated millions of dollars toward police associations for nothing; not to mention the large contributions to your mayor's campaign. You'll tell me what I want to know."

"It's okay, John. Tell him," the Mayor said.

Driscoll began to fill the man in on the details of the case.

"We were initially going on the theory that only one killer was involved. Now we know there are two. We think acting in tandem. Each of them slipped up once, leaving behind a telltale trace. We found the bloodied fingernail of one of the killers at a crime scene atop the Brooklyn Bridge. Remnants of human skin, detected under the fingernails of a later victim, confirmed a second killer. Then, DNA analysis unveiled something extraordinary. Our killers are twins. Male and female identical twins."

"No such thing!" said Shewster.

"We thought so, too. But our tests are conclusive. The female suffers from a medical condition known as Turner syndrome. It makes the pair genetically identical in all aspects but gender. It also makes them a rarity."

"Tell me more."

"Our first search encompassed the United States, where four such pairs were discovered within a time frame that would make them possible suspects. In order to diagnose Turner syndrome, a blood test called a karyotype must be done. But in all likelihood, no one would have done that at birth. It would have been done later in life. And it has to have happened after 1959, the first year they discovered the method to test for the syndrome. Based on their age, all four fall within that time frame too. We've already ruled out three sets of twins as suspects. Our investigation continues on the fourth while we continue our probe outside the United States."

"What's the hold up on the fourth pair?"

"There's reason to believe the pair had been raised on an Indian reservation outside of a small town in West Virginia."

"Where they picked up their penchant for scalping, no doubt."

"Our investigation is now focused on that reservation."

"The apprehension of these killers is Job One with this administration," said Reirdon. "Rest assured that every resource available to the New York City Police Department will be deployed."

"Save your speech for the tabloids. You still haven't explained how my daughter's body ended up with the apes."

An exasperated Reirdon glared at the man. "On with the details, John."

"These twins like to showcase their crime scenes. Forensic evidence indicates your daughter was killed just outside the baboons' compound and that her body was propped up on its protective fencing. We suspect that during the night her body slipped and fell from the fence."

Sadness returned to Shewster's face. The man's hand gesture entreated Driscoll to go on and so he did.

"We've detected a pattern. These twins have apparently chosen New York City tourist attractions as their killing fields. We discovered the first victim at the Museum of Natural History, a second on the Wonder Wheel at Coney Island. Another on the Brooklyn Bridge, a fourth aboard the USS *Intrepid*, and most recently, sadly for you, at the zoo. All the victims thus far have been either foreign tourists or, in your daughter's case, an out-of-towner. Each victim is felled by a forceful blow to the right side of the head. And, of course, the scalping. We're not sure how that ties in, but serial killers have been known to take trophies from their victims. This killer—"

"You mean killers," Shewster barked.

"We don't know they're working in tandem."

"Are these sick bastards playing some sort of game? Some sort of competition as to who can kill more people? And, if so, what would the prize be?"

"We don't know their motive," Driscoll said, flatly.

"Is it money they're after? Maybe the bounty I'm considering will turn them against each other."

"There's been no evidence of robbery. In many cases, crimes of this nature don't follow any standard of normalcy. They may be simply getting off on the act of killing."

An electronic purr interrupted the conversation.

"Driscoll, here."

The look on the Lieutenant's face confirmed what the Mayor feared most.

"Another one?" Reirdon asked.

Driscoll nodded.

"Where?"

"Central Park." He stood. "If it's all right with you, I'd like to get over there right away."

The Mayor agreed.

As Driscoll disappeared out the door, Shewster exhaled a cloud of cigar smoke and raised an eyebrow at Sully Reirdon.

Chapter 30

Hours before news of the latest murder broke, Angus, clad in Old Navy overalls and a blue polo shirt, slid into a fiberglass seat across from his sister. The all-night diner was near empty. It would be some time before the early morning rush of breakfast-hungry New Yorkers would descend upon the eatery. The only other night owl was a bulbous female patron seated diagonally across from the booth where the teens were hunkered down. She had stopped stuffing herself with corned beef on rye long enough to stare openly at Cassie's scarred face.

"And what the hell are you lookin' at?" Cassie asked.

The patron cast her eyes downward and returned to her meal. Cassie turned her attention back to her brother.

"Score?" she asked, eyes wide and expectant.

"Of course," her brother said with a grin, before disappearing behind an oversized laminated menu. "Hot fudge sundae for me! You?"

"Stack of blueberry pancakes on the way. Tell me! Tell me!"

Angus's face floated up balloonlike from behind the list of delicacies. "It all began with a stroll . . ."

Chapter 31

An anonymous 911 caller had brought the police to Strawberry Fields, a two-and-a-half-acre tear-shaped landscape inside Central Park. The well-manicured expanse had been dedicated to the memory of the slain music icon John Lennon, who lived and died a stone's throw away at the Dakota on West Seventy-second. The site boasted a bronze plaque listing 121 countries that endorsed the area as a Garden of Peace. Driscoll pondered the incongruity as he stared into the face of the city's latest victim, propped, marionette-like, against a bald cypress that marked the sanctuary's northern perimeter. Dead eyes, open and sullen, returned his gaze.

"She's been dead eight to ten hours." It was the voice of Medical Examiner Larry Pearsol, who had sidled up next to Driscoll. "No defensive wounds or evidence of sexual assault. ID has her as Antonia Fucilla, from Tuscany. What she's doing inside a New York City park, alone, after dark is what I want to know."

"She wasn't alone," said Driscoll, tracing a gloved finger along the linear head wound made by the killer's weapon. His frustration was escalating. He turned and barked orders at the flock of Crime Scene detectives. "I want every inch of ground swept within a hundred-foot radius. Cigarette butts, gum wrappers, food containers, the goddamn soil if it looks out of place. Anything! You find a snipped fingernail, I want it bagged."

"Whaddya make of the scalping?" asked Pearsol, eyes on the ravaged head.

"Serial killers are collectors, Larry. But I'm betting these scalps are more than just a trophy. These lunatics are doing something with them. Though I'll be damned if I can figure out what that is."

"The Indians used to post them on a stick."

"I know. Nineteenth-century machismo in the Wild Wild West."

Margaret approached, wearing a smug look. "The vic's got surprise painted on her face and my money says the killer put it there."

"These killers are no Picassos."

"They think they are. They're posing the bodies, right?"

"Right."

"Well, someone's supposed to get their message."

"Meaning?"

"Follow me on this one. The woman at the museum is shoved up the ass of a dinosaur. Our vic on the Wonder Wheel gets taken for a ride. They prop a guy from Kamikaze Central inside the cockpit of an American fighter plane for Chrissake! This pair is doling out humiliation. God knows what they had planned for the German on the bridge because the killing was interrupted and how they posed Miss Moneybags at the zoo is anybody's guess 'cause she did a Humpty-Dumpty."

"That'd take careful planning and a lot of smarts," said Pearsol.

"We may be dealing with psychos. But nobody said they had to be stupid. They've got an agenda, these two. I say it's spearheaded by vengeance."

"You may be right," Driscoll said, impressed with Margaret's insight.

"It's textbook. Ask any profiler and he'll tell you these killers are inflicting punishment to match the way they were punished. Look at her," she said, motioning to the murdered woman. "There's no evidence of a struggle. She knew her killer."

"That'd give us motive and would indicate the killings weren't random. You know? I think you are right! We've been looking at these attacks from the wrong side. Sure! The answer may lie in what the victims had in common. Margaret, I could kiss you."

"For now, I'm gonna settle for a pat on the back," she said, hoping her angst wasn't showing.

Chapter 32

"I had placed a call to the West Virginia Department of Health and Human Resources making an inquiry about this Raven's Breath ever being part of their foster care system. A Cynthia Travis there said she'd check into it." It was Margaret on the phone. She sounded excited. Driscoll listened intently to what she had to say. "The woman just called back, said she'd found no records in foster care but had run the name through other state agencies. On the line with her, by way of a conference call, was Pauline Curley of the North American Registry of Midwives. Her search shows a Raven's Breath as being a midwife in 1991, residing on the Catawba Indian Reservation outside of Oak Flat. Cedric's news article, which ID'd her as the pair's foster parent, indicated the twins were five in 1996. The numbers add up. She probably was the midwife who assisted in their birth!"

"Great work, Sergeant. I'd say it's time to have a powwow with the Indians. While I'm gone, I want you and Cedric to check into the backgrounds of the vics. We'll run with your theory. See if they share anything in common that would warrant a set of twins wanting them dead."

"On it."

Driscoll wasn't fond of flying. Once the aircraft came to a complete stop on a regional airfield outside of Healing Springs, Virginia, he stood and grabbed his carry-on luggage. Anxious to get on with the investigation, he stepped onto the tarmac and headed for the Avis Car Rental Booth to secure the Dodge Intrepid he had reserved.

Traveling north on Route 220, he paralleled the Allegheny Mountains. The sun had climbed high in the sky, casting shadows on the red clay and evergreen mix that made up the countryside. He crossed the border into West Virginia at a town called Harper. It boasted a convenience store, an Exxon station, a single-screen movie theater, and a bait-and-tackle shop. Driscoll followed the instructions of a gas station attendant and climbed the side of the mountain into Oak Flat, destined for the Catawba Indian Reservation, which spread for two miles beyond the northern edge of town.

It was nearing 3:00 P.M. when the Lieutenant parked the rental beside a pine cabin that appeared to serve as the reservation's produce market and general store. It also marked the entrance to the Catawba land. Driscoll stepped inside. On the far wall hung a four-foot stretch of leather that was adorned with a painted buffalo head.

"Welcome," the Native American shopkeeper said.

Driscoll took note of the necklace the man was wearing. A string of bear claws. Levi's and a well-worn plaid flannel shirt clung to the man's angular frame. Around his forehead he wore a red bandanna, the color of blood. What concerned Driscoll, though, was that he was loading a handful of bullets into a Winchester rifle. "Going hunting?" he asked.

"For deer," the man replied. "The name's Bill Waters." He offered his hand. "You?"

"Driscoll. I'm also hunting."

"On Catawba land?"

"For Raven's Breath."

"Why? Did she do something wrong?"

"She delivered babies. No?"

"Nothing wrong with that. What do you want with Raven's Breath? You're police, right?"

"Adoption service," Driscoll lied, not wishing to cause alarm. "I simply wish to talk with her."

Waters ran his hand down the carved wood of the Winchester rifle, then doused it with an oil-soaked rag.

"What is it you need to talk with her about?"

"Babies."

"I'm afraid you won't find her here."

"Where would I find her?"

"Many miles away."

"In which direction?"

"Down. Six feet. She's buried in Blue Ridge Cemetery."

"Oh, I see. I'm sorry."

Waters nodded.

"Someone must have kept records of the births. Do you know who that might have been?"

"Raven's Breath had a daughter. Taniqua. You can speak with her. She lives here, on the reservation. Look for a small house up the road with a thatched roof."

"Thank you."

The woman who answered the door appeared to be in her late thirties, sporting a denim shirt over faded jeans. On her feet, she wore a pair of hand-sewn moccasins.

"I'm John Driscoll," he announced. "Are you Taniqua?"

"Yes, I'm Taniqua."

Driscoll sensed her reserve. He had experienced it before, many times. But always as a policeman. How would someone from an adoption agency react? Dressed in khakis and an Izod? He'd have to wing it.

"I understand your mother was Raven's Breath and that she was a midwife."

"Yes. That's true."

"I'm from the Mid-Atlantic Adoption Agency. I'm seeking information on a set of twins your mother may have delivered."

The woman flinched. Driscoll caught it.

"Please, come inside." Taniqua walked inside the small house, Driscoll trailing in behind her. The woman sat at a loom and resumed her weaving.

"What is it you're making?" he asked.

"A shroud."

"Someone die?"

"No. But someone will this week. Their burial cloak must be ready." She gestured for Driscoll to take a seat. "What is it you'd like to know?"

She was deeply guarded now. Her eyes searched Driscoll's face.

"I'd like to start by asking you some questions about your mother."

"My mother? My mother is dead."

"I'm very sorry for your loss. I'm interested in some children . . ."

"Does this involve a white man's adoption?"

"Something like that."

The woman continued her weaving.

"We believe your mother was the midwife for a set of twins born sixteen years ago. A boy and a girl. Did she keep records of her deliveries?"

"No," she answered, but Driscoll read worry in her face. She used a set of shears to cut the end off a length of yarn.

"This cloak is for a baby," she sighed. "Our infant mortality rate is forty percent higher than the white man's. The nearest pediatrician is thirty miles away. But even he would be of little help now."

Driscoll read the sadness in her face.

After a moment, he continued. "The twins were Angus and Cassie Claxonn."

Taniqua flinched. Again, Driscoll caught it

"March 1991. You were what? Twenty? Twenty-five? Surely, you'd remember."

"I don't," said the woman.

Driscoll knew she was lying. He wondered why.

"These were twins, Taniqua. You must remember twins being born."

"The only thing I remember about my twenties was dropping out of school and getting high on peyote."

A silence passed between the two. It was Taniqua, oddly enough, who broke it.

"Maybe they were born at the hospital in Franklin," she said.

"Did your mother work there?"

"Yes," said Taniqua. "Your white twins must have been born there."

Although Driscoll was certain the woman was hiding something, he left her to her weaving.

Chapter 33

Driscoll headed over to Franklin Medical Center, where his reception wasn't warm. In condescending fashion, the administrator made it clear that employment records were confidential. As he stepped out of her office, an attractive secretary silently mouthed: "Never worked here," and handed him a flyer for Prilosec. On its back was scrawled "Sheryl—304-358-7038."

Climbing into the rented Dodge, he tapped the flyer on the steering wheel and grinned. He checked his watch. It was nearing five-thirty and he was hungry. What he needed was a solid meal before heading south to the motel holding his reservation for an overnight stay.

He headed east, toward Oak Flat, where he discovered that Main Street was a pit stop for U.S. Route 33. It featured a Mobil gas station, the Duck Inn Whiskey Emporium, and Luellen's Diner. He pulled up in front of Luellen's. Inside, the metal walls and a string of steel stools lining a Formica-topped counter reminded Driscoll of Norman Rockwell's "The Runaway," where a freckled-face truant was being treated to an ice cream cone by a policeman. Driscoll straddled one of the stools and looked around. A buxom gal, with

the name MaryLou embroidered on her apron, cast a wink at
the gent she had been flirting with and sashayed over.

"Hi there," she said, sliding a glass of water, a paper napkin, and a set of eating utensils onto the counter. "What'll
it be?"

"How's the beef stew?" Driscoll asked, looking at a
blackboard featuring the menu.

"Chock-full of garden fresh veggies."

He gave her a nod.

MaryLou poured a ladleful of the stew into a bowl and
placed it before Driscoll. "You'll be wantin' crackers with
that," she said, placing a handful of Saltines next to his meal.

Driscoll took out the area map he had been given by the
Avis attendant, palmed it flat across the counter, and found
Sugar Grove, where he'd spend the night. His actions were
watched intently by two of the locals, who were seated in a
nearby booth, sipping from bottles of Rolling Rock beer.

"Can I expect any traffic on Route 21 this time of day?"
Driscoll asked MaryLou.

"You are definitely an out-of-towner," she said. "Where
ya headin'?"

"Sugar Grove."

The sound of a whining dog interrupted them.

"Orville, that damn mongrel of yours is loose again."
MaryLou cast a glare at one of the beer-guzzling duo. "He
puts his paw through that screen door one more time, I'm
gonna shoot his ass off."

Orville bolted for the door.

His partner, who looked like the scarecrow from *The Wizard of Oz*, eyed the contents of Orville's beer bottle. After a
quick look outside, he downed half of what remained.

Orville returned from tying up his dog and eyed Driscoll
and his map. He glanced at his buddy and grinned, displaying incomplete rows of nicotine-stained teeth.

Sensing a scene, MaryLou glared at the drunk. "Go on.
Get back to your booth before ya get yourself into trouble."

Orville cast a threatening glare at Driscoll before following her instructions.

"Pay no mind to those two idiots," MaryLou said, eyeing Driscoll's designer khakis and Izod shirt. "What brings a snazzy dresser like you to Oak Flat?"

"I'm looking for a set of twins. Teenagers. A boy and a girl."

"What'd they do?" she asked, sensing he was either a cop or a private investigator.

"Plenty! We're talkin' one bad pair."

"It's them drugs, ya know. It's all the rage, now. Teenagers, huh? How old?"

"Sixteen or so."

"Well, I dunno if it'd help any, but a number of years back, maybe ten, there was a seta twins down here that fit that bill."

"Oh, yeah?"

"Two blond kids. A boy and a girl, like you said. Spittin' images. They lived on the Indian reservation. Cute little buggers, they were."

"You sure they lived on the reservation?"

"Sure as there're carrots in the stew."

Chapter 34

"Why'd you lie?" Driscoll asked, his eyes boring into Taniqua's.

The woman's face flooded with color. With a long exhalation, Taniqua surrendered to the inevitable.

"I'll tell you what you came to hear," she sighed. "Please, sit." Taniqua squatted on a prayer mat and faced Driscoll. "My mother was loved as a midwife. To her, every birth was special. To the tribe, she was its shaman. She talked to the spirits and they answered her. The mother of the twins you're looking for was a white woman, a drifter, who had come knocking on my mother's door, wanting an abortion. Said she was pregnant and that her brother had raped her. But the woman was near full-term, so my mother delivered the twins."

"Why'd you hold that back?"

"My mother didn't want to involve herself, or the tribe, in a white man's investigation of a rape. She assisted in the births and made no record of them. I lied because I didn't want to disgrace my mother."

Fair enough, Driscoll thought. "What became of the woman?"

"She disappeared after the babies were born."

"And the twins?"

"The birth of a set of twins to a Catawba tribe is considered an omen of good fortune, so my mother felt honored to raise them herself. But when they were going on seven, the woman returned for them. Said she and her brother were heading up north and had plans for the twins."

"What can you tell me about this woman and her brother?"

"Not much. I only saw the woman."

"Get a name?"

"No."

"What'd she look like?

"A very white woman. Blond hair. About my height. It was a long time ago."

"Was that the last time anyone heard from the twins?"

His question went unanswered. Not certain if he had been heard, Driscoll asked it again.

"Was that the last time—"

"It was," said Taniqua, sharply.

But something was astir in Taniqua's eyes. Driscoll waited.

"They've been sending me things."

"Things?" He felt a rush of adrenalin.

The woman's eyes locked onto Driscoll's as if seeking escape.

"Wait here." She stood up and disappeared into another room. When she returned, Driscoll's eyes widened at the sight of what she was holding in her hands. "I don't know what they mean." She handed her oddities to Driscoll.

The Lieutenant thought he had seen every butchery of the human body imaginable. But what he was now holding in his hands filled him with an unfamiliar mix of repugnancy and awe. He had located the scalps. Each had been stretched to fit a five-inch wooden hoop. The hair had been combed and their undersides had been scraped of all flesh. What was tattooed in their centers was a puzzlement.

Driscoll didn't know what to make of it. The zagging lines were sky blue. "Native American?" he asked.

"No," said Taniqua.

"Would it have been the custom to mark scalps like this years ago?"

"I wouldn't know."

"Why would they be sending them to you?"

"I don't know that, either. They came about a week apart in a padded envelope. 'Angus and Cassie' was the only thing written as a return address."

"Did you keep the envelopes?"

"No."

"Remember anything about the postmark? The city, maybe?"

She shook her head. "They're in trouble, aren't they?"

Driscoll didn't answer. "Are there any pictures of the twins?"

"There were. But they were burned with my mother and buried along with her ashes."

"All of them?"

"No," she said, sheepishly. She stood and disappeared again. When she returned, she produced a tattered black-and-white photo and handed it to Driscoll. "I keep it under my pillow."

There, captured in Kodak clarity, were the full figures of the pair as five-year-olds, standing side by side, holding a makeshift poster. It read: HAMESA RE YI HATCU.

Driscoll looked to Taniqua.

"It means, 'We Love You, Sis.' " She paused. "You're not from an adoption agency, are you?"

Driscoll smiled sympathetically, and the woman began to cry.

Chapter 35

Driscoll was anxious to decipher the meaning of the scalps' tattoos. He regretted not packing a laptop because his accommodations at the Sugar Grove Inn included access to the Internet.

Time to update Margaret. He punched in her number on his cell.

"How're things at Teepee Junction?" she asked.

"Didn't walk away with Tonto's autograph but we've got a positive ID on our twin killers and a dated photo to go with it. Number four on Cedric's list, Angus and Cassic Claxonn, have been mailing the scalps to an Indian woman on the reservation. I'm bringing them back with me. They hold a secret of their own."

"A secret?"

"Each one's been tattooed with a symbol of some kind."

"Native American?"

"That'd be too easy. I'm hoping the Internet will help me interpret their meaning. Where are we in finding a parallel between the victims?"

"There's very little listed anywhere on Shewster's daughter aside from her G-rated escapades with the highbrow socialites she ran with."

"Doubt there'd be a record of anything out of character had she been raised from the dead! Big money hides secrets."

"Tell that to the parents of Paris Hilton. We've got calls in to Interpol on the other vics from China, Japan, Germany, and Italy. They are all member countries. We're waiting to hear back."

"Good. What I want you to do now is get the names to the media. See if anyone can help us locate these Claxonn twins. Then I want you to run a check of reported rapes in and about West Virginia that would have occurred in 1990. We're looking especially for any involving incest."

Incest? Margaret's heart raced. "On it," she said.

Call completed, Driscoll unzipped his American Tourister carry-on and began to pack. Turning on the bedside radio, he heard an evangelist's voice: "Jesus saves! Repent you sinners! Praise the Lord, your God! The all-knowing Almighty who begs for your repentance. Turn your back, brothers and sisters on sinfulness and transgression, lest you become kindle for Satan and his disciples."

"Praise the Lord!" echoed Driscoll as he packed the last of his attire and headed for the door.

Chapter 36

Driscoll returned from his lawyer's office, where he had finally closed the deal on his house in Toliver's Point. Considering where he was in the investigation, he would have postponed it, but it had already been rescheduled twice. His lawyer warned him that any further delay could affect the buyer's closing commitment. Settling into his swivel chair, he peeled back the lid from his coffee container and logged in on the department's IBM desktop. His eye caught sight of his likeness on page one of yesterday's *Daily News*. The headline, emblazoned above his face, read: STILL THE BEST MAN FOR THE JOB??? Driscoll didn't know why he had kept the rag, suitable now for wrapping fish. Today's paper featured the photo of the youngsters, with CLAXONN inscribed above it. His capabilities were no longer for debate. Politically or otherwise.

"Goddamn you, Reirdon!" he grumbled, positioning the computer's arrow in the search field of the PC's monitor where he typed: SYMBOLS BLUE ZIGZAGS. The response was immediate. After a listing of four icon hawkers, including eBay, where you can get anything on the planet, twenty-four-seven, he learned from Doughtydesigns.com that blue zigzags are often used to illustrate one of the four elements: earth, air, water, and fire. In this case, water. Continuing his inquiry, he clicked on eRugGallery.com. They featured Serape blankets woven by the Navajo in the early 1800s, which included zigzags used as stripes. Blue was one of the preferred colors used in the weaving of the blankets. He made a mental note to check if the Catawba tribe was part of the Navaho nation. Scrolling further, a couple of fashion sites informed him that zigzag patterns were prevalent in the spring of 2005. But when his search led him to Wikipedia, the Internet's free encyclopedia, he learned that the tattoo was a genogram, commonly used to construct a family tree; it was also used to depict the family's health history and interpersonal relationships. Further search led him to a Web site for Northwestern University and instinct told him he had found what he'd been looking for. Academia unraveled the geno-gram's meaning: sexual abuse. He grinned. He had established motive.

As the computer made a whirring sound, Driscoll looked up to find Mr. Shewster standing in his doorway, holding a Dieffenbachia, adorned with a red ribbon banner.

"What's that for?" asked Driscoll. The banner on the small tree read: WORKING TOGETHER WE CAN BURY THE HATCHET. Driscoll found the fitting play on words amusing. "Great! You bring me a plant with poisonous sap?"

"According to my man in research and development, you're looking at the cure for multiple sclerosis. Give us another three years and we'll have it refined and capsulated. It'll be available in every Duane Reade."

"So, why give it to me?"

"To cure any hard feelings between us."

"Squawk! Squawk!" Driscoll's mechanical bird sounded.

"See? Your fine feathered friend knows a quality plant when he sees one."

Driscoll hit the OFF button on Socrates' claw.

"Some headline in yesterday's paper," Driscoll said. "If I

recall correctly, those were the exact words uttered in the Blue Room at Gracie Mansion."

"But today you're the toast of the town! Why look back? Wayward is the way of politics. Tsk. Tsk. Tsk." Shewster fanned out the small tree's plumage.

What was he up to? "Mr. Shewster, before we go any further, there's one thing we've got to resolve."

"And what's that?"

"You look me dead in the eye and tell me you had nothing to do with the fickleness of our illustrious Sully Reirdon."

"Lieutenant, you're holding on to baggage that is best left unclaimed."

"Dead in the eye," Driscoll repeated.

The businessman returned the Lieutenant's glare. "I had nothing to do with that headline."

Time froze. Shewster was the first to flinch.

"I'm only interested in catching the psycho who killed my daughter, or twin psychos, as you contend. It's been my only interest from the start. I needn't bore a lawman with the statistics of how many homicides go unsolved. With all due respect, even serial homicides! Take the Axeman of New Orleans, the Capital City murders in Madison, Wisconsin, the Frankfort Slasher in North Philadelphia, the Monster of Florence. Hell, the goddamn Zodiac Killer reigned for thirty years! I'll be damned if I'm going to stand by and watch these twisted twins do the same. I'm likely to be dead in thirty years! Let's face it. That early photo of Abigail's killers isn't the only likeness that's going to hit page one. You know it and I know it. All I'm asking is that you let a grieving man help. With my contacts, I can put together a team of physiognomy experts and graphic computer artists who can project their current-day likeness better than any civil servant the NYPD has on its payroll."

Driscoll studied Shewster's face. He saw a grieving parent looking for closure. The Lieutenant's own mirror had returned that look many times. "Couldn't hurt."

Chapter 37

WELCOME TO THE NEW YORK AQUARIUM

After he used his Discover card to gain admittance, a strong smell of fish assaulted his sinuses. He popped a stick of Doublemint into his mouth and listened to the voice that boomed over the site's loudspeaker: "Boys and girls, ladies and gentlemen, it's four o'clock. Time to feed the dolphins! Come join us in Pavilion Four."

The announcement caused a stir in the crowd. Families scurried toward the Big Top, where a school of dolphins were sheltered from the sun.

Joining the crowd, he climbed the steps of the bleachers, found a comfortable seat, and scanned the spectators. There were no sailor's caps to be found. Had he said baseball cap? There were dozens of those. Nah. That wouldn't be likely. It had to be a sailor's cap. He adjusted his. Although he felt somewhat like a dork, it was a British one, like he'd been asked. The Royal Navy issue porkpie cap stood out. Perhaps he'd be spotted first.

"Quite a show they put on," the woman beside him murmured, eyes fixed on the dolphins swimming in tandem. "Wow! Did you catch that, Brendan?"

Her four-year-old nodded. "Mommy, can I open my Cracker Jacks now?"

"Sure," she said, stroking the side of the child's face.

"Love that caramel corn, myself," said the man, feeling awkward, being the only adult without child. "Battery went dead on my digital," he lied. "Caught some good shots of the sharks, though."

The woman smiled. "A photography buff?"

"Do some freelance for the local papers. Work the zoos, the parks."

"Sounds like fun."

"Mommy, is this a peanut or a bug?"

While the mother examined the oddly shaped nugget, he scanned the bleachers. No sailor's cap. He checked his watch. He was sure they were to hook up at 4:00. It was now 4:20.

Ten minutes later, feeding time was over. He watched the crowd spill from the stands.

"It was nice chatting," said the woman, guiding her youngster down the steps.

"Same here," he replied.

What should I do? In about ninety seconds I'm gonna look pretty dumb sitting here alone.

He decided to find a secluded area and call the number he had used to arrange the get-together. He found a path that led to a fieldstone tunnel. There was no one else in sight.

Chapter 38

"The suspects have either changed their MO again, or they've gotten sloppy," said Margaret, who, along with Thomlinson, had been invited to a brainstorming session in the Lieutenant's office. "The ME says the victim was struck twice on the left temple before being scalped, not the right parietal like all the others. And it doesn't look like the perp stopped to pose the body. The vic was found curled inside a tunnel."

"Could be a copycat," said Thomlinson. "He'd know about the scalping from the papers."

"What do we got on the victim?" Driscoll asked.

"One Francis Palmer from San Antonio, Texas. Like Miss Moneybags, not exactly a tourist. He was in town for an Internet convention. Headed up a company that designed Web sites for entrepreneurial self-starters. The guy's got a prior, John. He was busted three years ago for child molestation."

"Now there's a connection. These twins have a beef with sexual abusers. That's evident by the tattoos on the scalps. That makes the killings far from random. We may be dealing with vengeful executions. Anything yet from Interpol?"

"On it," said Thomlinson, dashing out of the office.

"Why'd our guy at the aquarium get two hits?" Margaret pondered aloud.

"Crime Scene may have the answer to that one. It could be a simple one. The blood trail might suggest the first blow didn't kill him. He lunges for his assailant and whack! He gets it again. Whatever the reason, I don't think they're getting sloppy. And I don't buy into the copycat theory. I think they've turned their anger up a notch. The fact that the body wasn't posed says to me the killer was rushed—interrupted by someone approaching."

"Or he didn't want to spend more time with the scumbag than he had to."

Driscoll recognized revulsion in the Sergeant's voice. He fought back the impulse to take her by the hand. Seeking diversion, he picked up the black-and-white photo of the twins. "What turned you two kids into a pair of revenge-seeking killers?" he asked, staring into the eyes of the Kodak-captured innocents.

"My money'd be on the father," said Margaret, looking like she was about to spit.

Driscoll closed the door to his office. He knew Margaret intimately. Her past was no secret to him. He knew it'd just be a matter of time before this revelation of sexual abuse would stir unwelcome memories.

"Would it help if we talked about it?" he said, taking a seat on the edge of his desk.

Margaret slumped in her chair as if her body were a blow-up doll that someone had pricked with a needle. "Is it this case? . . . I don't know. I feel sorta stretched. About everything. So stretched, that I tried to reach my therapist from when I was a kid. She's the only one I know. And wouldn't you know it. The woman's dead. I gotta be honest with you, John, working with you, now, after the death of your wife . . ."

She stopped talking and scrunched her face. "You know I have feelings for you. That's a given. And I know you have feelings for me. I also know you need time to grieve. But it hasn't been easy for me to sit on those feelings. Especially since her death. Jesus! Look at me! You've lost your wife. Your emotions must be doing somersaults, and I'm complaining about pining. Grow up, Margaret! But that's the problem. When it comes to men, I'm like an eighth grader, for Chrissake! I needn't go into detail. We both know why. Just when I think I got a handle on things, this sexual abuse bombshell explodes in my face. It puts me back in Mary Janes and a training bra with my old man peeping through the keyhole to my bedroom!"

Margaret began to cry. This time, Driscoll took her by the hand. "I can have you reassigned. No one need know why."

"My emotional baggage is like lint. It's in my pocket no matter where I go."

"I have a therapist. I don't see her much. But she was there for me after Colette's accident. Her name is Elizabeth. You'd like her."

Margaret used her hands to wipe tears from her cheeks. Her expression was one of embarrassment. "Look at me. Some gun-totin' detective, huh?"

"A human gun-totin' detective," Driscoll said with a smile.

"I'm glad we had this time, John. I miss what we had."

"What we *have*," Driscoll said. "I'm just in for repair."

Chapter 39

The following morning Driscoll was seated at his desk, perusing the Crime Scene report from the aquarium, when Margaret sauntered in. She appeared out of sorts. After sitting down, she robotically reported that her inquiry into any reported rapes, between siblings or otherwise, in and around Oak Flat, West Virginia, during 1990, had turned up nothing. In retrospect, Driscoll wished he had given the assignment to Thomlinson.

"You okay?"

"Will be."

"My door is always open."

"I know. Thank you. I'll be fine. What I need now is distraction. What's that you're reading?"

Driscoll hesitated.

"It's okay, John. The incest inquiry is behind me. It'll help if I stay focused on what's to come."

He smiled at her. "You know . . ."

"You gonna tell me what you're reading or do I have to grab the damn file?"

"It's the forensics report on Francis Palmer's blood evidence. Their reenactment of the assault suggests he was stationary when both blows were inflicted to his head. I'm thinking something pissed off our assassin." Driscoll was about to help himself to a cup of squad room coffee when his desk phone rang.

"Driscoll, here."

"You've got mail," the caller said and hung up. Driscoll hadn't a clue to the caller's identity.

He powered on his IBM desktop and was immediately connected to the department's Web site. He clicked on his mailbox, eyes on the screen. There, superimposed under a red and white bull's-eye, was the face of a male adolescent with wavy blond hair, the color of hay, and piercing aquamarine eyes. To the right of the face was a small speaker icon that Driscoll clicked. The prerecorded voice of Malcolm Shewster sounded through the desktop's speaker.

"John, whoever or whatever you're pursuing is yesterday's news. This is our boy! My team of specialists is to be commended. You now have what you wanted from the start. The sister will have the same face, give or take a few curls. Take a good look into those eyes, John. He's out there and he's daring you to nab him. And nab him you will. Set your eyes on the prize. And, John, you may as well get used to looking at that face because this afternoon its hits every newsstand and newswire in the nation with something the city has left out. A hefty bounty. And that's only step one in a full-scale Shewster alliance. Over and out. For now."

Driscoll's eyes locked on Margaret's. "Alliance? The man asked me if he could have his team project a current-day likeness of the twins. That's all. What's with the hefty bounty and an alliance? I never agreed to any alliance."

"Usually, grieving parents are Lone Rangers."

"I know. So far the only alliance he's made is with *our* evidence and *our* investigation. This guy's made his fortune on the backs of people, not hand in hand with them. He's gotten himself very involved in this case. Just how far does that involvement go? The man's up to something. I'm sure of it. Which means you and I are gonna keep a short leash on him."

Chapter 40

It was Saturday, just before 8:00 P.M. on Fifth Avenue at East Fiftieth Street in New York City. Pedestrians were making their way inside Saint Patrick's Cathedral only to exit a few minutes later spattered by holy water. The avenue was getting ready for evening. Neon lights were slowly coming to life above store windows as taxicabs hauled sightseers to restaurants, movie theaters, and Broadway shows. A woman stood at Saint Patrick's southwest corner, perplexed by the endless flow of vehicular traffic. She seemed distracted, anxious, turning her head furtively toward the cathedral's entrance. She carried a finger-worn Polaroid of a man in a plaid shirt overlooking a cornfield. It had been protected by a frayed white napkin into which she now spit her gum. She tossed the napkin into a trash can, held the photo against her chest, climbed the steps of the cathedral, and slipped inside.

Compared to the hubbub on the avenue, the church was sedate; a welcome sanctuary. She walked down the center aisle, searching left and right for the man she had typed "hello" to eight months ago in a MySpace chat room. They had become virtual lovers, disclosing a mutual predilection for oddity and postpubescent teens. It was now time to meet and gratify their sexual longings together.

Her heartthrob was nowhere in sight. Where could he be? She checked her watch. It was nearing 8:10. They were supposed to meet at 8:02, the time they first met over the Internet. Could her Timex be running fast?

In the second row her gaze fell upon a gentleman who smiled at her as though he had known her all her life.

"My God, it's you!"

The man stood and moved toward her. "I was beginning to think you had changed your mind."

"I was standing outside trying to get up the courage to come in. I still can't believe we're going through with this. Oh, Alex, I do love you so."

"And I you," he murmured. "But I have a confession to make."

Puzzled eyes looked back at him.

"Tara, I think I've committed a sin. And of all days to commit it!"

"What did you do?"

"I defaced church property."

"Go on!"

"No, really," he said, taking her hand. "Come, I'll show you."

He led her behind the main altar into a darkened circular aisle, faintly illuminated by the candles that were burning before the altar of the Blessed Virgin.

"Look," he whispered, pointing to his handiwork on the Virgin's marble pedestal.

Tara's eyes widened as they took in the arabesque letters: A and T intertwined.

"Alex and Tara, about to start their flight of fancy. Right here," he whispered.

"Mmm umm."

"Don't worry. I used an erasable marker. One swipe with a sponge and we're history."

They stood solemnly before the carved image of the Madonna. There was no one else in sight. It was nearing half-past eight, the meeting time he had arranged with the gentleman on the phone for their threesome.

A stir in the darkness of the alcove interrupted their exuberance. Like a flutter of wings or the friction of cloth. Something moved, undefined, unidentified.

They heard a cracking sound, like the shattering of stone. Alex was felled by blinding pain. Then blackness set in.

Before Tara knew what had happened, she heard the sound again.

Chapter 41

Father Xavier Thomas, glistening in vestments of green and gold, stood majestically at the rear of the church, about to follow the procession of altar servers, lectors, and Eucharistic Ministers down the center aisle of the historic cathedral. The church bells were pealing. Their tolling marked 6:58 A.M. In two minutes, Mass would begin. The latecomers, skittering in the nave of the cathedral, were met by the soft smile of Father Thomas, a true New Yorker who was well accustomed to the chronic tardiness of his time-pressed parishioners.

At the stroke of seven, the organist began the refrain to "Let Us Go Rejoicing," number 308 in the missalettes. The procession proceeded down the center aisle and all attendees stood to welcome the presiding priest.

"Where'd ya hide them?" Cassie asked.

Angus, crammed in the crowded pew to her right, sang the hymn's lyric and smiled teasingly at her.

"You're not gonna tell me?"

He crooned louder, casting his accomplice a sidelong smirk.

The cleric and his liturgical assistants reached the main

altar, bowed before the Lord, and assumed their positions for the opening prayer.

A late parishioner, wishing not to disturb the assembly nor Father Thomas, snuck into the cathedral through the East Fifty-first Street north transept entrance. Instead of joining the faithful already seated, she scurried past the baptistery and circled around toward the cluster of altars in the ambulatory, behind the celebrant, intent on attending Mass there. And then she screamed.

"Bingo!" said Angus.

"Wow! What a setta lungs! That dame belongs in the choir," Cassie snickered.

Father Thomas, standing hopelessly at his pulpit, watched as the congregation flocked to the alcove behind him.

Propped like marionettes, in the third pew before the Blessed Virgin's altar, with blood oozing from their ravaged heads, the pair sat inert. Their lifeless eyes stared vacantly at the stained-glass window of Saint Michael spearing the dragon. Around their necks hung a heart cut from cardboard. On it, fingered in blood, was the inscription: "Ah, ah, unh."

Chapter 42

Cassie was the first to see it. She had been channel surfing, heading for *Judge Judy*, when it suddenly appeared. There, in Sony Trinitron color, was the face. Not an exact likeness, but close enough. They had laughed off the photo of her and Angus as kids, and their Claxonn name had stayed on the reservation. Their first names, Angus and Cassie, listed in the full article posed a slight threat, but as Angus said, "Who the hell in Carbondale, Pennsylvania, is gonna give a damn about a spree of killings in New York?" But what she saw on the TV screen now was a whole other story. How the hell did they do that?

"Angus!" she screamed. "We're dead meat! Get the hell in here!"

"Wassamatta?" her brother said as he ambled out of the bathroom, naked and dripping wet.

"Ssssh! You'll wanna hear this."

"What the . . ." he muttered, his eyes staring now at the tube. The newscaster's face was center screen. But there, in the upper right corner, was one that resembled his. "How'd they do that?"

"Ssssh! Listen!"

". . . Is this the face of the killer who has been terroriz-
ing New York City for the past twelve months? Someone seems to think so. An anonymous caller is offering
a million-dollar reward to anyone who can tell him the
whereabouts of this person or his look-alike sister. A
special number, 800-854-4568, has been established to
field all calls . . ."

"Are they shittin' me?" Angus said as his near likeness
once again filled the screen. "How the hell did they get that
picture?"

"Angus, we gotta get outta here!" said Cassie.

"How long they have that?"

"I dunno. They say it's in all the papers."

"A million dollars is gonna make for a lot more readers.
Holy shit! We coulda been spotted in New York! At the
freakin' aquarium! Or. Holy, holy shit! At the goddamn
church!"

"What are we gonna do?"

"Give me a minute to think, will ya? Just need a minute
to think." He raced from one end of the trailer to the other,
rummaging from drawer to drawer, collecting what he was
after: a pair of scissors, a disposable razor, and a can of
Gillette Foamy. Suddenly, he stopped and turned to face his
sister. "I've got an idea."

Chapter 43

Driscoll opened the door to his office and eyed the flashing icon on the IBM desktop. He clicked on his mailbox, saw he had one new message, and opened it. His eyes widened at what he saw. Immediately, he called for Margaret and Thomlinson to join him.

"I wanted another set of eyes to see this so I know I'm not dreaming. We got a message from Angus." He looked to Margaret, his expression said "you gonna be okay with this?" She nodded. Driscoll swiveled the monitor around for all to see.

"He's calling himself OddDuck-Ephebophilia-Chaser@ webster.com," said Margaret. "What the hell does that stand for?"

"A pervert with a graduate degree," said Thomlinson. "A pedophile goes after the young. An ephebophile prefers adolescents."

Margaret winced.

"What do you make of the odd duck reference?" Driscoll asked.

"All adults who prey on adolescents are odd ducks."

"From where we sit," said Driscoll. "But for him to label an abuser odd may have significance."

Driscoll read aloud. "Dear Lieutenant, I know you are looking for us. I'm writing to tell you our side of the story. You might call off the search. The scumbags we been killing belong in body bags. They are warped, disgusting pigs! They deserved to die in public toilets because they're made of shit. How would you feel if you was just a kid and your old man sold you to bastards like them so they could get laid, or jerked off, or eaten out, or even worse. Get to fuck you up the ass! All because we look the way we do."

Driscoll stopped reading and repeated the last line loudly. " 'All because we look the way we do.' That, my friends, is what's driving these two. This adds a major twist. Their true motive is revenge for unspeakable mortification and vile repetitive debasement."

He continued his recitation. "Me and my sister been swallowing more cum and lickin more pussy than you could in a lifetime. We both had our bodies felt up since before Cassie had tits! I'm talking since we were ten. Ten years old!!! How would you feel? Well the old man is dead now. He ain't dragging us odd-i-twins. That's what he called us. Angus and Cassie, his prized odd-i-twins. His days of dragging us from amusement parks to baseball fields are over. Selling us like we were alien creatures. The alien creatures are the ones we been killing, if you ask me. They been making the old man rich, paying him for all the shit me and Cassie had to put up with. It ain't fair. I don't know if you got kids. But if you do, how would you like it if some motherless sick bastard stuck his finger in them or sucked them off year after fucking year? They're freaky. Let me tell you. We had one prick that only wanted to get naked, lie down, and have me and Cassie have a pissing duel over him. We were eleven! Eleven freaking years old! We figured you got our picture from the reservation. Tell that bitch Taniqua and her mother we sent them the scalps so they'd know the blood of the freaks is on them too. They shoulda never let the old man take us. But, like I said. Dear Daddy is dead. Goody-goody We just didn't stop the business. Now, instead of us taking it up the ass we get to kill the scumbags. I hope you do have kids. Then you'd understand. –Angus."

No one spoke for more than a minute. It was Margaret who broke the silence. "Good for them," she said and walked out of the room.

Quiet returned.

"What's that about?" Thomlinson eventually asked.

"Issues," said Driscoll, making a mental note to ask Margaret if she'd set something up with a therapist. He picked up the phone and hit speed dial. "Communications. . . . This is Driscoll . . . I received an e-mail. Time sent says about two hours ago. Any chance we can tell where it came from? The IP address? Let me look. It's 68.219.43.34." Driscoll gave Thomlinson a thumbs up. "Good. I'll hold."

Driscoll listened attentively as the response from Communications filled his ear. After ending the call, he turned to Thomlinson. "The e-mail came from MegaBytes, a computer self-serve center, on East Eighth off of University. That's ten minutes from here. Get on the horn to the Sixth Precinct. Tell them what we've got. I want that place sealed and surrounded. The twins might still be there. I want it done now! When you're finished with the call, head over there, yourself."

"Yessir."

"I'll have someone reach out to this Webster.com outfit to see what they've got on Angus's OddDuck handle."

As Thomlinson headed for the door, Driscoll thought of Margaret and the inner conflict this case had stirred. Interestingly, her emotional havoc spawned his. On the one hand, he needed her to stay focused. To avoid subjectivity and help him put an end to the killings. Yet part of him wanted to guard her from the disturbing turmoil the investigation was delivering. Uncertain what he'd say, he picked up the phone and called her.

Chapter 44

The call prompted resolution, but not because of anything Driscoll had done. As soon as Margaret heard his voice, she apologized for her unprofessional outburst and pledged her assistance. "I'll try to keep my head on straight" was how she put it. Relieved, he asked her to check into Angus's online account.

Ten minutes later she was in his office to report that she had spoken to Paul Houston, head of communications at Webster.com. "They offer twenty hours of free Internet service per month. If you exceed the limit, they have you set up an account and arrange for PayPal or credit card payment. All you need is access to the Web to start. If you never go over the twenty hours, there's no ID, billing address, or phone number recorded."

"Cyberspace anonymity."

"You got it."

"We'll wait then to see if Cedric comes up with anything. We traced Angus's e-mail to a retailer that provides on-site computer rental. He's probably there now." A smile creased Driscoll's face. "Margaret, I'm proud of you. I know this case rouses a whole host of frightening memories. And I know resolving mental mayhem isn't easy. You're not alone with your wrestle with objectivity. If what is said in the e-mail is true, the twins have been through hell and that evokes my sympathy. Sadly, though, it doesn't alter the fact that they've murdered people. We have the obligation to stop them. If you need a break, even temporarily, the offer to have you reassigned is an open one."

"I know. And I must admit, sometimes, late at night, when I'm alone, it's tempting."

Driscoll fought against the impulse to hold her. For he knew if he did, he'd have a hard time letting go. "Have you called Elizabeth?"

A vacant stare said she hadn't.

"Whether we act on the transfer or we don't, you should call her." Again, the desire to embrace her. "Promise me you will."

She nodded.

Driscoll studied her face. It appeared she hadn't slept in days. She returned his steady gaze. He smiled, for he had found a way to caress her. With his eyes. His, holding. Hers, not letting go.

Until the ringing of a phone shattered the trance.

"Driscoll, here."

"They're long gone, Lieutenant." It was Thomlinson. "The e-mail was generated from here, all right. I'm looking at the particular computer now. I had the uniforms lock the place down like you instructed and Forensics will dust the PC, but I don't think it's gonna give us any more than we already have. There's a slim chance the twins are among this horde of customers. But I doubt it. I searched every face. They'd have to be chameleons. You oughta see this place. It's like the registrar's office at Columbia on steroids. Customers are going every which way but out with the uniforms at the doors. It's like a Toyota sell-a-thon commercial shown in fast-forward. I feel like I've been time-warped. Anyway, I spoke to one Aleeshia Smathers, the store's assistant manager. She's a college cutie with purple hair and facial piercings. I showed her Shewster's version of Angus. Negative for an ID."

"Any surveillance camera?"

"None."

"They use some sort of sign-in sheet?"

"Already had it copied. Running from last night through today. It'll give us the time each customer signed in and the time they left. The co-ed suggests we may come up with zilch, though. She says a lot of customers pay cash and sign in as SpongeBob Square Pants."

"Okay, Cedric. Have the uniforms get IDs from everyone, including the help. We'll run down each one. When that's done, head back to the house. We'll need to search the obits and resurrect one hell of a dad."

Chapter 45

The obituary search, though computer assisted, was morose, time-consuming, and going nowhere. The three lawmen were convinced Claxonn wasn't the name dear old dad left this planet with. A call to Taniqua only complicated things. She didn't know for sure what name the birth parents went by. Whether the father was actually brother to the mom was now in question. Taniqua believed that to be the case, but was uncertain if it was fact or something made up by her mother, who was a bit capricious.

"They offed the dad. Probably cut him up into pieces and scattered them into the four corners of some cornfield," Thomlinson said. "We're never gonna find him or any record of him. This pair may be strung out but they're not stupid. They're not about to add patricide to the list."

"It would help if we had a name," said Margaret. "Claxonn's not setting off any bells."

"The name is in the cornfield," said Thomlinson. "The chance of us pulling off a Lazarus is zero. We're gonna have to make use of Shewster's handiwork. There's a million-dollar target on that face. Somebody's gonna cash in. The only question is when."

Chapter 46

Driscoll had placed a call to the National Center for Missing and Exploited Children, hoping somewhere, in their vast database, there might be a reference to the twins. He had left his number with Douglas Glasser. Not only had Glasser made good on his promise to have someone call him back, but that someone was now standing inside Driscoll's office introducing herself as Susan Lenihan, a behavior analyst and licensed psychotherapist. Her friendly blue eyes returned the Lieutenant's evanescent ogle, which had not gone unnoticed by Margaret.

"Thank you for coming, Miss Lenihan—"

"Please. It's Susan."

"Okay, then. Thank you for coming, Susan. This is Sergeant Margaret Aligante and Detective Cedric Thomlinson."

"Please. Call me Margaret."

"Cedric."

"It's a pleasure to meet all of you," she said, extending her hand.

The four took seats around the Lieutenant's desk.

"I was expecting a return call," said Driscoll. "And here you are in person."

The woman smiled.

A bit too flirtatiously to suit Margaret.

"I've been following the story in the papers and on the tube with the rest of New York," Susan explained. "When I read about the man killed at the aquarium, Francis Palmer, his name set off an alarm. At first, I didn't know why, but I was sure I had heard the name before."

"He had been convicted of child molestation in Texas," said Thomlinson.

"That was the easy part. When I ran his name through our system, the conviction popped up. But our database focuses on child exploitation. So I dug a little deeper and realized why I remembered the name. Francis Palmer headed up his own company in Texas because seven years ago he was fired from a Web design and enhancement firm in Silicon Valley, California. The company monitored their employees' work computers. He was let go because they found he had been making frequent visits to Web sites dealing in prostitution. Child prostitution. He was never formally charged because the firm wanted to avoid exposure. But their director of human resources alerted our California branch office in Tustin, and a record was established. Although no further action was taken, the information remained in our database."

"How is it his name set off whistles?" asked Driscoll.

"That conscientious director of human resources called me for advice. Her boss had ordered her to delete all information related to Palmer. She knew if any investigative agency made inquiry, her company would deny ever having the guy on the payroll."

"Why'd she call you?" asked Margaret.

"Because she's my sister." Susan Lenihan blushed.

Chapter 47

The door to Driscoll's office opened, and Thomlinson stuck his head inside. "We've got news from Interpol."

"Let's have it," said Driscoll, as Thomlinson planted himself in front of the Lieutenant's desk.

"Interpol had their nets set for Guenther Rubeleit and Yen Chan, but had nada on Helga Swenson," said Thomlinson. "They based their suspicions on reports from overseas ECPAT centers." The detective was referring to a worldwide network of agencies established to End Child Prostitution, Child Pornography, and Trafficking of Children for Sexual Purposes. "The only thing in line with our evidence is an entry on file for Rubeleit. He liked to trawl the Web for amputees."

"Some assortment of deviants," said Driscoll. "That look on your face says there's more."

"It might make you think twice about ordering sushi." Thomlinson grinned. "It's about customs in Tokyo, where Tatsuya Inagaki hailed from. Seems Japan has an ECPAT agency too. It's in Tokyo and is called ECPAT Stop Japan. But the country's got its own code of ethics regarding the age of consent for sexual activities and how it applies to the law. This is straight from Interpol. It's Japan's Article One-seven-seven Penal Code applicable to the charge of rape. I quote. A person who, through violence or intimidation, has sexual intercourse with a female person of not less than thirteen years of age commits the crime of rape and shall be punished with imprisonment at forced labor for a limited term of not less than two years. The same shall apply to a person who has sexual intercourse, we're talking consensual now, with a female person under thirteen years of age. The article doesn't say what happens if the recipient of wanted or unwanted sex is male. You're gonna love this. They've got a dating service going on over there. It's called Enjo kosai. Girls of high school age, who don't wanna depend on babysitting money, can get paid to escort older men on dates. That doesn't necessarily mean sex is on the menu . . . but?" Thomlinson raised an eyebrow. "And so the boys aren't left home on a Saturday night, there's gyaku-enjo."

"And where does our victim Mr. Inagaki play in all of this?"

"On him they got zip."

"So, let's see, two of the four foreign victims have a sub-stantiated yen for teenagers. Excuse the pun. And on domestic soil we have Mr. San Antonio, Texas, himself, Francis Palmer."

The two lawman exchanged glances.

"Wanna flip a coin?" asked Driscoll.

"For?"

"To see which one of us gets to ask Shewster about Goldilocks."

Chapter 48

Driscoll, having lost the coin toss, had a quandary. A comprehensive investigation leaves no doors unopened. But there was no evidence to indicate Abigail Shewster had been into sex with sixteen-year-olds, bizarre or otherwise. He didn't feel comfortable broaching the possibility with her father. He'd likely deny it, and Driscoll believed a man of Shewster's influence could have buried such a degradation on Mars. There was also the possibility that his daughter was a player but had managed to keep her father, and everyone else, in the dark. He'd only pursue it if evidence surfaced to support such a scandal.

Telephones had been ringing. The department's Tip Line, linked to Shewster's 800 number, thanks to the ever-accommodating Mayor, had every Tom, Dick, and Harry spewing knowledge of who Angus was, and they were eager to cash in on the big bucks. In Ann Harbor, Michigan, he was the Domino's Pizza delivery boy. In Titusville, Florida, a lifeguard. In Nashville, an usher at the Grand Ole Opry. And in Albuquerque, the tour guide on a Hopi reservation. He was everyone's next-door neighbor. The irony was he might be one of them.

Driscoll summoned Thomlinson and Margaret to his office.

"The possibility is that the twins could be anywhere in the country," he said. "Coming in, making their hits, and hightailing it back home. Out of the forty-two calls that came in since the face made its debut, we've got three possibles in our neck of the woods. A night watchman's call from a halfway house over on Staten Island is one of them. He says one of the kids there had a meltdown when he saw the sketch on the tube. Number two is a clown from the Pie in the Sky Circus. Says the image is a good likeness to some guy they feature as The Thing, a circus hairy scary, of sorts. Without his costume and makeup, he's a dead ringer for our guy, says the caller. The third one has curiosity written all over it. A priest at Saint Barnabas Church in Brooklyn apparently broke the seal of confession by calling to say a member of his congregation confessed to the crimes."

"That's a new one," said Thomlinson. "Since when does a Catholic priest turn his back on a vow to help the police?"

"Good question. It's one I'll be sure to ask him."

Chapter 49

Saint Barnabas Church was a red stone building with three Gothic steeples towering over the southwestern entrance to Prospect Park, on a street lined with quaint boutiques and trattorias. The parish had gone through a gentrification that was underwritten by Keyspan, the local utility company. What once were tenements teeming with welfare recipients now housed dual-income professionals who traded mutual funds.

Cutting the Chevy's engine, Driscoll stepped out onto the sidewalk and proceeded toward the rectory, where the bell was answered by a matronly woman in a floral dress.

"May I help you?" she asked, in an Irish brogue.

"I'm Lieutenant Driscoll. I'm here to see Father Terhune."

"Father Terhune is it? Well, the good father is in his study preparing a sermon. It wouldn't be wise to disturb him."

"But we spoke on the phone. He'll want to see me."

"And I'm tellin' ya he left instructions not to be disturbed."

"Telling him I'm here would be the Christian thing to do, don't you think?"

"I suppose next you're gonna tell me you're an envoy from his Holiness, the Pope."

"Even the Pope would be in favor of you interrupting Father Terhune," said Driscoll, with a smile.

"You're a sly one, you are." She motioned for him to come inside and pointed to a chair in the corner of a richly furnished room. "Have a seat, why don't ya? I'll see what I can do."

Soon, Driscoll heard the sound of wheels in motion laboring down the corridor.

"Good afternoon, Lieutenant Driscoll. I'm Pat Terhune," the priest said, rolling his wheelchair into the room. "I see you got past my sentry."

"You're safe with her around."

"Right you are about that."

Father Terhune was clad entirely in black, save for an open clerical collar. A pair of horn-rimmed glasses framed kindly blue eyes set in a boyish face.

"Let me say it's an honor to meet you, Lieutenant. Your reputation for commendable police work makes you a hero to me and to all of my parishioners."

"Thank you," said Driscoll, handing Terhune the illustration. "Is this the youth you called about?"

"As sure as the day is long," said the priest.

"Would you know his name, Father?"

"Everett Luxworth."

"You're sure about this?"

"Quite."

Driscoll sat back in his chair. "Forgive me for raising the question, Father, but I'd be remiss if I didn't ask it. Doesn't the confidentiality of the confessional prohibit you from speaking out?"

A soft smile formed on the priest's face. "He asked me to call you."

"Luxworth?"

"The lad had been coming to see me, regularly, over the past few months. He considers me his therapist."

Their conversation was interrupted as the sentinel reappeared with coffee.

"Cream and sugar?"

"A touch of cream. No sugar," Driscoll said, annoyed at the loss of momentum.

"As I was saying, Lieutenant, Everett saw himself as my patient. We clerics handle our fair share of spiritual counseling, you know. In any case, he came to confession twice a week. He was troubled. He raised issues of self-respect and was seeking a way to get a handle on his anger. It was only when the image hit the newspaper and I confronted him with his likeness that he broke down and confessed to the killings. It was then he asked me to call the authorities. I told him I'm not here to sit in judgment. The church is not a law enforcement agency, I said. But he begged me to stop him. And told me if I didn't, he would kill again and that I alone had the power to save a soul that he was prepared to send to hell. It would be on my conscience if I didn't stop him, and the only way to stop him was to call the police. When he left the confessional, I felt it would be his last confession and that he would never return."

"And so you placed the call."

"Yes."

"Do you know where this Luxworth lives, Father?" Driscoll asked.

After staring at the Lieutenant for what seemed like minutes, he answered the question.

"Two-two-five Sussex."

"Thank you," Driscoll said, standing and preparing to leave. "Father, one last question. Does Luxworth have a sister?"

"I wouldn't know, Lieutenant. He never mentioned one."

Chapter 50

Driscoll wasn't banking on Father Terhune's information. He had met many a confessor on the job. And for some reason this one didn't feel right. Perhaps it was the absence of a sister acting in tandem. Driscoll wasn't sure why his instincts said no. But he'd have to track down the lead.

"Cedric, run an Everett Luxworth through the system and give me a call if you get a hit." Driscoll folded his cell phone and headed for the suspect's residence.

225 Sussex was a two-story frame structure in need of maintenance. A cluster of mismatched mailboxes, hanging haphazardly near the front door, suggested it might be a single-room occupancy home. Its peeling paint and eroding gutters suggested that here, gentrification had missed its mark.

Driscoll approached the house, which was marked by a steel security gate more suited for the rear of a boiler room than a multiple family dwelling. Of the six weatherworn mailboxes, only three had names on them. None read "Luxworth." Only two of six doorbells were labeled. Evans and Peterson. The word *super* appeared below Peterson, so that's the one he rang.

"Who's there?"

"Mr. Peterson?" Driscoll hollered. "May I have a word with you?"

Driscoll heard the shuffling of feet and the sound of another door opening inside the residence. In his mind he envisioned a balding man, clad in a soiled T-shirt, trudging along on falling arches. Peterson turned out to be a strikingly handsome man in his late thirties. He wore his well-groomed hair parted on the side. His eyes were Mel Gibson blue and he sported a mustache, trimmed in Clark Gable fashion. Clad in a shimmering white robe, he looked more like a movie star on a break than a superintendent of a run-down rooming house in Brooklyn.

"May I help you?"

"You Peterson?"

"That's me." The man spoke in a theatrical, effeminate voice.

"Everett Luxworth. He live here?"

"Yes. With me. But you just missed him. He went down to the florist not five minutes ago." The man smiled, showing off a dazzling set of pearly whites. "Love your suit."

Driscoll figured Luxworth to be this man's live-in partner.

"What is it you want with Everett?"

"My name's Driscoll. Lieutenant John Driscoll. I'm with the New York City Police Department."

"Would you like to wait inside?" Peterson asked, anxiety and curiosity piqued.

"That'd be fine."

The interior of the apartment was a far cry from the house's drab exterior. The living room, its walls papered in lilac and fern, was elegantly furnished with a satin ottoman, facing matching love seats, as its centerpiece.

"Would you like some rose hip tea? I just brewed a fresh pot."

"Why not?"

Peterson disappeared into the kitchen and returned with a Japanese lacquered tray supporting an earthenware pot and two clay mugs. He poured tea into Driscoll's cup and the two men took their seats, Driscoll on one love seat, Peterson on the other.

"Is Everett in some sort of trouble?" Peterson asked.

"I need to speak with him. Some routine questions."

"He is in some kind of trouble, isn't he?"

The door opened and Luxworth stepped into the room holding a bouquet of fresh-cut carnations. He resembled the sketch. Not an exact match. But the resemblance was there, nonetheless. Driscoll had a sinking feeling. He doubted the man was Angus.

"I didn't know we were expecting company," Luxworth said absently as he fussed with a Waterford vase. "There!" he said, happy with his floral display.

"Everett. Is there something you haven't told me?" Peterson asked.

"What do you mean?"

"This gentleman is Lieutenant Driscoll. He's from the police department and he's here to see you."

"Me?" Luxworth said, alarm in his voice.

"Perhaps we should discuss this in private," the Lieutenant suggested.

"We'll do nothing of the sort. Antoine stays right here!"

"Your call," said Driscoll.

"Everett, have you been playing with matches again?"

"Matches? No. But I've been known to carry a torch or two." Luxworth cast a sidelong glance at Peterson.

What was that all about? Was this guy an arsonist? Driscoll let the matter go unanswered, for now. "I'm here with some questions regarding the murder of several tourists in New York," said Driscoll, eyes fixed on the suspect.

"I knew I saw your face before. You're *that* Lieutenant Driscoll! From the newscasts. Oh my," said Peterson.

"That no-good son of a bitch of a priest," Luxworth muttered, his eyes brimming with anger.

"This isn't a game, Luxworth. Several people have been killed. Father Terhune says you're to blame."

"I didn't think he'd really tell on me! I wasn't serious when I told him to call the police."

"Told him what?" asked Peterson.

Luxworth collapsed on the ottoman.

"Your roommate confessed to a series of brutal crimes," said Driscoll.

"Everett, I thought we were beyond all that."

"I'm so sorry, Antoine. I'm so sorry," Luxworth sobbed.

"Sorry for what?" said Driscoll.

"Lieutenant, Everett suffers from depression. He has an inferiority complex as big as Texas! It makes him do anything—and I mean anything—to get attention. Even convincing a parish priest that he's the serial killer hunted by the police for killing those poor people. But my Everett wouldn't swat a mosquito. Everett, what am I to do with you?" Peterson cradled Luxworth in his arms.

Driscoll's cell phone sounded.

With his eyes fixed on the weeping Luxworth, Driscoll listened intently to what Cedric Thomlinson had to report. A minute later, the Lieutenant ended the call and turned to face Luxworth.

"Everett, just how was it you managed to kill all those people over the past twelve months if you were confined to the psychiatric ward of the Coxsackie mental health facility for setting trash cans ablaze? They didn't let you out until four months ago!"

"Thank you, God. Thank you," said Peterson. "And this time you're to take all your medication. The Lexapro, the Wellbutrin, *and* the Zyprexa! Is that clear, Everett?"

"Okay," whimpered Luxworth.

The Lieutenant chose not to dwell on the combination of

medication. From conversations with his sister's pharmacist, he had become familiar with the drugs and what they were used for. He said a silent prayer for Luxworth as he headed for the door.

Chapter 51

"Step right this way, ladies and gentlemen! Right this way! See the sword-eating Claudius and the tiger-faced lady! Right this way, ladies and gentlemen and children of all ages!" The circus barker stood behind his rainbow-colored podium at the entrance to the Midway, a corridor of wonders that led toward the circus's big top. "Our Midway is now open, ladies and gentlemen! And later tonight, our big top will open for the main event! A wonder of wonders! Not to be missed!"

The Pie in the Sky Circus was a traveling extravaganza that toured the East Coast, delivering weekends of joy and pleasure. Under three multicolored tents, it featured a "barrelful of clowns," a troupe of trapeze artists, and a host of animal acts.

It was a bright Friday afternoon when Margaret arrived on the fairgrounds outside of Lester J. Coddinton Elementary School in Cherry Hill, New Jersey. The caller to the Tip Line, a clown named JellyBeans, had told the police to look for a red and yellow camper, just to the right of the big top.

Margaret walked to the camper and knocked on its door.

No one answered.

Just as she was about to knock again, a voice sounded.

"Who ya lookin' for?"

Margaret followed the voice to the back of the camper, where she found a wafer-thin midget seated on a stool.

"You JellyBeans?" she asked.

"Nope. Ya lookin' for work. Are ya?" said the little man.

"No. I'm looking for a clown. Goes by the name of Jelly-Beans."

"Jelly's my friend. Whaddya want with him?"

"He's expecting me," said the Sergeant.

"He's expecting you, is he?" The little man squinted as if examining the Trojan Horse.

"That's right. We spoke on the phone."

"What's this all about?"

"It's personal," said Margaret, amused.

"I'm on to you Immigration people, ya know. Always buttin' in and stirrin' up trouble. You people make me sick."

"You gonna tell me where JellyBeans is or do I have to bust you for interfering in the investigation of a crime?" Margaret flashed the tin. JellyBeans! Good God!

"You callin' my friend a criminal? Come down off that high and mighty horse of yours, sister, and fight like a man!" The dwarf climbed down from his stool, not a simple task, and squatted, kung-fu style.

"You've gotta be kidding," said Margaret, laughter now erupting. "Look. I'm not here to arrest anyone. I'm just here to ask your friend a few questions. Like I told you before, JellyBeans is expecting me."

"Scared the pants off ya, didn't I?" the dwarf gloated.

"That ya did."

"Well if you must know, my bestest friend, Jelly, is sleepin' it off right here in this camper. He drank buckets of swill last night and the show goes on in less than three hours."

"Would it be asking too much to wake him for me? I'm asking this as a favor, mind you," said Margaret, fighting the impulse to squat down to the little man's level.

"Well . . . okay," said the dwarf. "Give him a minute to freshen up."

The dwarf disappeared inside the camper. Shortly after that, he stuck his head outside.

"Da-da-da-dah! His highness, Lord Jellsworth, will see you in his royal chamber! Step right this way." He held open a rusted screen door.

Margaret entered the narrow camper.

"Follow me!" the dwarf ordered, leading Margaret into what could only be described as the master bedroom. In miniature.

There, stretched across a diminutive bed, lay a second dwarf.

"Please, world, stop spinning," he pleaded.

"I'm gonna brew us some fresh coffee, Jel. It'll fix ya right up," the tiny man said. Then turning to Margaret, "How 'bout you, sweetums? Sorry, I didn't get your name."

"Margaret. And, yes, I'd love some coffee."

"Glad to meet ya," the dwarf said, exiting. "They call me Hot Stuff."

With a burst of energy, JellyBeans hoisted himself out of bed.

"Tough night?" asked Margaret.

"My birthday."

"Well, happy birthday! You're the one who called the police, right?"

"Sure did!"

"Feel well enough to tell me about this guy they call The Thing?" Margaret asked.

"He done it."

"He done what?"

"The killings. That's what he done. There's no hiding place for him now. Not with his mug all over the news."

Margaret took out the sketch and handed it to JellyBeans. "This the guy?"

"The spittin' image. Bragged about the murders, he did."

"Where can I find him?"

"Where he always is this time of day, the rascal. In his cage! Look for the red tent."

"And where would I find that?"

"At the top of the Midway."

Margaret left just as Hot Stuff reappeared laden with a tray supporting three cups of coffee and a box of Krispy Kreme doughnuts. The two would have to eat without her.

Outside, Margaret spotted the red tent and approached it. At its base, "The Thing" was inscribed on a wooden placard advertising the macabre oddity that was featured inside. Some curious thrill seekers had already gathered, waiting to be entertained by what was sure to be a ghastly experience.

The barker lectured the crowd. "The creature you're about to see once roamed the deserts of Arabia. He is the first of his kind to be captured alive. Do not trust your eyes, gentle visitor. For the manlike being is not human. He only assumes human shape to induce in you a sense of security and safety. Stare bravely into his eyes. Pay attention to his every move. For, if he feels you waver, he will change into an abomination, and before you can say 'Boo!' he will feed off your very flesh. Be warned, this exhibit is not for those of you with coronary weaknesses. Pregnant women, and children who suffer from insomnia, should likewise avoid entering these fright-filled halls." He pulled back a portion of the crimson curtain. "All other brave souls are now invited to enter. Once inside, follow the dimly lit arrows embedded in the stone floor. They will lead you to a wooden door that marks the entrance to his lair."

They lined up to enter. When it came to Margaret's turn, the barker asked, "Have you listened closely to the warning, madam? Do you believe in the supernatural?"

"I do." She lied.

"Are you prone to nightmares?"

"No. Are you?"

"Ghouls have been known to invade dreams."

"Can't be any worse than my day job."

"Enter, then, at your own risk," he cautioned, gesturing theatrically toward the opening in the curtain.

Aligante did just that and followed the illuminated arrows, which led through a winding corridor. Howling and yelping sounds echoed around her. Some twenty feet in, she came upon the door, which opened automatically. She ducked inside and found herself in a small auditorium that had stadium seating. The crowd that had preceded her had already taken their seats. Margaret joined them. An eerie silence filled the theater, broken intermittently by the giggles of wide-eyed children.

A drum sounded, sending a chill through the audience. Lights came on, illuminating a small stage. In its center stood the barker holding a cattle prod.

"Ladies and gentlemen, this is your last warning," he cautioned. "What you're about to witness will frighten the most courageous of men. Remember, The Thing is not of our world, nor, sadly enough, since his capture, his own. This creature belongs to a species long cursed by all of humanity, a living anathema to God. And mind you, he has not eaten human flesh since his nightly foraging in the Arabian desert, where he feasted on unfortunate nomads. But he can wait hundreds of years for his next meal. I further caution you, ladies and gentlemen, if you wear a cross, you are warned not to wear it inside your clothing. Display it boldly as an emblem of your faith. Your faith, the very essence of safe haven for you. An abomination for him."

Several members of the audience followed his suggestion.

"Ladies and gentlemen, I will now lower the house lights so The Thing will be unable to see you. It is important, from here on out, that you remain absolutely silent. For your safety, he must believe that he is alone. And now the time has come for you to meet the demon. The demon from hell."

Darkness ensued. A whisper of a melodious flute sounded as a yellow spotlight crept across center stage. As the light grew in intensity, The Thing became visible. The creature, appearing to be part lizard and part man, had batlike wings and a face like that of a gargoyle. It was perched on the branch of a tree, inside a large cage. Its left ankle was chained to the tree's trunk. The crowd was silent; not even a breath could be heard.

"Not bad at all," Margaret muttered, sliding a stick of Wrigley's into her mouth.

The barker approached the cage, drawing a snarl from the creature. He tossed what appeared to be a leg of lamb into the cage.

A child, invisible in the darkness, whimpered, causing the creature to fix his stare in the direction of the sound. Leaping, the creature smashed hard against the reinforced bars of his cage. He bared his teeth, let loose a screech, and flayed the air with his claws. His eyes glowed with light.

"Oh, my God!" the child's mother cried.

A clash of drums and a flash of light. A curtain came tumbling down, separating the beast from the stunned audience.

The house lights came on and the crowd, still spellbound, spilled down from their seats and milled toward the door they had entered. Margaret lingered behind and approached the barker.

"I wish to speak to the ghoul."

"Is your life so meaningless that you would risk such an encounter?"

"It is a remarkable act, I'll give you that. But an act nonetheless." She flashed her shield.

"Come with me," the barker said, begrudgingly, and escorted Margaret through a second maze of corridors. He knocked at a door, adorned by a paper star

"Open up. It's me," he said. "You have company."

"Why does he keep his door locked?" Margaret asked.

"Beats the hell out of me."

There was a shuffle of footfalls followed by the sound of the lock disengaging.

"You're on your own," said the barker.

"Whaddya want?" The Thing's voice snarled through a crack in the door.

Margaret produced her shield and poked it through the opening. "What say you and I get better acquainted?"

Margaret heard the chain fall. The door opened wide. She stood staring into the eyes of a wafer-thin figure, clad in a plaid bathrobe; his face was covered with cold cream. She thought of the sketch and tried to envision it covered in shaving gel.

"Who sent ya?"

"Why don't we step inside so we can talk?"

"Okay by me."

She followed him into a dark room where a votive candle burned, casting ominous shadows on the walls. In the far corner, a twenty-five-watt bulb barely lit a vanity, complete with a large mirror. Margaret inhaled the aroma of marijuana.

"Weed. That explains the infrared eyes."

"That's not my poison. Alfonzo smokes the dope. Not me."

"Alfonzo?"

"The barker," he said, using a towel to wipe away the facial cleanser.

Not a match, but close enough, thought Margaret, as his

face emerged. She placed a hand on her Walther PPK firearm.

It was as though he had read her mind.

"Ah! I know why you're here. You think I'm the serial killer who knocked off those tourists. Which one of the trained monkeys turned me in?"

"You're telling me you're not our boy?"

"I spotted the likeness on the tube and thought I'd have some fun with the wee folk. C'mon, do I look like a killer?"

"In the costume or out?"

Margaret eyed him cautiously as he reached under the vanity and produced a copy of the *Daily News* with the sketch on its cover. "Boo!"

"Murder isn't funny."

"Sorry."

Margaret studied him. He appeared to be a little older than their profile, and her instinct suggested his Thing routine was as far as he had ever gotten toward aggression, but she did have a job to complete. "You know you'd save us both a lot of time and bother if you'd be willing to give us a sample of your DNA."

"Blood, spit, or urine?"

"How 'bout you just say 'ah' and let me swab the inside of your mouth?"

"You're the boss."

Margaret collected the DNA sample. "You got a name?"

"Lance."

"Lance what?"

"Robert Lance."

Margaret used a felt-tip marker to label the DNA bag, then dated it and dropped it into her purse.

"That's it?" he said.

"What? You were expecting a nurse with a syringe?"

He shrugged.

"This specimen will do one of two things, Mr. Lance,"

said Margaret, heading for the door. "It'll clear you or guess what?"

"What?"

"You'll get that syringe. But they'll call it lethal injection."

Chapter 52

Driscoll had finally edged his way out of a parking space where two motorists had him close to bookended, when the call came in from Thomlinson.

"You're gonna love this one, Lieutenant. We just got a call from a sergeant at the Eighty-fourth Precinct. They had a visitor. One Samantha Taft, a salesclerk at a thirty-minute photo shop on Montague Street. Said she recognized Angus in the sketch. But there's more. Much more! You ready?"

"Ready."

"She's got his picture!"

Driscoll exited the Chevy near the corner of Montague and Henry streets, just west of Brooklyn's Borough Hall. Walking east on Montague, he found the shop. A bell chimed as he opened its door.

"May I help you?"

Driscoll's gaze fell upon a young woman whose scarlet blouse matched the streak of red in her otherwise jet-black hair.

"Samantha Taft?"

"Wow! You guys are fast! Cop, right?"

"You the one who stopped by the police station about the sketch featured on TV?"

"And you get right to the point. Double wow!" She scooted out from behind a free-standing device that resembled an MRI machine. "Got the sketch with ya? I'd like to see the two faces close-up."

"So would I." Driscoll leaned on the shop's counter, bringing himself eye level with the girl. "How is it you happened upon his particular picture? You must see thousands every day."

"The guy's face is plastered everywhere you look! Not just on television. You'd hafta be from Neptune not to have seen it. Anyway, we've got a sixty-day rule here. The owner of a processed film that hasn't been picked up after two months gets a call. You'd be amazed at the number of people who simply forget about their pictures. I would have brought it with me to the precinct, but it's not supposed to leave the store unless paid for." She reached under the counter and produced a white envelope with orange stenciling and embossed numerals.

Driscoll eyed the envelope. In the space for the customer's name and address someone, perhaps this young lady, had penciled in "Cash."

"Pretty tough to make a call on this one," he said.

"Yup! You can thank Harold for that."

"Harold?"

"Part-timer. Works the weekends. Not exactly the brightest bulb in the box, if ya know what I mean. That's what made me peek inside. Sometimes I'll spot a regular's face in the photographs. Then I'll have someone to call. But it wasn't some customer's face I spotted. It was your guy's."

Driscoll opened the envelope and retrieved its contents.

"He's numero twenty-two," she said. "The last shot before the pansies at play."

Driscoll raised a curious eyebrow at Taft's remark, then fanned the array of photographs. The dimly lit panorama of the New York City skyline came to life. And, just as the sales clerk had said, he found what he was looking for in photo number twenty-two, which he placed on the counter before him. It was a clear shot of a hooded Caucasian male running away, his head, though, clearly turned back toward the camera. The backdrop of the photo featured Brooklyn's skyline, which was of course what one would see if one were situated atop the Brooklyn Bridge, looking east. And, Driscoll knew all too well what the subject of the photograph was looking at. His handiwork. A fatally wounded man, taking a photograph that would speak for him from the grave.

Driscoll retrieved Shewster's sketch from his pocket, flattened it on the countertop, and compared it to the photo. Not an exact match. But close nonetheless. It would appear Malcolm Shewster's team was well trained. He turned his attention to the remaining photographs. The "pansies at play" shots featured a bevy of naked men having sex. In shocking detail.

"No other records for who might have brought this film in, huh?"

The salesclerk shook her head. But Driscoll already had an answer to the question. He'd first close the case. But after that, he'd have Margaret pay another visit to Mr. Drag Queen himself, Kyle Ramsey.

"I'll need to take the picture."

"Figured you would. But what the hell. It's not like anybody's gonna know it's gone."

Driscoll thanked Taft and left the store. It was apparent that Ramsey had stolen the dead man's camera. But Ramsey being at the scene was probably the reason the killer hadn't retrieved the camera himself. Judging from the photograph, the killer must have seen the victim aiming the camera at him, but the victim was no longer alone. Kyle Ramsey was now in the picture. The picture caught by the eye of a fleeing demon.

Chapter 53

Traffic was at a standstill on Chambers Street leading to the ramp for the Brooklyn Bridge, where a construction team had chosen rush hour to cordon off two of the bridge's three eastbound lanes. The congestion caused a tie-up on all connecting arteries. While Driscoll waited impatiently behind the wheel, he took out a pad and jotted down Samantha Taft's name and circled it in dollar signs. Malcolm Shewster may end up cutting her a check for a million in cash. Driscoll would make sure she got it. Unless Shewster had worked some loophole into the offering. His suspicion of the man was growing. It'd be just a matter of time before he discovered what role he played in all of this.

As if someone lifted a gate up ahead, traffic began to flow. The Chevy's low-fuel light had been on for awhile. He prayed he'd reach home before running out of gas. Seeking distraction, he ran through the case in his mind. The DNA, collected by Margaret from the circus fiend, had proved to be a no-hit. That realization caused him to glance at the copy of the *Daily News* that occupied the cruiser's passenger seat. The sketched face of one of the killers stared back at him. "End of chapter, my friend. I've got the real deal." He patted his breast pocket that contained the photograph. The silence that followed was interrupted by the sound of his cell phone.

"Driscoll, here."

It was Thomlinson again, with an update.

"Lieutenant, we just got a call from a Greyhound bus driver. Says the photo in the *Post* fits the bill for one of a pair of kids he's been transporting from Carbondale into the city for the past few months.

"Only one of a pair?"

"Says his regular ride-along might be his sister."

"Might?"

"The girl's face is disfigured."

And that's why no one called them in as twins. "Cedric, remind me to buy you a box of cigars."

It was close to six o'clock when Driscoll pulled his cruiser to the curb outside the Port Authority Bus Terminal. Tossing a police "Official Business" card onto the dash, he hurried out of the car and ducked inside. Following Thomlinson's instructions, he headed through the crowd for the northwestern corner and found the Greyhound Bus Lines customer service booth.

"I'm looking for Ted Clarkson. One of your drivers," Driscoll announced, flashing his shield to the rotund lady manning the booth.

"He in some sorta trouble?"

"No, ma'am. Just need to ask him some questions."

"Ted just finished his route. You're likely to find him in the busman's lounge. That'd be on the second floor. Take the escalator over there. When you get to the top, make an about-face. You'll be looking right at it."

Driscoll found the lounge. It was occupied by three drivers.

"Ted Clarkson?" Driscoll called out.

One of the men pointed to a door behind Driscoll marked "Men's Room."

In a minute, Clarkson came out. He was dressed in bus operator blue and sported a well-trimmed mustache. Being overweight must be one of the union rules, Driscoll reasoned. The buttons on the man's shirt looked as though they were about to pop. He appeared to be in his late forties, early fifties, but was probably younger, the extra poundage adding to his age. He had a gentle manner about him and a jovial face.

"Ted Clarkson?" Driscoll asked.

"That'd be me."

"I'm Lieutenant Driscoll," he said, holding out his shield and department ID. "You called about the photo?"

"You like doughnuts?"

An odd response, Driscoll thought. "Who doesn't?"

"C'mon. We can talk while we eat."

They found a Dunkin' Donuts shop.

"I'm hooked on their crullers," said Clarkson as the two men entered the store.

"Make it two crullers," Driscoll said to the slim blonde behind the counter. Driscoll smiled at the irony of finding a thin salesclerk serving up goodies to the heavyset Clarkson.

They sat across from each other at a Formica-topped table. Clarkson wrapped his chubby hands around the Styrofoam cup of coffee while Driscoll placed the suspect's photo on the table.

"Still look familiar?"

"Yup. That's him. Feel a little sorry for the girl. Her face bein' all scarred up and all."

Clarkson wouldn't be so empathetic had he gotten a look at their handiwork. "Tell me all you know about him and his tagalong."

"I'm figuring they gotta live somewhere near Carbondale. That's where they get on the bus. Every other week or so, for the past few months. They get on alone. They hand me their tickets and take their seats in the rear of the bus. It's near the beginning of the run so the bus is pretty much empty. Here's the puzzler. After they settle in, they take out this game board."

"Game board?" Driscoll felt the rush of adrenaline.

"Yeah, a game board. Sorta like Candy Land. Only this one sings."

"Sings? What does it sing?"

" 'New York, New York.' "

"Sinatra's 'New York, New York'?"

"That'd be the one."

The Lieutenant's mind raced. He envisioned the pair aboard the bus. If he reached out his hand, he felt he could touch them. Excitement filled him. He sensed closure. Not surprisingly, though, he also felt sadness. He thought of the twins and their wretched childhood. He wondered what he'd have done if someone had abducted his Nicole and subjected her to such cruelty.

"Tell me more," he said.

"One day, I smelled cigarette smoke coming from the back of the bus. 'Oh, jeeez,' I said. 'It's gotta be the kids.' I pulled over to the shoulder and went to see what they were up to. I find them smoking cigarettes, rolling dice, and moving these pieces around their board."

"What did the board look like?"

"Like I said before. Like Candy Land. You remember. The one with all the colors, where you moved your pieces around a winding track. Only this one had a map on it."

"A map of what?" Driscoll had the answer as soon as he heard himself ask the question. Of course, the city of New York!

"Wish I could help ya there, Lieutenant. I never looked at it up close." Clarkson took a bite of his cruller. "Anyway, I pointed to the 'No Smoking' sign. 'A five-hundred-dollar fine,' I said. You know what these crazies did? They used the tips of their fingers to snuff out the butts!"

Driscoll's eyes narrowed. "Anything else about these kids you can tell me?"

"Not much else to tell."

"They ever threaten anyone on the bus?"

"Nope." Clarkson downed the last of his coffee.

Driscoll stood up. He felt like an overwound machine. In his head he was already on the road to Carbondale. "You've been a great help. If you remember anything else, give me a call." He handed Clarkson his card, then headed for the store's exit, but stopped when he heard the man call out.

"There is something else, Lieutenant. I just remembered."

"And what is that?"

"Every night at the end of my shift I check the bus for lost items. I use my flashlight, ya know, 'cause the light on the bus isn't that good. One night I found this little metal statue. It looked like something I'd seen before, but, for the life of me, I couldn't figure what that was. Anyway, I found it near where the kids were sitting. It's probably still in the glove compartment of the bus."

"Let's go get it." Another rush of adrenaline.

They went to the depot, where Clarkson climbed aboard his bus and rummaged through the glove compartment.

"Here it is." It was a miniature figurine of a church with two spires. "Whaddya make of it?"

Driscoll wrapped his hand around the object like he would a trophy awarded him for winning a marathon. He was closing in. The unfamiliar mix of excitement and sadness swirled within him. "In my business, we've found that most serial killers are collectors. It lets them relive the exhilaration of their sport. This item was either bought or swiped from the gift shop where they committed their last murder. That, my friend, is Saint Patrick's Cathedral."

"Hmm. Never been there," Clarkson said, examining the tiny replica. "By the way, is it you I should call about the reward money after you nab the pair? The million dollars, that is. Or should I wait for another call from that other guy?"

"What other guy?"

"The guy who called me on my cell phone before you showed up. Said he was following up on my initial call."

"He give you his name?"

"Nope. I didn't think to ask."

"What'd he sound like?"

"Whaddya mean?"

"Did he have an accent? Sound old, young? That sort of thing."

"No accent. And I don't think he was old. But I was on a cell phone. You know how those things are. Reception ain't always that good."

"Whaddya tell him?"

"Not much. I was still on the bus. You're not suppose to talk and drive, right?"

"That's right."

"Well, I made it brief. Told him to call me after seven."

Driscoll looked at his watch. It was 6:38.

"What should I tell him when he calls back?"

"Tell him you already spoke to me and gave me all your information. I'll make sure you get the reward money when the time comes." Driscoll produced his card and gave it to the man. "If he presses you further, tell him to call me."

"That million's legit, right?"

"Yes. And if what you've told me leads to their apprehension, you have my word you'll get it." What he didn't tell him was that he might have to split it with Samantha Taft.

Chapter 54

Carbondale. Once the Pittsburgh of Sullivan County, it had been a bustling industrial town where men melted ore and forged steel. Proud smokestacks that had once billowed pitch into the Catskill sky now stood lethargic, their bricks covered with moss, their inner columns eaten away by rust.

Margaret and Thomlinson had spent the better part of the morning flashing copies of the photo to every storekeeper on Maple Street, the heart of town. The hardware store manager and a cashier at Toys on Maple both thought the teen featured in the picture was Angus. They believed he resided with a sister, but neither the manager nor the cashier knew where.

Driscoll, having left the Sheriff's office with nada on the pair, was now inside Weatherley's Hardware speaking with Fred Thurgood, the shop's manager.

"The kid's been in here maybe two or three times, tops," Thurgood said. "Paid cash every time."

"When was the last time he was in?"

Thurgood scratched the back of his head. A human computer at work, thought Driscoll.

"Hadda be a month ago. Maybe two."

"How is it you remember his name to be Angus?"

"Came in with a girl, one time. Poor kid must have poked her nose inside a meat grinder. Disfigured. Ya know? Anyway, she screamed out his name like a banshee. Angus! Must have spotted a spider or something."

"Get her name?"

"Nope."

"A last name for Angus?"

Thurgood shook his head. "Wha'd the boy do?"

"Plenty," said Driscoll. "Wha'd he buy?"

The storekeeper gave Driscoll a blank stare. It seemed to last a full sixty seconds. He then closed his eyes as if that would prompt faster recollection. The eyes shot open.

"An ax sharpener! That's what he bought. An ax sharpener."

Driscoll thanked the man, exited Weatherley's, and headed for Toys on Maple, where a second retailer had ID'd the photo. He was greeted by a haggard gent, bib overalls draping a frail figure.

"Help ya?"

Driscoll produced the photo. "You the one who ID'd this fella?"

"You must be the cop lookin' for Prudence. Followin' up on the brunette cutie, are ya?"

He must have met Margaret. The old codger. "Right," he said.

"I'll go get her. I won't be but a minute. You wait right here." He disappeared through a door at the rear of the store.

The sound of the woman's voice preceded her entrance. Driscoll's eyes soon focused on a redhead with dazzling green eyes. He figured her for twenty, twenty-one.

"Are you here to see me?" she asked.

"You the young lady who recognized the teen in this photo?"

"That's Angus. Where'd you get that?"

Driscoll caught something in the tone of her question.

More than recognition registered in those glittering eyes. "You sound as though you know him. Do you?"

The question broadsided her.

"No," she stuttered.

She was concealing something.

"You wouldn't be in any trouble if you did."

Driscoll watched her. Her blank stare was replaced with the look of agitation.

"I knew it! I just knew it!"

"Knew what?"

"That the cheating bastard would get himself into some kind of trouble."

"How old are you?" he asked.

"Seventeen."

Clarity surfaced.

"You'd be doing him a favor if you told me what you know about him."

"Can we talk outside?"

Driscoll spotted Old Baggy Bibs peeking from behind the rear door. "Sure."

When they reached the curb, the teen leaned against a parked Buick and faced Driscoll.

"Ya wanna hear it from the top?"

"Why don't we start with your name?"

"Sally. Sally Potter."

"Pleased to meet you, Sally." Driscoll extended his hand. "I'm Lieutenant Driscoll."

"Okay. What I know about him. First off, our relationship, if ya wanna call it that, was like being on a rollercoaster with a stranger. The guy was distant. Seemed to have difficulty connecting. And the rollercoaster part. One minute he was up. And I'm talkin' up! Like he was on some sorta drug. Then wham! The bottom falls out and he's down, 'I wanna kill myself' kinda down. I don't think he ever tried it, but with him anything was possible."

"Did you ever see him use drugs?"

"That's the thing. He wouldn't take a sip a beer, for Chrissake! I doubt if he was using. Never did with me. But the mood swings had me wondering."

"How long the two of you been seeing each other?"

"On and off for a few months. Like I said, it wasn't what you'd call a regular thing. Hell, we never even—" She stopped abruptly. Driscoll wasn't surprised. He'd found that most teens weren't comfortable sharing intimate details with adults. More so when that adult was a cop she'd just met.

"What don't we see in the picture?"

"Whaddya mean?"

"In it, he's wearing a hood. Did he keep his hair long or short?"

"Somewhere between the two. The photo hides it, but his hair is blond."

"How tall is he?"

"About five-eight."

"Any distinguishing marks?"

"You mean like moles or freckles? Things like that?"

"Exactly."

"No. He didn't have any. His complexion was better than mine."

"How 'bout the rest of him?"

She became flushed. "Um . . ." A half smile. "This is sort of embarrassing."

A fatherly smile told her he understood.

"He kept his clothes on," she said. "Always! Even when—" She stopped short again.

Driscoll waited.

"It could be ninety freakin' degrees out and he'd be in pants, socks, shoes, and a long-sleeved shirt. Buttoned. To the neck!"

What's he hiding? Driscoll wondered.

"Nothing was ever . . . what you'd call regular with Angus. Every time I turned around, he and his sister were either headin' outta town or coming back."

"Ever tell you where they went?"

"Nope."

"What'd she look like?"

"I guess like him."

"You never saw her?" Driscoll found that surprising. Surprising and disappointing. He watched as anxiety collected on the girl's face.

"He's in a heap of trouble, isn't he?"

"He could be."

Silence settled. But not for long.

"With his sister! Can you believe it? He dodged having sex with me. But he goes and does his goddamn sister!"

Driscoll believed that if Angus had gone through half of what he had claimed, elective sex would be the last thing on his mind, but he wasn't going to let Potter know what he was thinking. Instead, he'd rely on the adage about hell having no fury as a woman scorned. It'd just be a matter of time before she erupted. In the meantime, he'd light some fuses.

"You may have heard about the killing spree in New York City."

"Jesus! Is he wanted in connection with that?"

Driscoll's expression said "you tell me."

"Figures. The guy was whack city."

"Sally, you're in a position to help us stop the killings."

The teen narrowed her eyes. Driscoll sensed she was still reeling with jealousy and rage. He waited for that fury to ignite. His wait was short. With her eyes still tapered like a honing blade, she gave him up, feeling like she was a descendant of Judas Iscariot.

Chapter 55

Sally Potter wasn't much help in providing a last name for the twins. When asked, she said Angus told her it was LTB. At first, Driscoll thought the letters may have some Native American significance. That notion ceased when Sally explained LTB meant Like The Beef. Angus Like The Beef was clearly fond of games.

But she had told him where they lived.

The clapboard one-story house sat under a sprawling willow, fifty yards in from a dirt road, some six miles from the outskirts of town. Well hidden. Weathered plywood covered the windows and a 1962 Plymouth Belvedere was decomposing by its side.

The tall grass that helped conceal the residence was now matted down by a twenty-man Sullivan County SWAT team that was sitting tight and awaiting Driscoll's orders.

The Lieutenant, armed with an arrest warrant, radioed Thomlinson, who was in place with Margaret, some thirty yards away. On Driscoll's orders, two SWAT team officers, armed with a three-foot battering ram, stormed up rickety steps and charged the door. A barrage of armor-clad police-men hustled inside, machine guns at the ready.

In seconds, they swept from one end of the house to the other. Besides the chirping of a canary and the skittering of a calico cat, the place was deserted.

"Secure!" the team leader shouted.

Driscoll entered. In what appeared to be the living room, he spotted a padlocked door.

"Break that down," he ordered.

An officer, using a two-foot industrial cable-cutter, made short work of the padlock. When the door swung open, Driscoll stood staring at a set of steps that led downward. Three members of the SWAT team rushed past him and hur-ried down the steps. "Secure!" sounded within seconds. The Lieutenant descended into a small cellar. There was an open-ing behind the furnace that led into a windowless room where a faint smell of copper lingered. He recognized the scent. It was the characteristic odor of dried blood. Who or what was slaughtered in here? he wondered. In the center of the room was a table. On it sat a cardboard box with "New York, New York" scrawled in felt-tipped marker across its top.

Driscoll donned a pair of latex gloves and opened the box. It contained a game board. Its surface was a map of the city of New York. A snaking trail of one-inch squares mean-dering in and about the five boroughs. At the site of each landmark, the square appeared to be raised. He traced his finger along the path, beginning in the northwestern corner of Brooklyn, up and onto the Brooklyn Bridge. There, he de-pressed the square. Something metallic sounded, followed by Sinatra's voice singing "New York, New York."

"Who had made such a game?" he asked Thomlinson, who was now at his side. He turned his attention back to the game box and saw a velour pouch, stuffed in its own card-board compartment. He emptied its contents into his hand. Miniature representations of city landmarks crowded his palm. He had found more trophies. As if the scalps weren't enough. They included an inch-high tin replica of a carousel. Driscoll recognized it as matching the one on Coney Island's Surf Avenue, a stone's throw from the Wonder Wheel, where the body of the second victim had been discovered. There was also a silver charm bracelet, dangling an imitation sapphire. He was sure he'd be able to trace that one back to the gift shop at the museum. He fingered a two-inch brass-plated model of an aircraft carrier; surely from the Intrepid Sea, Air, and Space Museum. There was a small magnet characterizing Central Park, and a tiny orangutan; no doubt from the Bronx Zoo. Saint Patrick's Cathedral, the bus operator's find, was indeed missing. But, so, too, was any item relating to the murder on the Brooklyn Bridge. That he found odd. Still, he allowed the rush of adrenaline to warm him.

"Lieutenant, whaddya make of that?" Thomlinson was gesturing to an item, sitting on the floor, in the corner of the room.

The two lawmen approached. They stood staring at a small square package covered in newsprint that had been wrapped in such a fashion so as to showcase Angus's sketch. Smoke rings, which had been penciled in, spewed from his mouth. Driscoll and Thomlinson exchanged glances. Glances that read caution. They may have happened upon something they wish they hadn't.

"Everybody out!" hollered the Lieutenant.

Chapter 56

For Driscoll and the platoon of law enforcement personnel, it had been a tense fifty minutes, spent three hundred
yards away from the perimeter of the house. Some quelled
their anxieties by exchanging war stories while Driscoll pondered what his next move might be. The Lieutenant, knowing he was closing in, wanted to get closer.

His radio crackled, dispelling the stillness that hung in
the country air: "All clear."

Eager to find out what was inside the package, he and
Thomlinson drove to the house. Two officers, clad in blast
protective tactical body armor, were waiting there for them.

"It's all yours, Lieutenant, and many returns of the day,"
one of the officers said with a grin as he handed a box to
Driscoll.

The Lieutenant was holding a wooden coffer. Teak, he believed. On its exterior was an expertly carved Native American whom Driscoll recognized immediately as Sinister, the
same Manhattan tribe warrior featured on his and every New
York police officer's shield. "Cute," he said, before lifting
the lid.

Inside was a piece of clay pottery. It stood about three

inches tall and an inch and a half wide. Its body, supported by three fixed feet, resembled a bowl with strawlike stems protruding from its sides in the four cardinal directions. A small envelope was attached. Driscoll opened the envelope and retrieved a white card. He read from it. "Sorry we're not here to greet you. My face plastered across everything but the freaking Goodyear blimp told us you'd soon make a visit to Carbondale. Lieutenant Driscoll, you got to have a heart. Don't you think we suffered enough? This here's a Catawba peace pipe. We're hoping to share it?"

Chapter 57

Margaret fidgeted with her fingers as she studied the woman seated across from her. Elizabeth Fahey, psychotherapist extraordinaire, was what Driscoll had called her. Margaret hoped his accolade was appropriate. She was as he had described: an attractive redhead with sparkling green eyes and a gentle demeanor.

"You said on the phone you wanted to discuss some childhood fears that have resurfaced," Fahey said. "I think it best I get to know a little more about you. Would you feel comfortable with that?"

Margaret inhaled deeply. Then nodded. She was one tough cop but the thought of embarking on a journey of self-exploration scared her half to death.

Fahey crossed her legs, placed her hands on her lap, and smiled. It appeared to Margaret she was eager to listen. But was Margaret eager to talk?

"Where do I start?"

"Anywhere you'd like."

"Okay. I'm a police officer. I work with John Driscoll. I suppose you're aware of that since John referred me to you." Margaret caught herself editing her words. *Should I be call-*

ing him John? she wondered. *Focus. Make this more about you.* "I was raised in Brooklyn in a typical Italian family." She stopped abruptly. "Well, maybe, not typical. But Italian. Catholic Italian. We attended Mass on Sunday. I wore a new outfit on Easter. And attended parochial school . . ."

Margaret looked down at the floor and shook her head. The gesture did not go unnoticed.

"Sounds like an idyllic childhood."

Margaret knew better and was willing to bet Fahey did too.

"Look at me. I'm acting like those zealots who drape themselves in enough scapulas and Saint Anthony medals to choke a horse! Rambling about a childhood steeped in allegiance to the Catholic Church, Easter Sunday, and goddamn parochial school as if it would all protect me now. Hell, it didn't then!" Moisture coated Margaret's eyes.

"Define 'maybe not typical.'"

Margaret smiled. "We're there already! Wow! I've been hovering an inch above solid ground for over thirty years. You ask me for a snapshot of my life. And in less than a minute I stumble over the word 'typical' and wham! We zero in on why I'm here."

"We have?"

"I was in therapy once before. In my teens. It seemed to take a lot longer back then to get to the crux of the problem."

"I'm not sure we're there yet. But we're circling. What was so untypical about your family?"

Margaret felt like she had been asked to dive into a freshly dug grave. She'd been caught. On some level, she had hoped she could get away with hinting that her childhood was anything but ordinary and leave it at that. The mere notion of exploring it further shot splinters of fear through her marrow.

"Let's see. My cousin Tony owned a pizza shop. Both grandmothers dressed only in black. And that was long before it was considered voguish. We ate pasta every Sunday. I had four brothers and three sisters. And if that wasn't atypical enough, my father . . ."

Fahey was watching a woman desperately try to distance herself from her inner demons. It was not uncommon for a patient to use levity, in this case tinged with sarcasm, to avoid dancing with the devil.

"You were about to tell me about your father. What was he like?"

She had a delicate way of probing. "I like you, Elizabeth. I was told you were kindhearted. I'm finding that to be true."

Margaret had sidestepped the question. Fahey found self-preservation to be a curious mechanism. For many it was inborn. For others it was clutched after.

"That Lieutenant Driscoll! You've got to love the man. How do you and he get along?" the therapist asked.

There's no stopping this one. Margaret felt like she was being led through a minefield, but was comforted in knowing she wasn't making the trek alone. She also knew the course was skillfully plotted and designed to help, but an inner voice yelled caution.

"The Lieutenant is a gem. We get along famously," she said.

"A minute ago you called him John. He's your boss, right?"

Zapped again! Margaret searched Fahey's eyes for escape. Outmaneuvered, she succumbed to the inevitable. "He's part of the reason I'm here. I'm guessing this is way out of bounds, but has he discussed me with you?"

"Out of bounds? Hmm . . . what say we keep it in bounds by you discussing him with me. With emphasis on the part about him being part of the reason you're here."

Yup. She earned her title. Psychotherapist extraordinaire fit. "You know what's funny. I've got this sudden urge for a cigarette and I haven't smoked a day in my life."

"Some crave nicotine. Others, scotch. But it's a good sign. It means you're seriously considering the exploration of your inner self. The mind goes to great lengths to protect the journeyer. It's suggesting a sedative."

"Not a bad idea. You wouldn't happen to have a jumbo-sized Prozac on hand, would you?"

"I wish it were that easy."

Margaret felt dizzy. Trepidation was on the rise.

"At your pace, Margaret."

"I was hoping our hour was up."

"My Timex has a slow second hand."

Margaret exhaled sharply and stared at the therapist. "I don't know where to start."

"Anywhere you'd like."

"Okay. Here goes," she said, slapping the tops of her legs. "Since I've confided to you that my boss is one of the reasons I'm here, I'll begin with him. John and I have this thing going on. I'm not sure what else to call it. When we worked our last case, we realized we had feelings for each other and eventually let it be known. He was married. To Colette, who I'm betting you know was in an irreversible coma and was being cared for at home. He loved his wife. Adored her. And this man's moral fiber is forged in steel. The investigation called for us to work side by side for hours on end. One night, after a grueling day, we ended up at my apartment. It was supposed to be for a bite to eat. But I think we both knew we were flirting with trouble. After actually sharing a meal, one thing led to another and before we knew it, we were in each other's arms sharing a kiss. And then another. We knew what came next. At two in the morning, just as we were about to give in to passion, his cell phone rang. For a homicide honcho a call in the middle of the night is not unusual. But the call was from his wife's nurse. Colette had stopped breathing. Care to take a stab at what happened next?"

"He headed for the door?"

"Like the place was on fire." Margaret sighed and grew silent.

"Still jones'n for that cigarette?" Fahey asked.

"The scotch too!" She gave Fahey a crooked smile. "As it turned out, his wife had resumed breathing by the time he'd gotten home, still comatose, but breathing. But that put the kibosh on things. The next day, he told me he was filled with guilt and asked if we could slow things down. I got the sense he was hoping for a complete stop. The days that followed. . . . Who am I kidding? The weeks that followed were awkward. We weren't making any headway on the case, so that only added to the frustration. But the investigation gave us something to focus on, aside from our feelings."

"What feelings did you experience throughout this 'thing,' as you call it? He was married, no?"

"If you're wondering about my guilt, yes, I endured the shame of being the other woman, but what was really nagging me was something else. Something far more dreadful."

Margaret prided herself on being able to detect and decipher body movements, an attribute in her profession. Fahey had leaned forward in her chair. An inch. No more. Was she spreading a net for the freefall Margaret was about to take? She certainly hoped so.

"My father repeatedly raped me when I was a child."

Margaret expected the walls to reverberate. Instead, silence settled. But only for a moment.

"I'm very sorry," Fahey said. "Would it be all right if we talked about it?"

"I believed it was my fault, Elizabeth. Isn't that the damnedest thing? For years. My fault." Tears welled. "He was my father! A man who could do no wrong. He was even a cop, for Chrissake!" Margaret stared down at the floor as memories swirled. "He'd come into my room. Three or four times a week. Some nights he would straddle me; cover my mouth with his hand." Margaret looked up. Her cheeks were red, stained with tears. Her chin was trembling. She cast doelike eyes at Fahey. "Sometimes he would lay back and have me get him off. Said my hands were sent by God.

Lambskin wonders, he called them. Other nights he was more adventurous. Adventurous. I was eleven years old and my father is teaching me how to su—" Margaret choked; her face falling into cupped hands. She sobbed uncontrollably, while gasping for air.

Fahey had witnessed many a meltdown. She was always moved with pity. But her feelings of empathy were stronger this time. Undoubtedly because of the relationship she had with a central character in this woman's life: John Driscoll, a man whose life was likewise riddled by trauma, albeit of a different sort. She was proud to have helped Driscoll cope with his feelings of abandonment brought on by his mother's suicide, the untimely death of his daughter, and the prolonged demise of his wife. She had also been privy to the Lieutenant's struggle with his feelings for this woman and knew it was no stroke of happenstance that Driscoll had referred her. Strokes of happenstance were not accidental. They were, like everything other impulse, driven by the unconscious. Life may rock. But the id rules.

"Some cop I turned out to be, huh?" said Margaret, a handle on composure.

"A damn good one, I'd bet. Your abuse was the likely force behind your decision to become part of law enforcement. Someone to right the wrong was who you needed back then. And now, here you are. Like the song title suggests, everyone needs someone to watch over them. But more often than not, it takes time for that someone to materialize."

"I believe you're that someone to John."

Fahey was touched by the remark. "In his mind, that may be the case. But if he were to look closely, he'd realize he is his own protector. My role as a therapist is to help people discover their omnipresent power and provide them with tools to tap into it to effect and maintain good health."

"It must be a rewarding job."

"At times. Therapy is a process. Each individual goes through it at his or her own pace. So . . ."

"So sometimes you wait forever."

"Precise and succinct."

Margaret's expression soured. "I've got a feeling my pace is going to be like that of a snail."

"That remains to be seen. But you're off to a good start. We've established your relationship with your father for what it was. We may need to dredge up some stuff about that relationship you'll wish we didn't, but that's part of the healing process, I'm afraid. For now, though, I'd like to touch on your relationship with men in general."

Boy, she's good at keeping the nerve exposed.

"Judging from the look on your face, it would help if we talked about it."

Perceptive too. "Just how slow is that second hand on your watch?"

"Well, we're not going to resolve all of your issues in one session, but I'd like to spend some time putting them out."

"It'll be more like pulling them out."

"That speaks volumes," said Fahey with a smile.

"Thank you, Daddy!" Margaret growled, waving a fist in the air. "Does it always lead back to horrendous parenting?"

"In some cases back to the womb! It's only recently that expectant mothers have been made aware of the risks involved in picking up a drink or smoking a cigarette. And let's not overlook the mothers-to-be with emotional baggage of their own who seek relief from a variety of substances. Mother's little helper may becomes baby's little toxin."

Jesus! Margaret thought, deciding quickly to save the exploration of the back-to-the-womb part for another time. "You asked me about my relationship with men. Hello-o! Venus to Mars, come in please. I'll sum up my relationship in three words. Men petrify me!"

"That apply to John Driscoll as well?" Her boss, the perfect father figure.

"Especially to him! On the job, there're mostly men. Despite the efforts of Betty Friedan and Anna Quindlen, the wall of blue is still predominantly male. Focusing strictly on matters of law enforcement, I get along well with those I'm assigned to work with. Pair me up with one? It'd better be inside a police cruiser. Otherwise, Panic City. When it comes to relating to a guy outside of Platonicville, I'm an emotional idiot. I feel as adept as an eighth grader. I'd rather be thrown from a plane!"

"I've known some eighth graders . . ."

"Well, they didn't go to my school!"

Fahey was pleased. She had elicited some anger from Margaret. That was a good sign. Margaret would be visiting that emotion, often, in the months to come.

"I said men were part of the reason I'm here. I get a sense that we'll be talking about them for quite a while. But the other reason I'm here is more urgent."

"How so?"

"The case we're working on involves a pair of twin adolescent killers."

"Ah, the twins with the million-dollar bounty on their heads."

"They're the ones. I'm having a problem putting aside strong feelings of sympathy for the pair. We believe they're killing their adult victims to avenge years of sexual abuse. There's more to their motive, but the likelihood of them being sexually abused has stirred up not what I'd call a treasure trove. I'm rocketed right back to my bedroom as a child. Where I was abused! Where I was raped by my father! Their father apparently forced them into prostitution. I know I took an oath that calls for me to stop them. Arrest them. Shoot them, if it comes to that. The struggle I'm having is because I want to save them. I try to be objective. To focus on their crimes and not their dreadful life. But, if they walked in here right now and confessed, I'm more likely to take them home, secretly harbor them, and get them help, instead of slapping on the cuffs. I know my issue with men stems from my being abused. I've lived with that for a long time and I know it may take equally as long to resolve. But this is immediate. These twins are out there killing people and it's my job to arrest them as soon as possible. You sure you don't have a super-sized pill for a quick fix so I can to do that? The way things are going inside my head, I'm liable to put my job—hell, my life—in jeopardy by aiding and abetting this pair. The entire city sees them as demons. I see them as victims. I live with that every waking hour. John offered to discreetly arrange for a transfer. I got to tell you. I'm getting closer and closer to accepting one."

"What's stopping you?"

"I'd feel like I'd be running away from responsibility."

"What would your best friend suggest?"

"My best friend? I'm not sure I have a best friend."

"Then you'll need to become your own."

"Okay. And what would I tell myself?"

"Think about it. Suppose for a minute that your brother or your sister, or anyone who might fit the bill as a best friend, was driving a car, quickly approaching a T-intersection where they had to decide to turn one way or the other to avoid colliding into a house and injuring themselves. They can't stop. They must go one way or the other. Which way would you tell them to turn for their absolute safety?"

"I don't know if I could."

"Why not? Remember, they can't stop. If they don't turn, they're very likely to injure themselves. Perhaps fatally."

"I wouldn't be able to guarantee their safety because I don't know what's around each corner."

"Sort of like life."

"Right."

"And, although you're not sure what's around each corner, you would suggest that they turn, correct? Remember, there's that big house. And it's getting closer and closer."

"I'm not sure I'm getting this. Or how it relates."

"You're not necessarily supposed to. Therapy is a process. That's why we don't recommend the big pill. You see, you *would* tell them to turn. Turning right could present new challenges. Likewise, turning left is likely to present new, but different, challenges."

Margaret looked and felt befuddled.

"I'm afraid we need to stop now."

"Now?"

"It'd be a good time. Trust me." Fahey cast her a huge smile. "I would like to set up future appointments. Would you be open to that?"

"I think I'd better."

"Good. Check your upcoming tour schedule and call me. I'm here Monday, Wednesday, and Friday until six. I'd like to meet once a week. Would that work for you?"

Margaret nodded and stood.

"We're going to work at both issues together, Margaret. In the meantime, since you said you're not sure if you have a best friend, I'd like to apply for the job."

"That'd be nice."

"I'm glad you feel that way."

Margaret headed for the door.

"Oh, there's one more thing. Between now and the next time we meet, think about the advice you'd give the driver. Don't focus too much on which way you'd tell them to turn, but concentrate on why you'd instruct them to make the turn."

"I will." *I think.*

"Great! With today's session we're off to a good start."

Following an exchange of smiles, Margaret disappeared out the door.

Chapter 58

Driscoll was at his desk speaking on the phone with Susan Lenihan from the National Center for Missing and Exploited Children.

"There're some details of the case I want to run by you. As a behavior analyst, you're in a position to help."

"Be happy to."

"When I spoke to a young lady who claimed to be at one time our teen suspect's girlfriend, she told me a couple of things, one of which I didn't think fit."

"What was that?"

"She claimed he was sleeping with his sister. I'm no analyst, but I can't see a guy forced to prostitute himself for six years wanting to have sex."

"That would seem logical, but I'm afraid trauma victims don't always follow the dictates of what might be considered predictable behavior."

Driscoll was startled. "You mean he might be having sex with her?"

"It's possible."

"Please, make me a believer."

"Without having him on a couch, this is pure conjecture.

Children forced to prostitute themselves sometimes feel excessively guilty. They forget who the victim is. If they lean on themselves heavily enough, it could lead to raucous promiscuity and extreme hypersexuality, which may include incest."

"So, she may have it right. Interesting. She also said he had exhibited intense mood swings. One minute he'd be flying high as a kite, the next minute he's talking suicide."

"Mood swings that concurrent could point to a number of things. Bipolar affective and interictal dysphoric disorders immediately come to mind. With his forced lifestyle, he'd be at a higher risk for either than, say, your average high school student furtively exploring sex under the bleachers. Not only are you chasing after a pair of homicidal maniacs. They could also be two very sick puppies, both physically and emotionally."

"Thank you, Susan. This crash course in Behavior 101 was enlightening."

"We only covered two paragraphs of the first chapter. But you're welcome, just the same. If you want to fast-forward to chapter six, all you need to do is call."

Driscoll thanked her again and hung up. He thought he detected flirtation in her last remark. Not in what she said, but in how she said it. Or was he imagining things? He was newly single, out of the game for years.

Aligante entered his office and sat.

"Uh-oh. That look on your face says you'd like to sit down with the twins and smoke their pipe," Driscoll said. "I'm praying the gold shield in your pocket says otherwise."

"These kids have been traumatized, John. Far worse than me. They probably killed their father believing it was the only way out of their nightmare. Hell! I thought of killing my father. Often."

"But you didn't."

"No, but a voice inside me cheered at his funeral and suggested I set off fireworks."

"You call Elizabeth yet?"

"She sends her best."

"That's what I wanted to hear. Tap Cedric on the shoulder and ask him to join us. I'll let him tell you firsthand about the nugget of gold he and his contacts in LA found in a closet."

"One Detective Thomlinson coming up."

When Margaret reappeared, Thomlinson was at her side. After they took their seats, Driscoll spoke. "From the top, Cedric."

"My pleasure!" Thomlinson leaned back in his chair. Having an eager audience encouraged the man. He smiled at Driscoll, gestured to Margaret as though he were tipping his hat, and began. "The tracking of sex offenders in California falls to the responsibility of the state's Department of Justice."

"Why do I get the feeling I know where he's going with this?"

"Listen and learn," said Driscoll.

Thomlinson, amused by the chatter, continued. "Not only does the DOJ maintain the database but they also post most of it on the Internet."

"Most of it?" Margaret griped.

"The crimes that some of these sleazebags have been convicted of aren't considered abominable enough to warrant Web posting. They get to see their names in the registry but are spared the embarrassment of Internet stardom. Ah, California! Ya gotta love that state! Once a year, within five days of their birthday, the entire cast of misfits is required to renew their registration. A belated birthday greeting from Arnie the Governator, no doubt. As you'd expect, the offender must update his info pronto, if he moves, or, God forbid, becomes homeless. My favorite requirement is listed as penal code section two-nine-zero, subdivision f-three. It requires the degenerates to update the registry with any name change. They've got five days to do it or get a nastygram from the authorities." A grin formed on Thomlinson's smug face.

"I know that look," said Margaret.

"June 1998. A UCLA grad student gets nailed for oral copulation with a minor. It seems the poli-sci enthusiast lured a fourteen-year-old male back to her apartment to give him an up close and personal lesson on what she had learned in the Art of Good Fellatio 101. The recipient's name was purged from the record but our doer's was not. Does the name Shewster ring a bell?"

"I knew it. Abigail Shewster."

A broader grin formed on Thomlinson's face.

"Here comes the best part," said Driscoll.

"Gweneth Shewster," said Thomlinson.

"Who the hell is Gweneth Shewster?" Margaret searched his eyes for an answer.

"Gweneth Shewster. Date of birth August 12, 1976. Daughter to Malcolm and Penny Shewster of Holmby Hills."

"Whoa!"

"That's an excerpt from her obituary," said Thomlinson. "Made all the noteworthy papers. Even the *New York Times*. Sunday edition! Very modest funeral, though. Attended only by family. Gave daddy an immediate excuse to have the little darling's name deleted from the sex offenders registry. No sir. There was no further need to renew this lady's subscription."

"May I take it from here?" Driscoll asked.

"By all means."

"Malcolm Shewster slipped. I'm sure he isn't even aware of it. When I first met him in Sully Reirdon's office, he boasted that he was prepared to offer a large sum of money to the man who delivered the psychopath that killed his daughter, an only daughter. And he was correct. He only had one daughter. But no man buries an only daughter twice."

"Unless you're Malcolm Shewster," said Margaret.

"Precisely. He was powerless to force Gweneth's crime to

go unpunished. Part of that punishment included her name appearing on the sexual offenders registry. I'm sure he fought that armed with a bazooka. I'm guessing neither his money nor influence could sway the courts. But he's Malcolm Shewster. Orchestrating a fabricated death was not beneath him."

"Shortly after the burial, the Shewster clan, diminished though they were in number, relocated to San Luis Obispo," said Thomlinson. "Got themselves a new house, new surroundings, new neighbors."

"And gave birth to a twenty-two-year-old daughter. They called the newborn Abigail."

"Shewster was good at the game," added Thomlinson. "He had Abigail visit a plastic surgeon, pick out a new look, do something with her hair. Hell, he even threw in a boob job! The birth records were made to appear like any run-of-the-mill adoption. He might not have been able to stop the authorities from posting Gweneth's *nom de famille*."

"But he'd be damned if he couldn't remove it," said Driscoll.

"That's why California's penal code, section two-nine-zero, subdivision f-three is my favorite. It's the one that mandates the Department of Justice be informed of any name change." Thomlinson smiled and unpocketed a cigar.

Chapter 59

Margaret hurried into Driscoll's office to bring him up to speed on her ongoing investigation involving the duplicitous, somewhat clonelike, Shewster woman.

"Your boy Shewster shoulda been a bricklayer," said Margaret, using a dampened finger to blot out a stain on her skirt.

"Why's that?" said Driscoll, distracted by the flash of thigh her action produced.

"Because the son of a bitch who managed to have his daughter's dental records, from when she was six, mind you, come back with Abigail's name on them is also good at building walls. No problem getting at Abigail's, excuse me, Gweneth's cell phone. It was retrieved at the zoo. A tad banged up. The overgrown chimps must have played Frisbee with it. But her computer? That's a story unto itself. Despite the fact that the detective we flew to California was armed with enough paper to warrant the seizure of Michael Jackson's Neverland Valley Ranch, his efforts to retrieve the computer were stymied by a wall of high-priced lawyers. At one point, he toyed with the idea of getting Tom Cruise to do his *Mission: Impossible* dangling-from-the-ceiling trick to get his hands on it."

"You catch *Mission: Impossible III?*"

"Nope." *Jesus! Is he about to ask me out?*

"Me neither. Tell me he got the computer."

"Yep. It's on its way to Technical Support."

"And the phone?"

"Ah, the phone. Appears this West Coast socialite wasn't much of a chatterbox. A few numbers led back to California. Never more than two minutes. We're tracking them down. But the interesting calls, three actually, were made to and received from an eight-five-eight exchange. One outgoing six days before her body was found, followed by an incoming, three and a half hours later. The third call, outgoing, was placed the day before they found her in the cave."

"If the ME's right about the time of death, that last one was placed the day she was murdered. Let me guess. The eight-five-eight exchange is a disposable."

"You got it. The number-one choice of drug dealers from coast to coast. Who knows? These crazies may have one of those World GSM phones with an International Sim card. They *are* hooking up with globe-trotters."

"We're a long way from rotary dialing."

"Mr. San Antonio? Aka the guy who got whacked at the aquarium? Communications says he also called the eight-five-eight number. Once."

"They couldn't have both picked the number out of thin air. I'm thinking Web site."

"Me, too. But I'm be willing to bet when we get our hands on his hard drive, it's gonna show a lot of shopping at Disney.com. Remember, he was caught surfing rent-a-ho sites and got fired for it. And according to his résumé he took up designing Web sites for a living. He'd know how to cover his tracks."

"Probably used a laptop that's buried deeper than he is."

"Have Tech Support use industrial-sized crowbars on Miss Shewster's computer. We need to know her cyber secrets yesterday!"

Chapter 60

Cassie's body looked like the letter *C*. With her ass pressed against the worn couch in their new lodgings, she was digging at an ingrown toenail with a corkscrew. She had watched as Angus's inner demons took hold of him. The malaise could last a few minutes. Or upward of an hour. She would always try to keep him engaged. "We both knew the chance of them backing off was at minus-a-zillion. Even making it seem like you were a retard in the e-mail didn't help. To them we're still the bad guys. It's not like we were asking for a goddamn medal-pinning ceremony. But we did rid the world of a lot of degenerates."

"And we ain't done yet."

Angus felt as though he'd been swallowed whole; the walls of their refuge, becoming the hollow of the creature that had consumed him, making him feel trapped and vulnerable. He imagined he was under the scrutiny of an unseen snake, coiled and ready to strike. The predicament put the killing spree on hold. Others would likely resign themselves to their fate, praying that a mask of anonymity would shield them from further peril. But not Angus. Every fiber of his body demanded he exorcise himself, reclaim his weapon, and continue his righteous undertaking. His vengeance had become insatiable.

"Our game board. We shouldn't'a left it. Now we're gonna need a new one," said Cassie.

"Gaming is over."

"We're gonna stop?"

"Hell no."

"Jeeez! I thought ya really lost it. We'll hafta forget about the Web site. They'll be all over that. TwoNaughtyFreaks is officially shut down. Outta business. It's gotta show up on one of the stiffs' Favorites Lists. I'm thinkin' chat rooms."

Angus stood. That was a sign he was coming out of it. *Hang on, Angus. Fight it!*

"No chat rooms!" he said. "They're crawlin' with monitors. Ya think you're talkin' to a deserving target and it turns out to be J. Edgar Hoover."

"He died."

"Whatever."

"We can still use the phone, right?"

"Yeah, but we can't go out and hire one of those freakin' planes to write the number in the sky. That means another Web site. New name. New menu. No twins. You can bet your ass they're swarmin' around every twin site on the planet. I'll get ours routed through Nigeria. Driscoll tries to trace the IP address, he'll end up on Mars."

"Nigeria will cost a shitload of money, Angus. There's like sixty zillion sites. They can't monitor all of 'em."

"Oh yeah? Last month the freakin' NASA headquarters in D.C. was raided. They caught some high-ranking dude, right outta Mission Control, dealing in kiddie porn over the Internet. If they can trace a guy who knows how to disappear into outer space, they can locate anybody."

"You're watchin' too much CNN."

"And this new pope. Benenick—"

"Benedict, you idiot."

"Whatever. There's this old priest—"

"Don't even go there."

"He's like eighty-somethin'. Marsh or Marshall something. Outta Mexico. A big shot. A bishop, I think. Anyway, he gets called in by the pope for some nasty they say he did sixty years ago."

"So what's your point?"

"You know how far Mexico is from where the pope lives? The guy reaches clear across the planet after sixty years? That says nobody's safe. Think about it. The feds take down an astronaut for trawlin' the Web and the Vatican's main man calls for a replay on one of his own. No. Body. Is. Safe. That Driscoll guy tracked us down to Carbondale, for Chrissake!"

"We got outta there just in time. How'd you know?"

"'Cause Big Brother is everywhere."

"Carbondale?"

"Everywhere. And it's only gonna get worse. We're on the run now with a million-dollar bull's-eye painted on our asses. We gotta hurry and set up a new Web si—"

Holy shit! He froze in the middle of a freaking word. "Angus, are you okay? Angus?" He'd never done that before. Cassie thought he'd passed out with his eyes open. Until a smile said otherwise.

"I know that look. What is it? Whad'ya come up with?"

His smile broadened.

"Ya gonna tell me? C'mon, I'm bustin'!"

"We're not gonna need a Web site, Cass."

"No?"

"Not even a phone."

Chapter 61

The Mayor held the handset away from his ear and let Shewster rant. When it stopped reverberating, he returned to the line. "May I speak now?"

"Go ahead," Shewster barked. "But I'd better like what you're going to tell me."

"Rest assured the city of New York is not about to bargain with murderers. What the Lieutenant will get out of this is an intricately carved Native American trinket. Nothing more. I doubt very much that the kids themselves believed their peace-pipe gambit would garner absolution. They're good at playing games. Our belief, the Lieutenant and I, is that both the pipe and the e-mail were meant as distractions. Give them a chance to regroup. We also don't think they have any intention of stopping. They're nuts, for Chrissake!"

"Look, Reirdon. I want to make this point crystal clear. I don't want to ever read in the papers that you've collared these bastards. What I want to read is that they're dead. Dead. You got that?"

"I can't promise you that. C'mon. This isn't Dodge City. Vigilante violence is a crime."

"Not where I come from!"

"Mr. Shewster, you have to let . . . Mr. Shewster? Malcolm? Hello? Hello? Are you there?"

Chapter 62

It was nearing 6:00 A.M. Driscoll had just arrived, early for the morning shift. He put on a fresh pot of coffee, adjusted the blinds, and took a seat behind his desk. Pushing an assortment of the paperwork to the side, along with three messages from the chief of detectives marked "Update," he reached for the folder Margaret had left for him. It was labeled: INTERPOL. Opening it, he discovered she had highlighted the important information in yellow. He wasn't surprised to learn the pair from Germany and Yen Chan of Japan had contacted the twins on their disposable phone. What he was hoping the report contained he found on page three. Not only had Margaret highlighted it but also it was underlined in red. He smiled as he read the editorial she had penciled next to the twins' cyber link: "TwoNaughtyFreaks. Some name for a Web site. I'm sure they had the old man to thank for that one. —M."

His phone rang.

"Driscoll, here."

"You get it?" Margaret asked.

"Just opened it. Where are you?"

"Ten minutes out."

"Good. Thomlinson's on his way in, too. It's time for the three of us to discuss strategy. There's been a new development."

Margaret was already seated inside the Lieutenant's office when Thomlinson appeared at the door.

"Come in, Cedric."

Thomlinson did and sidled up next to Margaret.

"You may have already seen or heard about this." Driscoll passed them a copy of the morning's *Daily News*. Its headline read: JUSTICE SEEKER RAISES BOUNTY TO THREE MILLION. "I've read the article. It doesn't shed any light as to why an anonymous justice seeker has raised the ante. Shewster obviously wants them found in a hurry. But not necessarily alive."

Thomlinson raised an eyebrow.

"It's likely New York has its own vigilante in Shewster seeking revenge-seeking twins. That, according to the Honorable William "Sully" Reirdon, who called me last night, a tad concerned. Seems he got a call from the man. Shewster doesn't want them caught. He wants them dead."

"And we know why," said Thomlinson. "He doesn't want Abigail's fondness for kinky sex revealed by the twins."

"Kinky doesn't quite cut it," said Margaret. "It's perverse."

"Whatever you wanna call it, Shewster's got one foot on Gweneth's grave, the other foot on Abigail's grave, and he's looking to get the twins in his crosshairs," said Driscoll.

"Does Reirdon know that Shewster has both feet on one grave?" asked Thomlinson. "Or is it just us civil servants who know Gwen and Abie are one and the same?"

"I doubt the Mayor's aware. Just to play it safe, I left him out of the loop. He *is* a politician."

"That puts a sniper between us and the twins," said Margaret. "With no way of predicting which way he'll shoot."

"Nor do we know who that shooter might be," said Driscoll. "Shewster will have an infantry of yes-men to choose from. Now, although our new initiative falls under the heading of prevention, I'm not enlisting anyone from the department's Crime Prevention Section. The fewer people we involve, the better. We'll be shadowing a man who's got the home phone number of a horde of political honchos and he'll go to any length to keep his secret buried. When I met with the Greyhound bus operator who ID'd the kids as coming down from Carbondale, he told me someone other than NYPD had returned the call he placed to the Tip Line. Who that was will likely remain a mystery. But on whose behalf had he placed the call? Three million fingers point to Shewster. It could have been the man, himself, but I doubt it. When it comes to selecting someone to take down the twins, he may not use a phone. The likelihood is he'll call him at some point along the way, so we'll trace his calls."

"You'll need a warrant, no?"

"Why? The president didn't need one to eavesdrop on millions of Americans. Besides, this is a crime prevention measure. We're not likely to have to use it in court."

"It amazes me what these guys in the White House get away with. George Bush listens in on unsuspecting citizens, across the nation, and Bill Clinton gives new significance to the *O* in Oval office. Then claims it doesn't constitute sex." Margaret shook her head.

"Let's not forget JFK," said Thomlinson.

"Kennedy was lucky. Back in those days reporters kept their noses out of the bedroom."

"Too bad. Marilyn Monroe coulda used a paparazzi aiming a lens or two on her boudoir. Coulda prevented her suicide, or homicide if you think like a Republican."

"You guys finished?" asked Driscoll.

They both nodded.

"Good. I just got off the horn with Danny O'Brien over at

TARU." Driscoll was referring to NYPD's Technical Assistance Response Unit. "He'll get someone inside the hotel to tap the room's land phone wires. He's got a triangulater for his cell phone and a Global Positioning System for his Lincoln with your name on them. I'll leave it to you, Cedric, to get it attached to his limo, set up the parallel tails, and coordinate the tracking through encrypted radio communication with TARU. Any new players show up on his 'let's go visit' list, Danny will supply us with a GPS to tag onto them." Driscoll turned his attention to Margaret. "I want you to get back to everyone we've spoken to. Your friends at the circus. The night watchman from that halfway house on Staten Island. Father what's-his-name who introduced us to that halfwit Luxworth. Speak to the girl at the photo shop on Montague and our contacts in Carbondale. Touch base with the bus operator again. It couldn't hurt. We wanna know if any of them had anyone asking questions about the twins or their involvement. If they did, get all there is to know on who did the asking. And let's not forget Kyle Ramsey. You'll wanna meet with him in person. Let him know his photos are ready and, when this is all over, he can expect a visit from me."

"You know what's the best part of an operation like this?" said Thomlinson, his eyebrows doing a dance reminiscent of Groucho Marx.

"This I wanna hear," said Margaret.

"I mean, ya gotta respect a satellite-based navigation system that helped take down Scott Peterson for the murder of his wife. And I'm all in favor of a law that says we can use it at will to track the movement of a car 'cause its driver has no reasonable expectation of privacy while driving on a public thoroughfare. No. No breach of the Fourth Amendment there. And who's not to marvel over a designer ankle bracelet with a GPS chip for the likes of Martha Stewart?" His eyebrows did their dance again as he reached for a cigar. "No, I'm in favor of the operation 'cause it means I get to spend a couple of hours alongside the vivacious Leticia Hollander over at CyberCentral."

"For what?"

"To brush up on my hi-tech tracking skills."

"You dog. You've run hundreds of satellite shadows."

"She doesn't know that."

Chapter 63

While Buju Banton was making reggae magic with Bogle, which was blaring through Thomlinson's four-by-four's six Jensen speakers, the detective had his eyes fastened on the rear of Shewster's Lincoln that sat curbside outside Angelo's Salumeria on Mott Street in Little Italy. Thomlinson figured either Shewster or his limo driver had a yen for fresh mozzarella.

"Purchase complete," Thomlinson said, sitting upright, watching the regally dressed driver return to the stretch limo. "Buju, we're on the prowl again!" Turning the key in the Jeep's ignition, he resumed the tail.

Installing the GPS device to the frame of Shewster's vehicle would be a breeze. Two high-powered magnets would see to that. The challenge for Thomlinson was getting it done without being seen.

"This should take awhile," he said, watching the Lincoln glide in next to the Mobil gas pump. The driver got out of the car and inserted a credit card in the pump's slot and proceeded to fill the tank. Thomlinson glanced at the foot-high numbers posted under the Mobil red, white, and blue logo.

He shook his head. "Shewster's not gonna like that charge. No sir. Three sixty-nine for high test is liable to break the bank!"

He wouldn't swear to it, sitting a hundred feet from the station, but when the driver replaced the gas nozzle, Thomlinson thought he read $73.36 as the total purchase.

"No sir. Ol' Shewster's not gonna like that one bit," he said, reengaging the starter and falling in behind the gas-guzzling limo.

It was close to 7:15 P.M. before Thomlinson's unwavering pursuit offered an opportunity to do the deed. He'd been figuring the Town Car would disappear behind some high-wired security gate, which he would then need to outwit to get to his target. Though he was prepared for the possibility, the limo driver's appetite saved him the bother. He followed as the Lincoln turned right into the parking lot of a Red Lobster eatery on Sunrise Highway. He was willing to bet the vehicle didn't end up there too often when Shewster was seated in the back.

He watched as the driver got out from behind the wheel, closed the door, and used a key remote to activate the vehicle's alarm. Thomlinson thought that a good sign. Had he been going in for takeout, he may not have set the alarm.

Thomlinson loved defensive parkers. They always parked at the end of a row, away from other vehicles, in the spot furthest from the restaurant. Very often they took up two spots. That wasn't the case for the limo, but it was parked at the end of a row and a good distance from the entrance to the lobster lover's paradise.

Not only was the view of the limo obscured when Thomlinson sidled the Jeep next to it, but his body going horizontal, his armed stretching under the vehicle, went unnoticed as well.

Thomlinson looked at his watch. He hadn't eaten since noon and was tempted to go inside for a bite, but got back in the Jeep instead. Why? Because Detective Second Grade Cedric Franz Thomlinson was allergic to shellfish.

Chapter 64

When his cell phone rang, Driscoll was getting out of the shower. Wrapping himself in a towel, he followed the ringing to its source, tracking wet footprints across a hardwood floor.

"Driscoll, here."

"Catch you at a bad time?" It was Margaret.

"No. Why?"

"You sound annoyed."

"I'm not. Whaddya got?"

"I spent most of yesterday afternoon and part of last night getting back to our sources. It appears Shewster got into the game only when Ted Clarkson came into the picture. I spoke to the bus driver. After you left him he got a call from a woman."

"A woman?"

"Yup. Said she had been instructed to call him after seven P.M., which coincides with what he told you."

"Interesting. The call he had gotten before I arrived was from a man. Or so he thought."

"Guess Shewster's an equal opportunity employer."

"What'd he tell her?"

"You must of coached this guy good. He told her he had already spoken to a Lieutenant Driscoll and gave her your number. She got a little pushy. Said since a bundle of cash was riding on it, her boss required lots of paperwork, background checks, and follow-up calls."

"Cute. She tell him who her boss was?"

"Being stupid must have ranked high on Shewster's 'Don't You Dare' list. Clarkson got a little pissed off by what he called, and I quote, 'her you'd-better-buy-this-life-insurance policy-or-else attitude,' and told her again to call you."

"Glad I picked up the tab for the crullers."

"Crullers?"

"You had to of been there."

"If you say so. Anyway, his allegiance to you cut off any calls to our friends in Carbondale. No life insurance tactics applied up there."

"Do me a favor?"

"Sure."

"Stop by a Dunkin' Donuts shop, pick up a dozen crullers, and deliver them to Clarkson. Tell him there's three million more in the oven."

"You have coffee yet?"

"No."

"When you do, make it decaf."

Chapter 65

The officer who handled incoming calls to the Twentieth Precinct West Eighty-second Street was used to receiving crank calls. The Twentieth averaged fifteen to twenty a month. Considering the advances in telephone technology and the availability of caller ID, not to mention the capabilities of the police in that regard, you would think oddballs who liked to cry wolf would smarten up.

That's what Officer Stephen Turley thought he had received from a very excited female. She claimed to work at PC Haven, on West Fifty-seventh near Tenth, and said he'd been to the store. When asked who she meant by "he," she clammed up and said she didn't want to discuss it by phone, thought maybe she should talk to a lawyer. Mucho dinero was on the line, she told him, and she didn't want to foul up her chances of collecting the reward. When Turley asked what she meant by that, she said, "You're kiddin', right? Where're ya from? Mars?" That remark angered him. Rather than making it personal or go on listening to her gibberish, he told the loon he'd have someone look into it. After hanging up, he had a chance to think more clearly, without her punctuating everything she told him with "Oh! My God!"

According to his monitor, the call had come in from PC Haven. That much was legit. Roll call for the past couple of months had included a directive to be cognizant of the murderous spree of a set of homicidal twins with a huge bounty on their heads. Not that he needed to be reminded every morning—he was a native New Yorker and was well aware of the twin psychos and the reward offered for their capture. Nah. Couldn't be, he thought. But after replaying the conversation in his head, he decided better safe than sorry. She had called the right precinct for Fifty-seventh and Tenth. He called it in to Dispatch.

He stared at the phone, lost to thought. He'd been to that PC Haven. He tried to fit a face to the caller. Nothing. No big deal, he thought, when the responding officer returned to the house, he'd find out who it was that suggested he came from Mars. He picked up the newspaper, and being a sports enthusiast, went directly to the back.

The patrol car, empty of its two police officers, sat at the curb outside the office supply retailer.

Inside, a crowd of employees had encircled a chubby redhead whom the two officers were questioning. Her name tag read "Rita." Her beefy hands were clutched to a newspaper.

"He was here! I checked him out! Oh, My God! Three million dollars! Oh, My God!"

"Can you describe him for us?" one of the officers asked.

She placed the newspaper on the checkout counter and smoothed it out with her palm. "Him!" she said, pointing to the hooded Angus. "Only he was wearing glasses when he came in. He's not in the picture. But, I'm tellin' ya, it was him! Oh, My God! Oh, my God!"

"What'd he buy?"

"A computer. An HP Compaq nc4200 WiFi Notebook. The PM 760 model. On sale!"

One of the other employees ran to get the weekly flyer.

"Was anyone with him?"

"Nope."

"How'd he pay for the notebook?"

"Cash. Funny thing, though. The bills smelled like horses."

"Horses?"

"Yup. I was gonna ask him if he hit it big at the track or somethin', but the look he gave me said NFW."

The officers exchanged glances.

"No f'in' way," a store clerk explained.

"We got that. What kind of look?"

"One I'll never forget. Like he wanted to kill me."

Chapter 66

Driscoll was in the elevator going down for a late lunch when his cell phone rang. He didn't bother answering it because the reception was zero inside the mechanical lift. He checked the screen. The caller was Thomlinson. He'd return his call when he reached the first floor.

His beeper sounded. That was rare. He checked it. Again, Thomlinson.

Depressing and holding the illuminated button for the first floor, he continued his descent. He knew his action made no difference. But in his adrenaline-fueled state, he did it anyway.

Stepping off the elevator, he retrieved his phone. It rang before he flipped it open.

"Driscoll."

Thomlinson got right to the point.

"The Twentieth took a call from a very excited cashier IDing Angus buying a notebook computer in a local PC Haven store. According to the cashier, he was alone. Paid cash. And get this. The cashier says the money smelled like horses."

"Horses, giraffes, or zebras—I got a good feeling on this.

Grab your jacket and meet me in the lobby. Tell everyone to get ready to move. Is Margaret there?"

"Right next to me."

"Good. Bring her with you."

Chapter 67

"What's in the bag?" Cassie asked, as Angus climbed the stairs to the loft.

"A computer."

"A computer? I thought we weren't goin' with a Web site."

"We ain't."

"Then why do we need a new computer? What's wrong with the one we got?"

"You see any freakin' online access cable coming through the wall?" Opening the box, he gave the user's manual a perfunctory scan and placed the notebook atop a chest-high barrel near the window to the street. He plugged in its AC adapter cord and turned it on. Not once did he look at his sister.

"You said we didn't need a Web site. Didn't even need a phone. Then you promised you'd clue me in when you figured out what the hell you were doin'! What's with the freakin' computer?" Annoyed, she rummaged through the PC Haven bag, finding the receipt. "You went across town? Angus, this is New York freakin' City! Ya think nobody here reads the papers? This is the television capital of the world, for Chrissake! What's this?" She had discovered what else was in the bag. A smile lit her face as she retrieved it.

"That, lovee, is a Beretta Tomcat. Be careful. It's loaded."

"Wow! Now, this is cool." Her eyes ogled the pistol. She passed it from hand to hand. "Why do we need it?"

Turning his attention from the notebook, he looked at her. "You wanna get Driscoll off our backs, right?"

"Of course."

"Good! We're not gonna use a Web site. Not gonna need a phone."

"I'm lost, Angus. You wanna bring me all the way into the loop?"

He shushed her, staring at the active matrix screen, its icons coming to life. "We just need to find the right target," he said with a grin.

Chapter 68

Racing along West Fifty-seventh Street, Driscoll spotted the department helicopter hovering above the northern tip of Clinton Cove Park, a few blocks ahead. Three miles south sat the Intrepid Sea, Air, and Space Museum, where victim number four, Tatsuya Inagaki, had been discovered.

After crossing Tenth Avenue, he pulled alongside a blue and white patrol car in front of PC Haven. Three others, their emergency lights ablaze, were double-parked across the street, along with a pair of unmarked cruisers from the Twentieth. He, Margaret, and Thomlinson got out and disappeared inside the electronic retailer, anxious to meet with Rita Crenshaw, the young lady who had reported spotting Angus.

Inside were a bevy of police officers, a cluster of excited employees, and a handful of curious customers. But no Rita Crenshaw.

Chapter 69

Malcolm Shewster was seated directly behind his chauffeur when the limo swerved seemingly out of control, hit something, then continued on. He depressed a switch, bringing down the privacy glass separating him from his driver. "What happened back there, Eddie? I thought for a minute we were about to buy the farm."

"Sorry, sir. It was either swerve hard or take a crater in the road full-on. We hit a smaller one in the process, though. I am sorry, sir."

"No need to apologize. It sounded like we lost something. A wheel cover, perhaps?"

"That would be unlikely, sir. The tires are mounted on aluminum-alloy wheels. I'll take it in to the service center, though. Let the mechanics take a look. If you'd like, I could pull over and give the undercarriage a—"

"We're pressed for time. Continue on. The young lady was told to expect us at precisely 1:15." Lost to his thoughts he added, "You know it's been a long time since I met a young lady at her workplace. Well, near her workplace, in this case."

"Those must have been the days, sir."

"Some memorable moments, Eddie. To be sure. It's sort of strikes me as ironic, though."

"How's that, sir?"

"Eddie, we've been together, what, fifteen, sixteen years? I feel we can speak candidly. This will take us back a good number of years, but the last time I met a young lady during her lunch hour, I had something other than food in mind. It took a great deal of coaxing to have her join me in the backseat of my automobile, where we could explore other ways of killing an hour. If you know what I mean."

"I believe I do, sir."

In the reflection afforded by the Lincoln's rearview mirror, Shewster caught the fraternal smile that had erupted on his chauffeur's face. "I suppose some customs haven't changed all that much over the years. Nor will they ever."

"I'd say you're right on both counts, sir."

"The ironic part, Eddie, is that I'm already in the backseat and the young lady we're going to meet will have no qualms whatsoever about joining me. Of course, we'll be back here talking, instead of . . . well, you know."

"Of course, sir. We're approaching the intersection, now. You said she'd be in front of a Duane Reade on the northwestern corner. Is that correct, sir?"

"That's right. I'm told the young lady's name is Rita. I'm looking forward to meeting her. We'll have much to discuss. Yes, Eddie, the backseat has always been a comfortable place for me to conduct business. Back in the day, in a different fashion, of course, but I'm sure this afternoon's rendezvous will be a rewarding experience nonetheless."

The privacy glass slid up as Eddie pulled the limo to the curb in front of the drugstore where a generously proportioned young woman appeared to be waiting.

Eddie lowered the passenger-side window. "Rita?" he asked.

"That'd be me."

Eddie smiled, got out of the limo, and came around to open the rear door of the Lincoln.

"Hi," a cheerful voice sounded from within. "I'm Malcolm. Come on in."

Chapter 70

"Whad'ya mean she stepped out?" Driscoll barked.

Josh Gribbens, an embarrassed precinct detective, searched the Lieutenant's face seeking sympathy. He found none. "Her supervisor said she ducked out to pick up a prescription. The Crenshaw woman told her she'd be right back."

"She wasn't instructed that none of the employees were to leave? Especially Miss Crenshaw?"

"This woman—her supervisor. She's a bit of a flake."

"Which one is she?"

Gribbens offered to introduce Driscoll, who declined, saying, "Just point her out," which he did.

Driscoll and Margaret approached the woman, who was clad in a red apron and was standing near the entrance to the store. She was a buxom blonde. Driscoll thought she resembled Billie Burke, the actress who played Glinda, the good witch in *The Wizard of Oz*. Her chest-high name tag, which seemed to jut itself forward as he drew near, read "Adeline."

Oh, boy! thought Margaret.

"Is there anything in particular you two are here to purchase?" asked the woman, casting a gentle smile. "We've got fourteen aisles. Everybody gets lost. I'd gladly assist you to the correct one."

She even sounded like Billie Burke, with her whispery voice and gentle intonation, thought Driscoll.

Oh, boy, oh, boy! thought Margaret.

To the woman's astonishment, Driscoll produced his shield and introduced himself. He didn't introduce Aligante. This pleased the Sergeant. She let her shield do the talking and left it at that.

"Silly me," said Adeline. "Here I thought you were newly-weds looking for an entertainment center."

Margaret's eyes crossed.

"I'll bet you're here to see Rita," the woman said, as though the thought just descended from a cloud.

"That's correct, ma'am. I'm told you know where she is."

"I did. But now I don't." The edges of her lips curled downward. Her eyes were fixed on Driscoll.

"Well, Sweet Adeline, care to expound on that?" said Margaret.

Driscoll sensed he was in the middle of a cross fire. The woman's immediate response, a curt smile and the look of guile, confirmed that. Fearing an all-out cat fight, he took to the questioning.

"When was it you last saw Miss Crenshaw?"

"About fifteen minutes ago."

"Were all these policemen here?"

"Yes."

"Did anyone of them speak to you?"

"Oh, yes. They asked the same question you did."

"And how did you respond?"

"By explaining that Rita had stepped up the street to pick up some medication and that she'd be right back."

"And that was fifteen minutes ago."

"That's right." The little-girl look reappeared on her face. She shifted her feet. Driscoll was certain she was trying to get Margaret out of her field of vision.

"And the thought never occurred to say anything to any of these officers?" Margaret asked, brusquely.

"No," she answered flatly, her eyes still fixed on Driscoll.

Adeline's attention was drawn to an anorexic-looking female dressed in a PC Haven apron. She checked her watch. "Sarah, what are you doing here? Shouldn't you be at lunch?"

"I switched with Rita."

"What?"

"She said she was going to tell ya."

Judging from the shock that filled Adeline's face, Rita apparently hadn't. Driscoll wondered why.

"Great! Just great!" Margaret griped, throwing her arms in the air as she walked away.

"Boy, oh boy, am I happy for you," said Adeline.

"Oh, yeah? Why's that?" Driscoll, though annoyed, didn't see the benefit in blasting the airhead.

"I had you two as newlyweds. Count your blessings."

Driscoll shook his head, did an about-face, and sought to speak with Sarah. He turned and asked a final question. "Does Rita have a cell phone and would you have the number?"

The woman shook her head. Driscoll thanked her and headed off to locate Sarah.

"If I give you my number, would you call me?" Adeline called out.

Driscoll turned and looked at the woman. He said nothing but a host of emotions erupted. Being single is gonna take time getting used to, he thought.

"Well," said Adeline, "now that it turns out you're not married to Miss Sunshine, and you're not wearing a ring, I thought . . . maybe . . ."

Driscoll smiled, but decided it'd be a better idea to find Sarah.

Chapter 71

Although the announcement over the store's loudspeaker brought the young lady to Driscoll, Sarah wouldn't have been hard to find. Not only did she appear anorexic but also her hair was filled with shocks of blue, and she sported rainbow suspenders. Cracking chewing gum added to her appeal.

After a check of the industrial clock hanging above the store's entrance, Sarah said, "She's not due back for another thirty minutes."

"Would you know where Rita was headed?"

"'Fraid not."

"Got her cell number?" Driscoll asked.

"She doesn't have a phone."

"Okay. Is there a particular luncheonette or coffee shop nearby that would be a usual spot for her?"

"Not any I'd know about. She often buys a hot dog and a soda from Sam, though. He's got an aluminum stand near the bus stop on Tenth."

"Would she bring it back here?"

"Never seen her do that. She often heads for the library

around the corner on Fifty-eighth. You're not supposed to bring food in, but no one says anything. You might find her there. She's got red hair and keeps the work bib on."

Chapter 72

"May I see it?" Shewster asked, the limousine continuing its meandering cruise inside Central Park.

As thoughts whirled inside Rita Crenshaw's head, one of them being *I'm gonna be riding behind my own chauffeur soon*, she reached her pudgy paw inside an oversized bag and fished around. "I know I was instructed to bring it . . . oh, here it is . . . but for the life of me I don't understand what for," she said, handing Shewster a photocopy of the merchant's portion of Angus's notebook computer purchase receipt.

"You just leave that to me," he responded, eyeing the SKU item code and barcode displayed on the image, before stuffing it into his pocket, which he patted down.

"Won't the police need that?"

"Yes, they will. It's sure to help track down these murderous demons. We need it for our accountant. There's quite a hefty reward involved, young lady," he said with a smile.

"I'll say! I've already got it half spent!"

"Do you, now?"

"Oh, my God!" the girl gushed. "This is getting so real!"

"Real it is, Rita. But there's work ahead for the both of us.

You see, your telling me all about your encounter, in the same detail I'm sure the police will require, will hopefully lead to the capture and conviction of these demons. Although I'd like to be in a position to give every caller with a concrete lead the windfall money. For there's no denying it. I am rich. But let's face it. We do get a lot of calls. So, it's only fair that the money be disbursed after the devils are caught."

"I understand."

"Now, that doesn't mean you stop dreaming about how you'll spend the reward money, because your information has been the most promising. It's sure to help with a conviction."

Rita felt like she had just lost her virginity to Brad Pitt. Move over, Angelina!

"Now, tell me all about his visit to the store."

She took a deep breath.

"I was stuffing reams of copy paper into one of our bags for a lady customer who had bought four, I think. Okay four copy papers, two bags of PC Haven rubber bands, a box of blue stick pens, and a box of professional letterhead with number-ten envelopes to match. She told me she was working on getting a book published. Said it's not what you write that counts but who's willing to read it. I wasn't sure what she meant by that and was about to ask. But then I saw him."

"For the first time, right?"

"Right. He was next in line. I didn't get a good look but enough of one to tell me he was getting annoyed with all the time I was taking with the lady. What's with the male species? Don't they know we girls are chatty? Oops. Sorry. You're one of the male species. I didn't mean—"

"It's okay. Go on."

"Anyway, when I got through with the lady, he plopped down the notebook computer on the counter. And right away says, 'How much?' Like I'm a freakin' mathematician. There's tax involved, ya know? So I scanned the box and the register came up with the answer. 'One thousand six hundred and eighty-two dollars and ninety-eight cents.' I said. He reached in the pocket of his jeans. I'm expecting a credit card. Seventeen hundred is a lotta money. That's when I got a good look at him. Damn, I know this guy, goes off in my head. From where, I hadn't a clue. So I really studied him. Who do I know wears retro black glasses? I think that pissed him off a little 'cause he made a face. A frightening face. Back away, Rita, back away, I said to myself. Now, no credit card. Cash. The guy fished out a wad of it. He took off the glasses and counted out seventeen hundred dollars. I really had a chance to study him. His eyes were on the cash. So I figured what the hell. Before I knew it, the sale was over. His notebook was bagged and he was headed for the door. I forgot to tell him about the rebate, but when I hollered out 'Hey! Hey, you!' he continued walking. A little faster, now. I wasn't about to follow the guy outside, rebate or no rebate. He gave me the creeps. Oh, yeah. His money smelled like horse doo-doo."

"Horse manure?"

"I thought so. Anyway, I was glad the guy was gone. But I still had the nagging feeling that I knew him. Then, wham! It hits me. The paper. The guy in the front-page picture! Me and the girls were reading about him before the store opened up. Believe me, a three-million-dollar jackpot attracts a lotta readers. I ran to the back room. Grabbed the paper and there he was. He didn't look like the sketch so much, but damn, the photograph was dead-on. The only thing ya got wrong was the hair. Seein' him close up, it looks jet black."

"What other distinguishing characeristics?"

"No visible tattoos or scars. No accent. Old-is-new-again glasses. Baggy blue jeans, a striped red and green polo, gray running shoes, Nike, you think." Rita glanced at her watch. "I gotta get back to the store."

"I'll see to that." Shewster hit the switch bringing down the privacy glass. "Eddie, Miss Crenshaw here needs to report back to work."

"Phew," said Rita. "We sure covered all the bases. You really make a girl work for her money."

The privacy glass was still down. Befuddlement flooded Eddie's face.

Chapter 73

Driscoll stepped outside the library. He hadn't found her.

On his trek there, he noted a few shops around the store she may have gone to. The Beanery on Tenth was a possibility. If she's the library type, she'd probably like the atmosphere of a trendy coffee shop, he reasoned. It was also a type of place where someone wouldn't feel uncomfortable eating alone.

Driscoll checked his watch. Ten minutes to go. What the hell, it was on the way back.

The Beanery was just as he imagined. A crowd of people, median age being about twenty-five, was sitting at small tables sipping a variety beverages; some eating lunch. A refrigerated display offered an array of pastry items along with an assortment of salads and sandwiches.

Driscoll didn't know if it was a chain. It reminded him of a Dean & DeLuca on University, north of Washington Square Park.

A quick scan revealed no one clad in PC Haven red. And the only person with red hair was male.

She was due back soon. Although he could have used a quick bite, he needed to head for the store.

His cell phone sounded as he was about to exit.

"Driscoll, here."

The voice of Lieutenant Matthew White at NYPD's Computer Investigation and Tech Unit sounded in his ear. This must be important. He took a seat at an empty table, listening to what White had to say.

"We got inside the four hard drives, Lieutenant. Those belonging to the German and Chinese victims that had been forwarded to us from Interpol along with the two from our stateside departed. We're gonna dig deeper, but I wanted to let you know we got in and give you a heads-up on where we're at. We had to have a translator involved. That slowed us down a bit. I'll start with the overseas drives. They tried to erase the histories of Web sites visited, but their Favorites lists offer a quick link to the twin's TwoNaughtyFreaks Web site. There doesn't appear to be any way for contact online. The twins have a phone number, 858-734-6523, flashing across the top of the site in red. I suppose that's how they're hooking up?"

"You got it. They're using a disposable."

"Sex trafficking in the twenty-first century."

"We show them having links to a number of Asian and European online outlets that offer all sorts of sexual enhancement gadgetry. We're talkin' some really weird stuff. Redefines kinky. No records of any purchases, though."

"I'm sure that if they bought anything they'd pay cash at a retailer. They probably did their window-shopping online. These two have handles?"

"HankySpankyOne and LazyOldFreak."

"Original," said the Lieutenant.

"Moving on to Francis Palmer. He was a big fan of freshwater fly fishing, according to the Web sites he frequented. His Favorites List supports that too. He paid his bills through South Texas online banking. He did a fair amount of shopping over the Internet. Had accounts at Amazon, Best Buy, and a number of others that appear innocuous enough. We'll know more when we get a complete list of his purchases. Mr. Palmer did have a flip side."

Driscoll leaned his head forward as though his action would raise the volume. Perhaps he'd been wrong about a Web site designer knowing how to cover his ass. Or the guy could have been plain stupid.

"Seems Palmer made room on his Favorites List for other pleasures. He was a big fan of Nero. Not Nero Wolfe, mind you. Nero, as in Nero Claudius Caesar Augustus Germanicus, aka, emperor of Rome. And from the looks of what Palmer tapped into, Nero had a passion for orgies. According to his findings, at Nero's first-century hothouse, nothing was off-limits. Didn't matter if you were heterosexual, bisexual, or had a hankering for the younger set, which is where the emperor reportedly leaned. Palmer was fixated on a figure from Greek mythology. Priapus, to his friends. A well-hung fertility god. Here's Priapus talking. Palmer had highlighted it in red. 'I warn you, my lad, you will be sodomized; you, my girl, I shall futter; for the thief who is bearded, a third punishment remains. If I do seize you, you shall be so stretched that you will think your anus never had any wrinkles.'"

"Quite a guy."

"Palmer?"

"Priapus."

"You ready for Palmer's handle?"

"Ready."

"AwwShucks."

Margaret said we'd find him in Disney. "AwwShucks as in Winnie the Pooh land?"

"'Fraid I'm not much of a fan of the Pooh Man. That Barney guy neither. On to the USA. I'm sorry to report that Miss Shewster wasn't much of a computer fan. No collection of hero worship like Palmer. There was an unopened e-mail in her mailbox. It was from her father. He wanted to know if she needed money, how things were going in therapy, and if she was still going to the meetings. Made me wonder if she was in some sort of recovery program."

"She shoulda been."

"Not much else. No frequent visits to any particular dot-com. And a very short list of favorites. Three. Victoria's Secret. Tiffany & Company. I'll let you tell me which site held the third spot."

"TwoNaughtyFreaks."

"On the mark as usual, Lieutenant."

"Make my day. Tell me Abigail Shewster had an exotic Internet handle."

"Not by my definition of exotic. It was GwennyPenny."

Driscoll ended the call, checked his watch, and was about to exit the café when his beeper sounded. Unpocketing it, he discovered it was Aligante. Retrieving his cell phone, he accessed her from his address book and hit SEND.

In a matter of seconds, she was on the line.

"Where are you?" she asked.

"Just around the corner on Tenth."

"I tried to reach you on your cell. What's wrong with your call waiting?"

"Damn! I was on the line with Lieutenant White from Tech Support. He had a ton of info for me. I guess I got too engrossed in the call to hear the beep. Why? What's happening?"

"Plenty."

Chapter 74

Driscoll was seated at a table in the back room of PC Haven. Across from him was an extremely elated Rita Crenshaw who, upon his arrival, had announced she was going be a gazillionaire.

It took the Lieutenant a couple of minutes to get her to focus and stop saying "Oh, my God! Oh, my God!" When he finally succeeded, he told her he was aware she had an exciting afternoon and asked her for her patience while he asked her some questions.

"Fire away!" she said.

"Miss Crenshaw, would you mind if I called you Rita? I don't want this to feel like an interrogation." The Lieutenant needed her to feel comfortable speaking with the police. God only knew what Shewster led her to believe.

"Sure. You can call me Rita."

"Thank you, Rita. I'd like to know what brought you and Mr. Shewster together."

"I spotted the picture of that Angus fella in the newspaper. Three million dollars is a lot of money! I wasn't sure what to do at first, but considering the guy was wanted for murder, I called the police. After that, I called the eight-hundred number in the paper. Some guy. I never did get his name. Anyway, he seemed very interested and asked me first for my full name and phone number and then asked why I was calling. I described the guy, Angus, who had come in to buy a laptop computer and that I checked him out."

Her attention was drawn over Driscoll's shoulder. When the Lieutenant turned, he saw another young lady, in a PC Haven bib, standing outside the room, waving to Rita while yelling, "Way ta go! Way ta go!" Rita responded by shouting "Whoo-hoo!" He was glad the interruption didn't prompt another round of "Oh, my God!"

His eyes found hers.

"That's Cindy. She's my backup."

"Sounds very happy for you."

"She's a sweetie!"

"Seems everyone is nice around here. Please, go on."

"Okay. Getting back to the guy who took my call. I told him the customer was a dead ringer for the photo on the front page of the *Daily News*. Except for the color of his hair. Even with the hood the photo looks like someone with light hair. I told him aside from that, he's the guy! Then I told him he paid seventeen hundred in cash for the notebook. His voice perked up. He sounded even more interested. Anyway, he read back my name and asked if the number I gave him was a work number. I told him it was. He then asked if it would be okay to call me at work if he needed to. I said yes, 'cause my supervisor, Adeline, is okay with that."

I'll bet, thought Driscoll.

"Five minutes later she tells me I have a phone call. I says, 'Nah. Nobody works that fast.' But guess what?"

"He called you back."

"Not him, but another man who said he'd been given the message. 'Is this Rita Crenshaw?' he asked. I nodded. Go figure! I was excited. He asked again. And I blurted, 'Yes! Yes!' He asked me where I worked. I gave him the address. He then asked if I would meet him on the corner of Tenth and Fifty-sixth, in front of the Duane Reade. Said something about not having a permit to drive a stretch limo on West Fifty-seventh. Who knows? But when he said 'limo,' I said, 'Step aside, Britney.' It wasn't like he was someone I met on the Internet. It is broad daylight. I figured a guy who could afford to shell out three million wouldn't be driving a Chevy."

Driscoll felt offended, but quickly dismissed it.

"I was told he could be here in five minutes. Yikes! I almost asked him if he'd have the money with him. I don't think I did. At least I hope not. So, before I knew it, I had switched lunch with a coworker and was on my way to meet him."

"Did you tell your supervisor about it?"

"I think so," she grew silent and began counting on her fingers.

Driscoll watched. It appeared she was going over some sort of checklist, perhaps about the events that had rapidly taken place. She leaned in, conspiratorially. Driscoll noted she was blushing. "I don't want to sound disrespectful," she said. "Adeline's a sweetheart and I believe I told her I was meeting someone for lunch in front of the drugstore. But, between you and me, if you looked in her right ear, you'd see out her left."

"The men who you spoke to, what'd they sound like?"

"Whaddya mean?"

"Did they sound young? Old?"

"I know where you're going. It wasn't Mr. Shewster I spoke to during either phone call. They were all business when they spoke. Malcolm's more of a codger."

Oh, boy!

Thirty-five minutes later, after he had thanked Rita for detailing everything she remembered about both her likely encounter with Angus and her entire conversation with Shewster, Driscoll rejoined Margaret and Thomlinson. They informed him that Forensics had arrived to sweep the place and that a team of officers was going door to door seeking any further information on Angus. He headed for the door.

Two questions gnawed at him: Why hadn't he gotten a call from Danny O'Brien telling him that their electronic shadow had followed the Shewster vehicle when it ventured out for the rendezvous? And why was Shewster so fixated on the PC Haven receipt for Angus's computer purchase?

Just before he got his foot out the door, Adeline brushed past him. He'd been a cop for a long time. She was either taking something out of his breast pocket or putting something in. Because her awkward sleight of hand hadn't been missed by Margaret, Driscoll, as a courtesy, would wait until he was alone to see what the lady had passed him. He believed he knew what he'd find. Adeline was no artful dodger. The Lieutenant never kept anything in that pocket. Until now.

Chapter 75

When Driscoll returned to his office, there were three messages from Danny O'Brien, the TARU technician, staring up at him from his desk. He picked up the phone and called.

"TARU," a voice answered. The Lieutenant recognized it as that of Steve Halley.

"They finally let you out from under, Steve?"

"We all need a breath of air now and again, Lieutenant. Even short timers like me. I take it when it's offered. I'm awful sorry to hear about your wife. You holding up okay? How's your sister?"

"She and I are fine. Thanks for asking."

"If you ever need another soul to turn to . . ."

"I know. It's nice to hear it."

"Hold the line. I know Danny's been eager to talk to you."

"Thanks."

The Lieutenant had a great deal of respect for Halley. He'd lost a son to leukemia a dozen or so years back. After burying the boy, he went home and poured every drop of liquor on hand down the drain of the kitchen sink. His cabinet was well stocked. He rescued two lives that day. His and his wife's. Bleak are the days of a whiskey widow. Bleaker are the nights of a mother who buries a child she bore. He no longer had Sean. But he'd be damned if he'd continue to steer his wife to an early grave.

The booming of voice of Danny O'Brien sounded in the Lieutenant's ear. "Hi, Lieutenant. I know you've got a long list of people to explain to. I want to help you do that. We followed the limousine down Fifth and into the park. According to the GPS tracking device, midway through the park, the vehicle stopped. Then sat there. We figured his car broke down or blew a tire. Though unlikely, he may have been meeting someone there. We sent an Aviation copter over the site. Couldn't make out much through the cluster of trees. We had a blue and white enter from Central Park West and cruise through. Zip! No stationary car. But the GPS still had him sitting there. The patrol car continued through, then turned around, and circled back. Nada. But they reported a patch of rough road. A series of potholes, right about where we had the GPS sitting. We believe we know what happened. Although the unit wasn't sighted at the scene, there are sewers on both sides of the roadway. We had the Environment Protection Agency dispatch a truck. They dredged both sewers, eventually finding the GPS in the northern drain."

"You got another unit? One with Krazy Glue?"

"We've got the next best thing," said O'Brien. "Sorry about—"

"No need to apologize, Danny. Some guys have all the luck."

"And excellent timing."

"The guy's crafty. I'll give him that. But he hasn't perfected the art of disappearing. Not yet."

Driscoll hung up the phone and leaned back in his chair. One mystery had been unraveled. What Shewster was going to do with a PC Haven receipt still had the best of him.

Chapter 76

It was nearing three in the morning. All Angus heard was the tapping of keys and his sister's snoring, which sounded, for the most part, like a muted motor with a rough idle. But her sudden guttural outbursts were annoying the hell out of him. Had he been in bed, he'd grind his heel into the fleshy part of her thigh. That shut her up in a hurry.

Right now, though, he wasn't in bed. He was pounding away on the notebook. He'd slept very little over the past week. His ass ached from its constant contact with the hard wooden stool he had placed next to the barrel that supported the laptop. His eyes hurt from peering into the dull luster of its twelve-inch screen. But he was on a mission, a tedious, time-consuming one that required intense concentration. Therefore, he would not, could not, tolerate her snoring. So he puckered his lips and let loose a high-pitched whistle every time his sister snorted like a wild boar that had its testicles shocked by a Taser.

It always prompted the same response: "What? What is it? What?" with his sister nearly leaping from her skin.

And it always worked, allowing him to return to the mundane and irksome task at hand. He had learned much about the Lieutenant over the course of the last seven days. But he was yet to find what he was looking for.

Chapter 77

"Jesus H. Christ! There it is again! Where the hell is that high-pitched whistling coming from?" Cassie grunted, eyes half open, spotting Angus quietly pecking away at the keys. A pencil behind his ear. A pad of paper at the ready. His gaze riveted to the screen.

"Angus, didn't ya hear that?"

"What?"

"That freakin' whistle!"

"I ain't heard a thing. Go back to sleep, Lovee. You must be dreaming."

She muttered something intelligible, dislodged a wedgie, and let her head hit the pillow.

Was I dreaming? Maybe.

"We're never gonna get back home," Cassie whispered, huddled next to her brother in the last pew of the church. "Not to Carbondale. Not to the loft. They musta cloned that Driscoll guy. He shows up everywhere! The guy probably walks on water."

She looked around the church. There were a handful of visitors, some lighting candles, some standing before one of many statues, the rest seated. They all looked the same. Same height, same clothing, same sinister look on their face, skeleton-like. They were humming. "We're running outta places, Angus. We're gonna hafta move to another planet!"

"If you'd like."

Huh? Why was he so polite and agreeable? "We might need another country."

"That's a can-do."

"Yeah, right. Like we're gonna be able to hail a taxi, say 'JFK, please.' You know what kinda security they got at airports these days? And the last time I looked, JFK was still in New York City! They probably got dogs there that look like Driscoll. We're screwed, Angus. Unless Scotty can beam us up to the Starship* Enterprise, *we're screwed.*"

"Look on the bright side. We have each other."

"Jesus, Angus, you're creepin' me out."

"Ya know what I always wanted to do when I grew up?" *he whispered.*

"I got this one! Trade in your feathers and become a cowboy."

"Cute. You're so adorable. I always wanted to become a millionaire, silly."

"Go on! They laid off security at Fort Knox?"

"Lemme show ya. Hand me the phone."

Sitting on the pew was a phone. Not a cell phone. A freaking landline phone. Cord and all! She was leaning over trying to figure out what it was connected to when she heard Angus speaking on it.

"1-800-854-4568." *She heard him say as though it were voice-activated.*

"Hey, that number rings a bell," *she said.*

"Cute, times two, Cass. Ooooo. I could just squeeze ya." *He gave her cheek a pinch.*

She was stymied. Still wondering where the phone came from, she began to stare at Angus, who was now dressed in a suit, a bow tie, and a straw hat, the phone to his ear.

"Hello," he said. "I'd like to speak to Mr. Shewster, please . . . Oh? . . . Well, I think he'll make an exception in my case and take the call . . . okay. If you insist. Ya got a pen? I wanna make sure you get the message down just right. Good! Here's the message. Tell him Abigail was still wearin' the strap-on when we propped her up on the pole. . . . That's right. Pole. Strap-on. S as in Sam, T as in Texas, R as in Roger—you got it? Strap-on. What's that? Sure. It's 858-734-6523. . . . Nah. He'll know who it is. Tell him it's a toll-free call. Not to worry. It won't cost him a cent."

Angus hung up, put the phone on the pew, and said. "See, Cassie. Now I'm gonna be a millionaire. Actually a millionaire three times over! Boy, oh boy! I can't wait. Why I—

A high-pitched whistle sounded.

"What? What is it? What?" she screamed, bolting upright in the bed. Wiping beads of perspiration from her brow, she spied Angus, still seated at the computer. "Only a dream. Thank God. It was only a dream."

Laying back down, she heard the pounding of her heart and the tap, tap, tapping of keys.

Chapter 78

Malcolm Shewster was good at a lot of things. Through the years he had mastered the art of baiting a hook for deep-sea fishing. It is an art, he'd been told. Not merely a skill. He was also adept at setting steel traps for catching critters. And he took pride in the fact that he could take down quail with a twenty-eight-gauge shotgun without inflicting injury to anyone standing nearby. He even possessed the dexterity needed to lasso a calf.

Admittedly, he was a younger man when he acquired and honed these skills, but he had discovered he could capture just about anything, if he put his mind to it.

As Friedrich Gernsheim's Concerto in C minor, Op. 16, emanated in absolute clarity from the fifth-generation iPod, Shewster was scanning the PC Haven receipt onto his computer.

He swayed his hands in maestro fashion, waiting for the image to appear on his own notebook, a Pegasus 330.

"Voilà!" he said, pleased with the transfer, which he quickly minimized so as not to interfere with his online conversation with Kyle Rogers, an associate of sorts, and CEO of Bengal Enterprises in Los Angeles, California. He, like

Shewster, was an ambitious industrialist. He was also a man in demand. It was only last year that he'd been asked to chair the board of trustees for a nationally based corporation. He accepted the designation graciously, promising to comply with the record-keeping and disclosure requirements of federal law. The corporation he was asked to help govern wasn't going to turn into another Enron or Tyco International. No sir. As long as he was in at the helm, no stockholder or employee of PC Haven, Inc., need worry. He was a man of conviction. A man of character. A man who knew the intricacies of corporate America.

One of those intricacies involved favors.

"Ready when you are, Malcolm."

By simply tapping on a touchpad, Shewster placed the image of Angus's purchase on the WiFi expressway. Before the pharmaceutical mogul powered off, Rogers was viewing it.

Chapter 79

"Lieutenant, we're all at the mercy of physics," said Danny O'Brien, leaning against metal shelving inside TARU as Driscoll examined what the tech had placed in his hand.

"You think this has a better chance of staying onboard?" Driscoll examined the black device that looked like a cigarette holder Hitler might have used. "It feels so light."

"Cedric tagged the Lincoln with a Qicktrack. It's a good GPS, but maybe too heavy for a chauffeur who likes to ride the rumble strips. What you've got in your hand is a Protrack. Granted, it's lighter. Thinner too. But those are pluses. Cedric will need more time and a ratchet, but I think he'll be able to wedge it between the limo's fuel tank and its support straps."

The technician disappeared. When he returned, he handed Driscoll a three-eighths-inch drive ratchet set and a laptop.

"What's with the laptop?"

"It's configured to work with the Protrack."

"You mean I can follow him myself?"

"If you want to."

Driscoll looked pleased.

"One more thing, Lieutenant."

"What's that?"

"You might want to hold on to Cedric's cigars when he tags the vehicle. He's gonna be working under twenty gallons of gasoline."

Chapter 80

A knock sounded at the door to Shewster's suite. Muttering something unintelligible, he went to answer it.

"Hmm . . . showdown time, huh?" he said to Driscoll, who looked like he'd come to conduct a hanging. "I'd figured you'd drop by sooner or later. Come in. Come in. We're not going to air our grievances in the hall."

Driscoll barreled past the man and entered the room. "You're crowding me, Shewster. I'm an inch away from arresting you for interfering with a police investigation."

"C'mon. We both know that's not about to happen."

"No?"

"You reach for a set of cuffs, Lieutenant, and you'll be back to pressing a uniform."

"You threatening me?" Driscoll asked, looking like he was about to put Shewster through the wall.

"Sit down."

"I don't know who the hell you think you're talking to. I'm not some goddamn—"

"Please, Lieutenant. Have a seat," Shewster said, motioning toward the sofa. "It hasn't been my best day either. You can put away the sword. I'll tell you what you came to hear."

Driscoll didn't move.

"Please. No more threats. Miss Crenshaw wasn't as big a help as I thought she'd be."

"What's with the store receipt?" Driscoll asked.

Shewster sat down. "Do you like cookies, Lieutenant?"

Driscoll thought he'd stepped into an episode of *The Twilight Zone*. "Suppose we cut to the chase," he said.

Shewster gestured like he was telling a child it was okay to cross the street and offered a smile.

The Lieutenant straddled a wooden chair, facing him.

"Good. Good. See, we're making progress."

"I didn't come here to be toyed with, Shewster."

"What we're both seeking, Lieutenant, is one and the same."

Yeah, right. "What's with the store receipt?"

The business man used the palms of his hands to massage his face, his fingers to rub his eyes. He then looked squarely at Driscoll. "You know as well as I do anonymity isn't always as Webster defines it. Thanks to the Internet and to the resourcefulness of tech-literate people, privacy is another word that has an asterisk next to it."

"PC Haven. Rita Crenshaw. The store receipt. You wanna tie those into where you're heading?"

"My plan to help the police apprehend these killer twins is to include a Web site, for use by folks who prefer the Internet for communicating. Not everybody trusts Ma Bell anymore. The site will enable the net-only enthusiasts to stake their claim to the bounty. There will be a blog to keep visitors up to date on the latest developments in the chase. If I were the target of that chase, I'd be checking that blog every hour. That's where the PC Haven receipt comes in. Sure, any owner's manual would give me the specifications and capabilities of the notebook this killer purchased. But I'm a businessman who deals in products. A variety of products. Pills, syrups, inhalers, vaccines. Each one designed for a specific purpose, but each one unique. I'm the type of adversary, Lieutenant, who needs to know everything about his opponent. Right down to the dates on the coins he's carrying in his pocket. Like I said, an owner's manual would give me the notebook's capabilities. What it's not going to tell me is how vulnerable it is to privacy invasion. More to the point, that generic manual is not going to tell me how vulnerable *his* notebook is. I need to know every miniscule detail of the workings of that particular computer. Right down to whether the guy who installed its hard drive had a hangover at the time!"

"And a store receipt's gonna tell you all that."

"I'm a resourceful man. Placed in the right hands, the receipt's SKU and barcode will help reveal the computer's path from assembly line, to packing, to shipping, to—hell, you know where I'm going with this. If the damn thing was dusty when our young predator carried it to the cashier, I'll know about it."

All this from a store receipt? "Frankly, Shewster, I'd say that's a stretch." What Driscoll didn't tell him was that he thought he'd had gone off the deep end.

"He killed my daughter, Lieutenant. The word *stretch* doesn't exist in my dictionary."

Yup. He's lost it.

"Once I know that computer better than Hewlett-Packard, the rest is child's play. Are you familiar with the word *cookie* in a purely computer sense?"

"If you're talking about a means for, say, a retailer to tag onto a Web site visitor, I'm familiar."

"Were you aware that if used properly, a cookie can establish the visitor's Internet Protocol address and gather sufficient personally identifying information to uniquely ID and locate a particular person, or in this case a pair of twins?" It appeared to Shewster as if Driscoll was weighing the possibilities. "If the police academy is using a twenty-first-century syllabus, it may not be such a stretch."

"Some view such activity as illegal or at least deceitful. I'd hate to see some liberal lawyer convince a similarly slanted jury that it's actually entrapment. That could lead to an acquittal."

"There'll be no acquittal."

There'll be no trial is what you mean. "When were you going to share this with me?"

"I no longer see the need. Do you?"

"Am I to interpret that to mean I've been informed through this conversation?"

"You got it."

"The launch of this new Web site? When's that happening?"

"That depends."

Cagey bastard. "On what?"

"Any big-game hunter studies all aspects of an expedition before turning the key in the caravan's lead vehicle. No?"

"I'm sure he does. I'm just hoping the twins are the only ones who view this savagery as part of a game, Shewster. Not the game hunter himself."

Shewster stood, signaling the conversation was over. "I have a suspicion we have more in common than one would imagine, Lieutenant."

"How's that?"

"I sense neither of us likes to being threatened. Veiled or otherwise."

"Your suspicions are just shy of the mark. I never use a veil."

Driscoll checked his watch as he exited the plush hotel and headed for his cruiser. When he opened the door, the vehicle's dome light illuminated Margaret's face.

"The GPS get planted?" he asked, sliding behind the steering wheel.

"And then some," came a voice from the backseat. "Now, how 'bout that cigar?"

Chapter 81

Driscoll, Aligante, and Thomlinson were sitting inside the Lieutenant's cruiser, parked a hundred feet from the hotel. They had no reason to go anywhere. The electronic shadow was keeping track of Shewster's limo, which was moving, but hadn't gone very far. The GPS configuration on TARU's laptop featured a map, currently displayed as a grid of the local streets surrounding the hotel as well as the area where their subject was now circling.

"What the hell is he doing?" said Margaret. "This is his third trip through Central Park!"

"Maybe he's a nature fanatic," Thomlinson said from the backseat.

"Then he'd be sitting in his hotel room watching *National Geographic*," said Margaret.

"Don't encourage the man, Margaret. Cedric's prone to wit."

"He's leaving the park."

Driscoll started the car. There was no need to tailgate Shewster. The GPS was doing a good job of that. The Lieutenant would simply tag behind at a safe distance.

"Whaddya suppose he was doing circling the park?" Margaret asked.

"I'm bettin' he was talking to someone on his car phone."

"Aren't we tapped into that?"

"No. TARU determined he was using a hard-wired line. They'd have to get inside the car to properly tap it. We're only on the hotel landline and his cell."

"Any guess as to who he might have been talking with?"

"Don't know. But if we keep our eyes fixed on the laptop, he may lead us to him."

"I'm glad he's on the move," Margaret griped. "I was getting dizzy watching him circle."

Chapter 82

When Cassie opened her eyes, she found she was alone in the bed. It didn't surprise her. It was like Angus gave up sleeping. For the past week and a half, she had fallen asleep while her brother labored on the notebook. At first, the constant tapping was annoying. It was an effort to fall asleep. Last Tuesday, she had wrapped herself in bedding and headed down the stairs to stretch out in the old recliner. She had escaped the tapping sound, but the coils in the recliner stabbed her, and after a few minutes the noxious horse smell forced her back up the stairs to the loft.

"We're gettin' the hell outta here," she had griped, only to have Angus tell her, "We'll start looking tomorrow. Can you hold out 'til tomorrow?" She said she could. But goddamn it! They were still in the freaking loft!

She eventually grew accustomed to the tapping. As a matter of fact, it had become soothing. Like those audiotapes of babbling brooks or waves hitting the shoreline.

Cassie had also become accustomed to waking up to the sound. How the hell Angus could spend night after freaking night pounding away on the laptop was beyond her. And why? When she asked him, he'd wave the gun and shout

"Bang! Bang!" She thought he had lost it. What could be so interesting on the goddamn computer?

But when she awoke this morning, she thought they had finally moved. There was no tapping of keys. Angus wasn't sitting on his stool. And the place smelled like eggs and bacon.

"What the . . . ?"

Swinging her legs over the side, she pressed her fists into the mattress and got up.

That's when she spotted him.

Angus was standing at the stove and flipping eggs.

"How come you're not typing, and what's with the cookin'? You never eat breakfast."

Something isn't right. What the hell is going on? Is this a dream?

She covered her ears, certain the whistle would sound. It didn't.

"Angus? What gives?"

"Found her," he mouthed.

"What? Speak up for Chrissake!"

"I found her!" he hollered.

That she heard. "Found who?"

He lowered the flame under the pan and headed for the laptop. Only he didn't just walk there. He crouched down and slithered toward the unit. When he got there, he bolted upright, pouncing, like the laptop was prey. Grinning, he pointed at the screen and said, "Her."

Cassie hurried over. What she saw was the black-and-white image of a woman's face. "Who is she?" she asked, studying the image like it was a specimen in a cage. "She looks familiar. Do we know her?"

"Not yet."

"Whaddya mean 'not yet'? Why does she look so familiar?"

Angus depressed the laptop's down arrow, raising the photo. The woman's name appeared below it.

Cassie's eyes widened. "Wow! Way to go, Angus!"

Chapter 83

Driscoll was heading down Ninth Avenue. The laptop Margaret was monitoring had placed the Shewster vehicle a safe distance ahead, traveling south. Ten minutes ago it had passed the cutoff for the Lincoln Tunnel and its driver had headed for West Street, where he made a left and continued south.

"A man on a mission," Thomlinson remarked.

"What kind of mission?" asked Driscoll.

"He's passing Ground Zero. Still heading south." Margaret raised her head and looked to Driscoll. "I hope you're up to date on your E-ZPass account. He just went under the overpass, which will take him into the Brooklyn Battery Tunnel."

"Call Dispatch. Have them alert Highway Two." The Lieutenant applied pressure to the gas pedal, glancing at the fuel level gauge.

"You want Highway to assist?"

"No. Just let them know we're tailing him through their borough. We don't want him stopped."

Chapter 84

The F train twisted hard to the left after exiting the underground station at Carroll Street, just east of Red Hook in Brooklyn. The screech of metal resonated throughout the subway car, as lights flickered within. Daylight then greeted the train as it climbed toward an encasement of steel girders supported by massive concrete columns that formed a bridge over the Gowanus Canal.

The woman was having an exceptionally good day. Now, if she could only discover how to string them into a week, a month, a year. She adjusted the leather strap of her shoulder bag, preparing to exit the train three stops ahead at Ninth Street in the Park Slope section of Brooklyn. She had resided in the upscale neighborhood most of her life, occupying the third floor of a four-story brownstone on Sixth Street. Thanks to urban gentrification, the rent for the one-bedroom apartment had quadrupled over the years, but so had her income. A tradeoff. It allowed her to remain in the neighborhood, where she had amassed a trove of wonderful memories. If she closed her eyes, she could still experience the feeling, the very smell, of her first-grade classroom at Saint Saviour's Elementary. Just last week she marveled at the panorama of pure visual delight at Brooklyn's Botanical Garden. The Slope, as it had come to be called, featured a host of fine restaurants to accommodate everyone's palate, an expansive array of boutiques, and a number of cozy coffee shops along its main thoroughfare, Seventh Avenue.

After a brief interlude of sunshine, the train descended underground again, delivering her to the Slope at Ninth Street, where brilliant early evening sunshine greeted her. Her brownstone sat a mere three blocks away.

After her trek, which included a quick stop to purchase a small bouquet of fresh-cut irises, she turned the corner and headed south, hoping to be home in time to catch her favorite show on Food Network.

But because someone had other plans, she never got to see what went into the shepherd's pie.

Chapter 85

Police chatter continued to emanate from the cruiser's radio as Driscoll and company continued tailing Shewster. After sailing through the Brooklyn Battery Tunnel, the limo continued east. When it buzzed past Kennedy Airport, Margaret looked up from the laptop. "In another five minutes, he'll be crossing into Nassau County. You want me to let the chief of detectives know we're heading out of the city?"

Their crime prevention effort wasn't exactly in sync with department regulations. "We'd better run silent," said Driscoll.

"You got it."

"How's a guy from California know his way around New York? We haven't hit one traffic tie-up or construction bottleneck yet!" said Thomlinson.

"The day is young, my friend."

At the five-mile marker on the Southern State Parkway, Driscoll brought the Chevy to a complete stop behind a procession of red brake lights.

Margaret believed that if anyone, passenger or driver, raved about the good fortune of hitting no traffic, an immediate tie-up would materialize. "You had to make a remark about no traffic problems, didn't you?" She shot Thomlinson a glare.

Though tempted, Thomlinson figured now wouldn't be the best time to light a cigar, certain Margaret would have some superstition about that as well.

"Where's our friend?" Driscoll asked.

"About a half-mile up. He appears to be moving slowly. Let's hope that means we'll also be rolling soon."

It didn't.

As Driscoll's cruiser crept along at a snail's pace, Margaret charted the course of the now free-rolling limo.

"How'd he get through?" asked Thomlinson, taking note of flickering red and yellow lights in the distance.

"He probably passed the crash site before the emergency vehicles arrived to restrict access to lanes."

Twenty frustrating minutes later they, too, were rolling. What Driscoll had lost in distance, he hoped to make up for in speed. With siren blaring and emergency lights ablaze, he rocketed past cars clearing the middle lane.

"The limo stopped," said Aligante.

"Where?"

"He exited the parkway a mile into Suffolk County near the intersection of Bosley Road and Anderson."

"Anderson what?"

She tilted the laptop, seeking a better view. "It just says Anderson."

"Get Suffolk PD on the line. Find out what's there."

Fifteen minutes later, Driscoll, Aligante, and Thomlinson exited a garden supply center at 2276 Anderson Drive. None of them looked happy. After a brief conversation with the owner, it had been determined that a man matching Shewster's description had pulled up in a stretch limo, came into the center, and had purchased a cemetery blanket. The owner, Carl Phillips, had helped him with his selection, which was intended for the grave of his sister, Muriel, who, according to Shewster, had died three years ago while a resident at a nearby assisted-living center. All indications were that Shewster was headed for Saint Thomas's Cemetery, four miles east. The laptop had him coming to a stop at Withers Road and Degraw Place in Sayville.

"That'd be the cemetery," Phillips told them.

That prompted Margaret to use the laptop to access the Web site Interment.net, where the burial of one Muriel R. Shewster was recorded. It indicated she had been interred precisely three years ago today. Driscoll asked Thomlinson to call Saint Thomas's. When he did, the gentlemen who answered said, "That's odd. You're the second person inside of twenty minutes to ask about Muriel Shewster." It came as no surprise when Thomlinson was informed that the other inquirer said he was the deceased's brother, Malcolm, and was seeking directions to her grave. His description matched that of Shewster's.

The three climbed back into Driscoll's Chevy.

Quiet prevailed during their trip back to the city.

Chapter 86

Driscoll was annoyed. *Jesus Christ! What was I thinking? Three officers? I used three officers chasing the goddamn pied piper? Next time, if there is a next time, one of us will trail the limo. How hard could it be to monitor a laptop while driving a car, for Chrissake? And this Malcolm Shewster. The man was full of surprises. He had a heart.* Or so it seemed.

A knock sounded, dispelling the Lieutenant's self-deprecation. Looking up, he found Thomlinson shadowing the door to his office, sporting a huge smile.

"Cedric, you hit it big at Keno?"

"Better. You're gonna love this," he said, stepping inside. "Department of Corrections called. One Mr. Oliver Novak, a resident of Cell Block B in Sing Sing, says he recognizes the faces in the photo."

"Faces? Our photo shows only Angus."

"Ready?"

"Okay. Out with it before your face shatters from that grin."

"He recognized Angus and Cassie from their photo as

kids on the reservation. Claims to have met them. Now . . . are you really ready?"

Driscoll looked like he was getting annoyed again. Cedric sensed it, so he ended the suspense with a whisper, "Says he knows the father."

Chapter 87

Driscoll, northbound on the Henry Hudson Parkway, was heading for the Ossining Correctional Facility in Westchester County. Considering the traffic flow, he'd likely be there in forty-five minutes. The fifty-five-acre fortress known as Sing Sing, a name derived from the Indian words *Sint Sinks*, meaning "stone upon stone," sat on a rocky hillside overlooking the Hudson River. Oddly enough, it was part of a residential town where neighboring homes sold for upward of $500,000. So close, yet so far, he thought—probably in sync with the thoughts of the nearly two thousand inmates.

Oliver Novak was doing a stretch of twenty years to life for attempted murder. Driscoll was certain the three-time convicted felon would be looking for something in return for the information he claimed to have on the twins' father. There wasn't much he could offer though to a three-time loser, outside of a softer pillow.

It was nearing two o'clock when he pulled the Chevy into the prison's administration building's parking lot, where he flashed his shield to the gatekeeper before heading for the six-story tan brick structure. Was it his imagination or was he actually hearing the wails of Ethel and Julius Rosenberg, who had been convicted of espionage and executed on the site? Or the faint voices of President Abraham Lincoln, Mayor Jimmy Walker, or the actor James Cagney? They, too, had visited the maximum-security prison. Amusement ebbing, he put his flight of fancy aside and checked his phone to see if his sister or anyone else had tried to reach him. He was a distance up. There may have been trouble getting to him live. With his world in order, he got on with the reason he had come.

Novak was not as Driscoll had imagined. His freckled face and crooked smile suggested he be cast in a remake of the *Hardy Boys*. Had this man, cloaked now in prison green, met the right talent scout, he may have turned his back on savage butchery. His attempted-murder rap stemmed from an assault with a machete. The sliced and diced woman survived, saving him from lethal injection.

"Driscoll?" Novak wanted to know, taking a seat across from the Lieutenant at a metal table.

"You eyeball a couple of kids from a dated Polaroid in a downstate newspaper but miss my mug on page two?"

"You look better in the paper."

Do I, now? "I'm told you knew the twins."

"Their old man, too. I figure that's gotta be good for something, no?"

Why alert the police? Driscoll wondered. *He could have called Shewster and laid claim to $3 million. That'd be a whole lot of something.* "I don't know how current your newsstand is, but we already know who the twins are."

"Yeah? Then why ya here?"

"You tell me. You're the one who called."

"If the police department has ID'd the twins, why is their lead investigator here and not sitting before a judge and a jury with the twins lawyered up like O.J. Simpson?"

"News flash, Novak. Johnnie Cochran's dead. It'd still take a lot of money to hire the remaining Dream Team. And where would a pair of sixteen-year-olds get that kind of money?" The expression on Novak's face said he was aware he had slipped somehow. But it was too late to take back his remark. "Look, Novak, you placed the call. That tells me you've got something to say. So say it."

"What do I get out of it?"

"You must have me confused with the genie inside Aladdin's lamp. The police department's not a financial-aid office."

"I'm not after money. If I thought the king's ransom they're advertising in the paper could get me outta here, I wouldn't have called you. Besides, I'm sure who ever is fronting the money would figure out a way of not having to pay a three-time convicted felon." He smiled. "There are other forms of compensation."

"Inmates can still be charged with extortion, my friend. And here's another news flash. If you don't start talking, I can make life a little more challenging."

"This is a freakin' prison. They got bars on the windows. How more challenging can it get?"

"Oh, I dunno. . . . How about a stretch in Special Housing? Or maybe a new roommate. One who doesn't waste time soaping up after he tells you to bend over."

"Yep. Much better in newsprint. It hides your ugly side." After a bit of reflection, Novak opened up. Driscoll figured it was the prospect of no soap. "Their old man's name is Sanderson. Talk about an ugly side. This guy's a real prick."

He's speaking in the present tense. Could Sanderson be alive? "Yeah, like coming after a thirty-three-year-old woman with a machete makes you an Eagle Scout."

"That dyke had it coming. She led me around by the dick for three years while she was screwing my sister-in-law."

Driscoll was surprised. They usually swore they were framed. "Nice group of company you ran with. This Sanderson guy have a first name?"

"Gus. Gus Sanderson. A prince."

"Sounds like he fit right in with your stable buddies."

"You know the guy?"

"No. Should I?"

"But you said stable."

"Yeah?" *As in where people like you should sleep at night.*

"C'mon. You're shittin' me. Stable. Like in horses. Right?" The look on Novak's face was one of disbelief.

"So?"

"Sanderson was a hansom cab driver. Made a livin' carting tourists back and forth in Central Park between the Plaza Hotel and the Tavern on the Green. When he wasn't loaded and beatin' up on his kids, that is. He did some carving job on the girl's face, huh? Musta been tired of seeing double."

Driscoll lunged across the table and grabbed Novak by the throat. "Your sense of humor just pissed me off!"

The prisoner's face flooded with color. He gasped for air, leaning precariously backward in his chair until Driscoll released his hold.

"What's the big deal?" Novak managed, choking on his words. "You figure they're killing people. Aren't you? You forgettin' who the bad guys are?"

Was he? Or had the vision of a girl's face being butchered forced a memory of his daughter's mangled body entangled in the twisted metal of the family van?

"Lighten up, Lieutenant. You nearly killed me, for Chrissake! Lighten up already."

"Talk."

"I'm afraid to now."

"Tell me about Sanderson."

"As long as you stay focused, I will. Jeeesus! I thought it was lights-out back there."

"Start talking about Sanderson."

"Like I said. He ran a horse-drawn carriage in the park."

"How is it you knew him?"

Novak looked over both shoulders and leaned in to within inches of Driscoll's face. "This stays here, right?"

"Depends on what 'this' is."

"Look. I'm a three-time loser. I'm never gettin' out. But if Sanderson finds out it was me that turned on him, it's goodnight Elizabeth. I may be behind bars, but that don't mean I'm protected from the likes of him."

"Talk."

"Does that mean we have a deal?"

"DAs cut deals."

"C'mon, Lieutenant. You know what I'm askin' for."

"Talk."

Novak looked defeated. He took a deep breath and held it. But when he finally exhaled, his words flowed like water. "Sanderson wasn't just cartin' tourists around the park. Once a week, one of those tourists dropped off a package. The package contained a half-pound to a pound of methamphetamine—working man's cocaine. It came from a variety of sources. Some cooked right here in the USA. Some from other countries. At the end of the day, Sanderson would head to his stable, on East Sixtieth Street, under the FDR Drive. After tending to his horse—Teener was her name." Novak grinned at the notion. And Driscoll knew why. "Teener" was street slang for meth. "After settling Teener in for the night, Sanderson would climb the stairs to a loft he had built over the stable. There, he would cut the meth with either baking soda or vitamin B_{12}. One time he used lye. Said he had a score to settle. Remember, we're talkin' one mean son of a bitch. Back to the story. After depositing a sixteenth of an ounce of the stuff, Teener. The horse. A sixteenth, get it? Anyway, after depositing the speed into mini-press-n-seals, he'd call me."

"Why you?"

"I was his distributor."

Driscoll leaned back in his chair and reflected on what he had just been told. He had his suspicions, but he still wasn't sure why Novak was turning on Sanderson. "The guy into anything else?"

"There was a rumor he had a Web site. For what, I haven't

a clue. But it musta been another way of making money. It'd be an even bet he's still using it. That guy could squeeze mercury out of a dime."

"And the twins? How'd they play into this?"

"Beats the hell outta me. All I can tell ya is they were attached to him like a Vise-Grip. The guy'd go to take a piss, and they'd hafta tag along."

"So they knew about the loft?"

"Musta. Where he went, they went." Novak scratched his head. He looked puzzled. "You're really liking them for the killings?"

"You know otherwise?"

"No. Nothing like that. It's just that when I knew them, they were nice kids. I don't think either of them was a fan of the leash, but from what I saw, they were both nice kids."

"One more question, Novak. Why tell me all this?"

He grinned. "Sanderson was one cheap bastard. Had tons of money. All of it cash. Stashed it under the floorboards in his loft."

So that's where they were getting the money for their killing spree. Sure, the Crenshaw girl said the bills smelled of horses! A perfect place to store it, too. Right in the middle of their killing field.

"I doubt if Uncle Sam ever saw one nickel of the money. But a lot of that cash was mine. He cut me off when the judge pounded the gavel. Why go and do that? He coulda easily got it to me in here. But he didn't. So, my compensation is seeing to it the guy gets busted."

Revenge. Powerful motivator. "You said the stable was on East Sixtieth under the FDR?"

"Looks like a two-car garage. Sits across from a small park on Marginal Street. Painted battleship gray, the last time I saw it. Had a rusted sign hangin' overhead. 'No Vacancies.'"

The man grew silent.

"That it?"

"I doubt you'll need more."

The prisoner whistled, as he watched Driscoll stand, summon a guard, and head for the door.

As soon as Driscoll stepped outside the building, he called Margaret. "The con thinks their father's still alive. Says his name is Gus Sanderson and that he operated a hansom cab inside Central Park across from the Plaza. Give the media a heads-up on the name and put a call in to the sheriff's office in Carbondale. See if they have anything on a Gus Sanderson, then send someone up to the park."

"On it."

"I'm betting the father's dead and that the twins are holed up inside a stable on East Sixtieth under the FDR. It'll resemble a two-car garage. Some sort of loft up top. Painted gray. Call it in to Manhattan North. They're to have the Nineteenth Precinct cordon off the area. No one moves in or out. The FDR skirts the river. Have the Harbor Unit send up two boats. And get a hold of Aviation. I want two choppers circling. They spot any pair in the vicinity, they're to point them out so someone can intercept. Anybody comes within five hundred feet of that stable is to be intercepted as well. Let's hope they're home this time. I'll be heading back with full lights and siren. Forty-five minutes. An hour, tops. If there's no movement, I wanna be there when we go in."

"You got it."

"Where's Cedric?"

"Sitting on Shewster."

"Good. Fill him in on what's going down."

"Will do."

Driscoll hesitated, not sure how she'd react to his next order. But he gave it. "I want a SWAT team onsite. Shooters in position." He was sure he heard her take a breath. He held his, waited two seconds, then heard her say, "Done."

Thoughts collided inside the Lieutenant's head as he raced

south on the Henry Hudson Parkway. Although Novak raised the possibility that Sanderson might still be alive, it'd be unlikely the twins would seek refuge in their father's building if he were still in the picture, and every instinct told Driscoll that's where they were. But were they alone? These two were psychos. Angus said the old man was dead but he didn't say buried. Driscoll hoped they hadn't pulled a Norman Bates or a Jeffrey Dahmer. Then there was Novak, who had confessed to pushing drugs. That couldn't go unreported. *Put an end to the killings first,* wisdom suggested. *The inmate's not going anywhere.*

Chapter 88

"You'd like to see the sights of old New York, would ya?" Timothy Alfreds beckoned to a strolling couple, in his best histrionic cockney. The closest he'd come to London's East End, though, was his being born on East Seventeenth Street, long before Starbucks opened at both ends of the block. Alfreds felt the accent added to the flavor and tranquility of the horse-drawn carriage ride through the park.

While he was fluffing the passenger pillows behind him, he heard a woman's voice. When he turned about, a gold shield and a police ID were six inches from his nose.

"Jesus! What now?"

"I'm Detective Butler. I'd like to ask you a few questions."

Detective First Grade Liz Butler was part of Driscoll's task force. She was a no-nonsense, top-notch police officer who was good at retrieving information. From anybody.

Although Alfreds was suspicious of all investigators, he was relieved she wasn't from the Department of Consumer Affairs, or worse, the Department of Citywide Administrative Services, who had the annoying habit of sending out an inspector to examine the carriage, its license, the laminated card that displayed the maximum charges, along with the horse. They did this, without notice, once every four months.

"It's always a pleasure to help the authorities," said Alfreds. "What is it you'd like to know?"

"Gus Sanderson. You know him?"

Butler caught his answer before he spoke it. The twitch of his left eye said he knew Sanderson. It also said Alfreds would weigh his words. There was a simple remedy for that. All men loved a flirt and she'd know when to turn it on.

"You're looking at the only friend he had in New York," said Alfreds. "He and I worked this circle for the past seven years."

Her knack at gravitating to just the right person boggled her fellow officers. She claimed she was gifted. "The only friend he had in New York? As in past tense?"

"I guess we're still friends, but I haven't heard from him in a while."

No twitch. "Why's that?"

"He headed south."

"South Carolina? South America?"

Alfreds grinned. "You never met Gus. Am I right?"

"What gives me away?"

"Gus wasn't much of a traveler. He knew a hundred ways of making money. But a thousand ways to keep it."

"No crime in that. How far south did his buck take him?"

"Pennsylvania."

Alfreds was becoming less reticent. Butler was pleased. "Why Pennsylvania?"

"We," he said, motioning in the direction of a handful of drivers, "have a friend there."

"You and the other drivers?"

"Me and the other horses."

Cute. "What kind of friend? Two footed or four?"

The man smiled. "You're quick-witted. And it suits you."

"Thanks," said Butler, extending an open palm to the man's horse.

"It might take Molly a minute or two to warm up to ya. The time would be cut in half if you had an apple in that hand."

"Passed a few fruit vendors on the way up. None of them looked like they could make it through the alphabet. I hate it when I have to use my hands to illustrate what a pound of grapes looks like."

"You've got a way with words, too. I'm guessin' all your denim is made in America."

"They fit better." Molly was nuzzling against the tips of the detective's fingers. "Who's your friend in Pennsylvania?" Her question was directed at the horse.

"If you had an apple . . ."

"No apple, Molly. Sorry."

"There's a farm just west of Philly. Miller's Farm," said Alfreds. "Molly, I see you've made a friend. Any room for Molly in your Mounted Unit, detective?"

"Not without a sex change. The department only uses gelded males."

"The Mayor know that?"

"You didn't hear it from me, but the commissioner held back that nugget until Sully Reirdon assured him he'd stay on as top cop. What's at the farm?"

"The farm?"

"Miller's Farm. You said it was outside of Philly."

"Right. Sanderson in Pennsylvania. Most of the carriage horses in New York work a nine-hour day. On the streets, there's just asphalt. Hot to the touch in July, cold in December. The city says if the temperature is over ninety degrees or below eighteen, the horses are not to be worked. Otherwise, we're out here, rain or shine. Sanderson brought his horse to Miller's to have her roam on grass, trot, lie down if he wants to. Anything but pound asphalt. Believe me. It's like being sent to a fine spa. Without that kind of break, the horse's life span is cut in half. His horse's name is Teener. A dappled gray Appaloosa. A beautiful animal."

"These temperature regulations. When you're not permitted to work, where do you bring the horses?"

"Same place where they spend their nights. In their stables. New York's got five major ones. A couple of them house up to seventy horses. They're up in the Hell's Kitchen area, between Eleventh and Twelfth avenues, from West Thirty-seventh to West Fifty-second."

Butler was stroking the side of Molly's neck.

"Where does Molly bed down?"

"Shamrock. On West Forty-fifth."

"And Sanderson's horse?"

"No four-by-six for Teener. Sanderson had his own stable. A single. On the Eastside somewhere."

"Not a fan of overcrowding?"

"Like I said, I'm probably the only friend he's got in the city."

"He piss someone off?"

"I don't think so. He was a hard man. Kept to himself. Stayed out of everyone's business. And didn't invite many into his. That rubbed a lot of the guys the wrong way. Most of them are regulars. So we see each other every day. Like family," said Alfreds.

"I take it Sanderson wasn't much of a family man."

"He had his own. Two kids. A boy and a girl. They used to work the carriage with him. Probably brought in most of the cash. Sanderson dressed them up as Indians. He told the strollers Central Park was originally built as an Indian reservation. The kids were the only ones still around. Might seem a little corny. But we see people from all over the world. Many of them think the old Westerns on Nick-at-Nite are reality shows. His Two-Little-Indians package was a draw. A gimmick to attract customers. One of his hundred ways to make a buck. It worked pretty well. Sanderson had many repeat customers."

"You said the kids worked the carriage. What's that involve?"

"Part of the attraction was to give his customers a chance to ride with a pair of real Indians."

"Where'd they sit?" Butler could live without knowing and would have preferred it that way. But this was an investigation, not a casual conversation.

"Nobody sits up front with the driver. The city is big on that rule."

"So they sat in back?"

"Alongside the customers."

"Could get a little tight back there, no?"

"Don't even go there. These were kids. With their dad right there with them."

"Tell me you never saw them share a blanket."

"That'd be a lie. It gets plenty cold. It's an open-air carriage."

"What'd these kids look like?"

"Indians."

"No. Not how they were dressed. What did their faces look like?"

"Indians. That was part of the show. They were coated in war paint."

"You never saw their faces?"

"Not without the paint."

"How is it you knew Sanderson went to Pennsylvania?"

"His son told me?"

"Angus?"

"That's not the name I knew him as. His father called him Titus."

"When did he tell you?"

"Back a month and a half. Maybe more."

"Here?"

"Nope. Haven't seen the kids for over four years. They must be in their late teens by now. As they got older, Sanderson stopped using them. It was no longer cute."

"You must have seen his face when he told you two months ago his father was heading out of town, no?"

" 'Fraid not."

"He was still wearing makeup?"

"Doubt it. He called me at the stable."

Chapter 89

"The resemblance is uncanny," said Angus, studying the woman's face. "You'd think *they* were twins."

Terror filled his captive. And it was heightened by the rag's metallic taste and the bite of the wire that bound her wrists and ankles to a hard wooden chair.

"You still haven't told me how you found her," said Cassie, taking her turn scoping their prize, indifferent to the plea her eyes conveyed.

"It wasn't easy," Angus said, shooting the hostage a glare. "I'm probably gonna hafta see a freakin' eye doctor because of you. I spent over a week scouring the Internet to track you down!"

"Next time I wanna see how it's done," said Cassie.

"There'll be no next time."

"Then clue me in, damn it!"

With his eyes still fixed on the woman, Angus caved. "The Web, Lovee, is a veritable feast for need-to-know people like me. There's birth records, public deed listings, frequent flyer accounts, and motor vehicle records." Angus was beginning to sound like a broken record. The monotony was making him dizzy. He leaned his face into that of his captive. "Guess where I found you," he said.

"She's not gonna answer you, Angus. You're better off just telling me."

"Death records."

"She don't look dead to me," said Cassie. "Not yet."

The woman's heart thumped, as tears welled, perspiration collected, and nausea set in.

"You ever read a memorial?" Angus asked Cassie.

"Nope."

"They're like the freakin' medal of honor of obituaries. They're filled with all sorts of stuff. You learn all about the dead person's hard work, loyalty, and dedication. They also throw in the date the person died. Maybe a membership in a lodge. And in the end, it tells you about the relatives. Emma Stiff, survived by . . ." He turned his attention to the woman. "That's where I found you."

"It's a good thing you didn't become a schoolteacher," Cassie said. "You're not very good at explaining things. I'm freakin' lost."

"The memorial was on a Web site for some art student's league. It was for a Colette Driscoll, wife of Lieutenant John W. Driscoll, NYPD. Said she was survived by a sister-in-law and it featured her name. A unique name. Hyphenated. Discovering where she lived was a breeze after that." Angus positioned himself behind his captive.

Cassie grinned. The woman fainted. Angus propped her head back up.

"Lovee, meet Mary Driscoll-Humphreys. Lieutenant Bloodhound's sister."

Chapter 90

Cassie was the first to hear it. She rushed to the window, spotting the helicopter. And not just any helicopter, a police helicopter. Correction. There were two.

"Well, Angus, you were right to call him a bloodhound."

Angus was astonished. "He's outside?"

"I don't know if he is, but a shitload of his friends are." Cassie did the Wicked Witch melting bit, descending out of sight.

Angus huddled beside her.

"You said not to worry. Nobody saw you graze his sister with the car."

"Like I said. Nobody saw me." Angus chanced a glance outside. What he saw didn't make him happy. He slid back down. "Okay, his sister. I got outta the car. Did the 'I'm so sorry. I'm so sorry' routine, and finessed her into letting me drive her to the hospital to make certain she was okay. The gun pointed at her head made for a quiet ride."

"You came directly here. Nonstop."

"Just to mail the camera's memory card. Pulled to the curb. Hopped out. Mailed it, and climbed back in. Not once was she out of the crosshairs."

"And the car. Nobody saw you hot-wire the car?"

"C'mon. Do I look like an idiot?"

Cassie thought about the question. She was tempted, but she chose not to offer her opinion. "Outside of strip searching the bitch to see if she's packing a LoJack, what're we gonna do? We got an army of cops out there!" She shook her head. Considered the possibilities. "I'm tired of running. And tired of hiding. Sure, we got his sister, but that might really piss him off. We could end up dead! Maybe it's time to turn ourselves in."

"We're not giving up. They don't get to win!"

"The cops?'

"No! The ones who liked to come on your face 'cause it's disfigured. The one who wanted his balls licked while he peed. The one who tied a belt around your neck. Made you howl like an alien while he screwed you up the ass. You forgettin' when that bastard carved you up, raped you, and left you screaming? Strapped to a table, screaming. You forgettin'?"

As Cassie collapsed on the floor, Angus thought about what she'd said. Her warning that they may end up dead, kept repeating inside his head. He considered their options. *We might have Driscoll's sister, but there is a freaking horde of cops outside and they all have guns. Could there be a trigger-happy shooter among them?* A police shooting in the Bronx a few years back popped into his head. He couldn't remember the victim's name, but while reaching for what turned out to be his wallet, over forty police bullets were fired. Half of them struck and killed the man. Bits and pieces of a more recent shootings came to mind. Something about a man being shot and killed by police, hours before he was to be married. If he wasn't mistaken, that incident also included a hail of police fire.

He retrieved his cell phone, hesitated . . . but ultimately placed the call.

Chapter 91

"Who is this?"

"No time for games, Shewster. You know who this is. Otherwise, you wouldn't have let them forward the call."

"You pissant. You kill my daughter then have the balls to call me?"

"And those balls are about to get bigger."

"Do you realize who you're talking to?"

"Your daughter was a moaner, dickhead. Insisted I holler 'Gwennypoo! Gwennypoo!' while I did her doggy style. Got myself two handfuls of hefty hooters while I was at it. Between you and me, I think Daddy's little girl had a boob job. I should tell you, our rendezvousin' don't involve actually doin' it anymore. But she had such doelike eyes. And she brought a camera! That was a first. We had our first threesome! Cassie is quite the photographer. *Hustler* might wanna buy these babies. I can send you some shots, if you'd like. You can tell me if you agree. There's thirty-six in all. My personal favorite is the one your daughter insisted Cassie take while she—wait! Hold on! Hold on! What am I doin'? That'd ruin the surprise. I got a question. Your Gwennypoo go to some sorta contortionist school? That girl wiggled like a worm."

Shewster said nothing.

"I'm figuring you wouldn't want the newspaper buzzards to get their mitts on this stack of photos. So, here's what your afternoon will look like. You're gonna have the police pick us up in one of those choppers they launched. Then we'll need a plane."

"You're out of your mind!"

"Have your pilot top off the tank. We'll be going to Quebec. Half the people there speak nothin' but French. They keep their noses in a wine list, not the freakin' *Daily News*! Even if he found us, Driscoll would have a tough time convincing the Royal Mounties to give us up seein' as we're gonna get jabbed with a needle back in the states. News flash! Canuck law prohibits our forced return if we're likely to be executed. Why do New Yorkers get their rocks off on capital punishment? I'm bettin' Driscoll's a big fan. He'll be packin' a pair of syringes monogrammed especially for us."

Silence from Shewster.

"Gwennypoo! Gwennypoo!" Angus howled. "Me, I'm not much into any more than three positions. Wait! Make that four. Your daughter taught me a new one. She was a real hottie under all those conservative clothes she were. Did you know she had both nipples pierced with little silver charms? One was a baby's shoe. The other one, I couldn't figure out. Tasted like maple syrup. Yessir, a real hottie. I'd bet she'd give Peter Pan a woody."

Not a sound. But Angus knew he was still on the line. He'd wait him out. *Ten, nine, eight, seven, six, five . . .*

"Where are you?"

Chapter 92

Thomlinson hadn't quite gotten over the stiffness in his lower back from the cemetery run. Driscoll's Chevy was roomy—as long as you were seated up front. That's why he was now in a super-sized GMC Yukon. Fleet Services had wired this baby up with XM satellite radio. Thomlinson was known to the crew as "a frequent flyer" of this particular vehicle. That being the case, Pokee, one of the technicians, had the receiver set to XM101 when he handed Thomlinson the keys.

His eyes were on the entrance to Shewster's hotel. His thoughts were on what he imagined was going on at the loft. But his ears were lost to the sound of Bob Marley's "Jammin'." The prolific songwriter may have left this planet in 1981, but thankfully, he hadn't taken his music with him.

His cell phone dispelled his rapture.

"Two of your key players just hooked up by phone," said an excited Danny O'Brien from inside TARU. "We put Angus on East Sixtieth near the FDR when he got through to Shewster. Their conversation was not what I'd call G-rated. You want me to play it back?"

"I'll have to settle for the gist," said Thomlinson starting up the Yukon. "Shewster just flew out of his hotel."

By the time Shewster's limo crossed Park Avenue, heading east on Fifty-ninth, Thomlinson had been brought up to speed on Angus's demand for an airlift out of the country and Shewster's assurance that he'd arrange it with Driscoll. But both he and O'Brien had a question. Thomlinson wanted to know what Shewster meant when he told Angus not to do anything rash. He'd personally see to it that Angus and his sister were long gone before day's end. Not to worry. They'd never see Driscoll again. O'Brien's inquiry involved whether Thomlinson and the Lieutenant were aware of what Abigail Shewster had hidden up her sleeve. Her pink sleeve. He also asked who Gwennypoo was.

Thomlinson's response was succinct. "Don't lose the tape."

Chapter 93

Angus had rummaged through Mary Humphrey's bag, securing what he'd hope to find: a ladies' compact. He'd snapped it apart and had the mirrored portion affixed to the end of a wooden stick that measured approximately eighteen inches. It was grooved at one end. Cassie had supplied it.

"Where'd this come from?" he asked her.

"You don't wanna know."

Although the mirror was small, when Angus planted himself below the window and held it over his head, he could survey the area outside, which was littered with an assortment of police vehicles and a bevy of police officers apparently in position. For what? he wasn't sure. He adjusted the view. "Will ya look at that? They've got shooters on the rooftops across the street and I doubt they're hunting geese, unless there's a flock perched above us. Their rifles are all pointed this way."

Angus watched as a dark blue automobile came to a stop several yards from the loft. A smile lit his face when a man in a dark suit got out. He summoned Cassie.

"Driscoll?"

"That's him. He's even bigger in person."

Cassie watched through the mirror as a woman joined him and pointed to the loft. "That lady cop is with him now. They're making some hand gestures to the other policemen. Another glance up here. Now they're talking."

What Cassie didn't know was that Margaret was filling Driscoll in on Liz Butler's conversation with Timothy Alfreds. Margaret reported that Butler couldn't swear to know if Sanderson was dead or not. Though she wished he was. But she was certain Sanderson had been serving up some real treats for his riders since the twins were ten. Margaret closed by telling Driscoll that the Carbondale sheriff's office didn't know there was anyone living in the house but the twins.

Cassie thought the conversation between Driscoll and the Sergeant looked innocuous. She turned and faced Angus. "You think Shewster had a chance to speak with Lieutenant Bulldog about our travel plans?"

"We'll soon find out. She awake?"

"Oh, yeah! You don't hear that whimpering?"

"I hit the off switch an hour ago. Pull the rag out and hold the phone to her mouth."

"What's the number?"

"She'll know it."

"She'd better," said Cassie, dislodging the gag, Beretta firmly in hand. "No funny stuff, lady, or the next time your brother gets to see you you'll be in a box. Start punchin' numbers!"

"Driscoll has a bullhorn in his hand," reported Angus. "Whaddya think'll happen next? Horn to mouth?"

"Nope. Phone to ear."

Chapter 94

Thomlinson had a pretty good idea where Shewster was headed. What he wished he knew was whether he had called anyone on the way. And if he had, what'd they talk about?

The laptop had him turning right at the FDR. He had apparently come to a stop a half block south. That'd put him between East Sixty-first and East Sixty-second. Why two blocks from the loft?

Thomlinson turned at the FDR, spotting the limo behind one of those trucks similar to the ones the city sends out to repair faulty streetlights. They were parked on the right side of the street approximately one hundred feet from the corner, in front of a single-story commercial structure, its security gate down, as was the case for the row of similar structures on either side of the street. The limo's engine was idling. It didn't appear anyone had gotten out. Thomlinson pulled in on the left, put the vehicle in park, and watched. Could Shewster be on the phone? He wasn't driving. If he needed to place a call, that wouldn't require him to pull over. Why had he? And why two blocks away?

Shewster's car continued to idle. Thomlinson continued to watch. He unpocketed his phone, intent on calling Driscoll, but the cherry picker atop the utility truck made him look up. Standing on the roof of the single-story structure was a man in dark clothing. Sharpshooter? From this distance? Thomlinson doubted it. He wasn't holding a rifle. In fact, he wasn't holding anything. That's when he spotted the tripod to the man's right. What appeared to be mounted on it caused Thomlinson to draw his weapon, bolt from the Yukon, and charge down the street hollering like a madman. This action prompted three reactions: the driver of the utility vehicle bolted away from the curb, Shewster's chauffeur did the same, and the man on the roof disappeared.

When Thomlinson rounded the corner on East Sixty-first, the only person he happened upon was a locksmith who was closing his shop, toolbox in hand. Despite the fact that Thomlinson was breathing heavily, wearing a disheveled suit, and had appeared out of nowhere brandishing a gun, the locksmith was quite accommodating—after he'd recovered from a rapid pulse, a surge of adrenaline, and a thunderous heartbeat. When color finally returned to the locksmith's face, the detective gained access to the shopkeeper's roof. A bit of high-stepping from roof to roof brought him to within inches of what had caused the ruckus.

Thomlinson had come across a variety of weapons during the course of his crime-fighting career. But there were always surprises. And not having served in the military, today was the first time he'd ever seen an Mk19 automatic grenade launcher.

Chapter 95

Margaret and Driscoll had helped each other shoulder a fair amount of stress over the years. Both on the job and off. Here was a man who had only now buried his wife after losing her six years ago. Margaret was heartbroken when he confided to her that sitting beside his comatose wife was tantamount to kneeling before her open casket. My God, a six-year wake! How he managed to get out of bed in the morning was beyond her. She realized she wasn't helping matters by dragging her own demons into their on-again, off-again relationship. Through it all, they had discovered their connection was similar to that reportedly experienced by twins, where unexplainable and extraordinary bonds exist. Ironic, considering their current case.

That's why the second he said hello to whomever had just called, she knew he'd been invited into a nightmare.

"You okay?" she asked as he ended the call. "You look like you're about to be hanged. Who was on the phone?"

"My sister."

"What's happened?"

"She's been abducted."

"Abducted? By whom?"

Driscoll pointed to the loft.

"The twins?"

"They're holding her hostage."

"Jesus Christ! What'd she say to you on the phone?"

"That he's holding a gun to her head." His eyes targeted the second-story window, then sought Margaret's. "She asked me the oddest question, even for her. She wanted to know if I would be the one getting them to the airport."

The Lieutenant's phone sounded again.

"Yes?" he blurted, his heart pounding.

"Lieutenant? That you?"

Chapter 96

Driscoll's caller was Thomlinson. The sight of color returning to the Lieutenant's face had Margaret somewhat relieved.

In his conversation with the detective, the perplexity involving the helicopter was quickly resolved as Driscoll was apprised of Angus's demands to set it in motion this afternoon and of Shewster's promise to comply. With that being said, Thomlinson offered a more precise version of what Shewster's afternoon looked like. So far. "What I wanna know," said Thomlinson, "is how Shewster, within fifteen . . . twenty minutes tops, had an automatic grenade-launcher set up within two blocks of the loft. Granted, the crowd of power players this guy's got in his pocket would fill the Super Bowl, but a freakin' military assault weapon *and* a cherry picker? C'mon! Merlin the Magician couldn't pull that off."

"Merlin didn't have speed dial on his Rolodex. Where are you now?"

"Outside Shewster's hotel."

"He's probably contemplating Plan B. Any further word from Danny?"

"Zip."

"You don't know it yet, Cedric, but I owe you a very personal debt of gratitude." Before Driscoll could explain, their conversation was interrupted by the sound of gunfire.

It came from the loft.

Chapter 97

In kaleidoscope fashion, a slide show of images flooded Driscoll's brain. Catapulted haphazardly through time, he witnessed blood washing over Colette's hand, obscuring all but a glint of gold that was the curve of her wedding band; he watched his mother leap into the path of the oncoming commuter train; he listened to his daughter crying out to him while her mangled body was encased in the metal of their family van. Hearses materialized, only to vanish like the edges of a dream. As his family plot beckoned, he heard the sound of a woman's voice.

With his sight suddenly returning, he discovered Margaret was holding his cell phone to her ear. Her voice, a faint whisper grew in intensity.

"Okay. Your brother made his point. It's loaded and it works. Just bring her to the window so we know he didn't shoot her, then hand Angus the phone."

Driscoll glanced up to see the look of total bewilderment on his sister's face. Retrieving the cell phone, he spoke to Angus calmly and clearly. "The chopper is sitting at the heliport, just south of us, at East Thirty-fourth Street. We're

waiting for Mr. Shewster to arrange clearance for the depar-
ture of a corporate jet from JFK."

"What's the hold-up?" Angus asked.

It was the first time the Lieutenant had heard him speak.
His voice was not as Driscoll had imagined. "There's no
hold-up. Ever since 9/11 federal regulations requi—"

"We're leaving the freakin' country. Not coming in. He's
got twenty minutes."

The line went dead and his sister disappeared from sight,
as though she were on wheels.

"Any truth to that?" asked Margaret.

Driscoll's expression didn't make known Shewster's
attempt to lob a grenade, but Margaret clearly understood
there'd be no plane. "We've got twenty minutes. Get on the
horn to every utility that operates in Manhattan. Within the
next five minutes, I want a team of eight men with jackham-
mers tearing into the asphalt under the highway, toward Fifty-
ninth. The loft has no window facing south. I don't want the
twins to see them. Then dispatch a team from Special Operations Division. No slackers. Let's move!"

"Yessir!"

Driscoll approached Lieutenant Ted McKeever, the SWAT
team commander.

"How ya holdin' up, John?" McKeever asked.

"I'll feel a lot better when she's sitting inside a patrol car.
He's given us twenty minutes. Any of your shooters get a
bearing on him?"

"Once. Too much of a chance of the wrong person getting
hit, though. You sure his sister's with him? Nobody's spotted
her."

"She was Margaret's last caller. When I got on the line,
she put me on with her brother."

"He did a fair amount of pacing when he was on the
phone. Any chance of getting him on the line again?"

Driscoll hit the return button, hoping he'd come up with a

reason why he was calling by the time Angus answered the phone.

"Ready to roll?" said Angus.

He wasn't standing.

"The Mayor's on the line with Homeland Security. It won't be long, now."

"Good. Here's how this is gonna play out. I count six shooters perched across the street. They come down. Mount your car on the sidewalk, rear door open and butted against the door to the stable. One driver. Not you. We get clearance on the plane. Cassie, me, and your sister will get into the car. Head directly to the helicopter. Make sure we hit no traffic. If I see so much as a skateboarder that looks like a cop, you'll be calling a funeral director to arrange your sister's wake."

The line went dead. Not once did Angus stand.

"How many shooters up there?" he asked McKeever.

"Six."

"Well, he tagged them all."

Ten minutes later, Driscoll's cruiser was on the sidewalk, its left rear door open and butted. The six sharpshooters were not only down from their perches, they were lined up in the middle of the street, weapons at their feet. To the on-looker, it appeared the Lieutenant and his idling team were waiting for clearance from JFK. But while Con Edison's air-compressed hammers ripped into asphalt, coupled with the noise of hovering helicopters, a team of Special Operations technicians were using a Sawzall to cut through the rear wall of the stable.

Chapter 98

Angus, suspicious of the racket, tried calling Driscoll on his cell phone, but he couldn't hear himself over all the noise. He was in the bathroom, door closed, hoping to hear more clearly, when the noise abruptly stopped.

Stepping back into the room, he heard the sound of feet storming up the stairs. He dove for Mary's ankles, grabbing hold just as Driscoll and Margaret appeared with guns drawn. On his knees, his pistol jabbed into Mary's rib cage, Angus smirked as he stared down the barrel of the Lieutenant's semiautomatic.

Cassie had managed to position herself behind Driscoll's sister, but Margaret's weapon was bearing down on her. As the twisted twins scoped the fashionably dressed Driscoll and the casually clad Margaret, the two officers witnessed, for the first time, the cruelty that indelibly marked the pair. Cassie's face looked as though it had been carved with a blowtorch. Beady eyes peered through jagged slits, surrounded by twisted shards of flesh, the color of burning charcoal. Layers of blubber-like flesh draped her narrow neck. She stood no more than four-foot-five. Her ears sat unusually low on either side of her head. A flat, shieldlike chest threatened to burst through the tapered blouse that clung to an anorexic body. In stark contrast, Angus displayed boyish good looks and wavy blond hair. Driscoll wondered what lay hidden behind his shirt, buttoned from waist to neckline. Hadn't he labeled himself an odd-i-twin?

"Here! Feast your eyes," Angus said, as if reading the Lieutenant's mind, ripping off the garment, exposing horrific scarifications. A collection of gargoyles, a distorted unicorn, irregularly shaped tombstones, several primitive amphibian and ophidian creatures surrounded an odd figure, its upper half, Goth, its lower, paranormal. Hues of bistre, raw umber, taupe, indigo, and Prussian blue bled haphazardly, producing the ominous and all-encompassing imagery that was his body.

"Enjoying the freak show, Lieutenant?"

"This is the end of the line, Angus. I'd prefer to see everyone walk out of here alive."

"But we're not alive," said Cassie. "We have no souls. They were stolen from us."

"You're the thieves," said Margaret. "You took away life."

"Depraved life," said Angus.

"What'd you do with your father?" Driscoll asked.

Angus looked to his sister and chuckled. "He's fertilizer."

Driscoll caught Mary's perplexed gaze. He offered a prayer for her and all present, before beginning what he believed to be their only way out of the stalemate. "You're vicious, Angus. Subhuman. You know why I say that?"

Angus didn't appear to care.

"Evil people kill. And there's no doubt you're evil."

Angus squinted, looking as though he were trying to decipher a riddle.

"But vicious people are menacing. They take pleasure in watching their victim suffer. They'll take a stick to a stray cat. String up a dog. You know why you fit, Angus?"

"The next victim I'm gonna kill is your sister if you don't stop badgering me."

"Vicious people kill because they're callous."

"Don't press your luck, Lieutenant."

"Vicious people kill the helpless. You know what that says about scum like you?"

Margaret was now anxious. She redirected her weapon on Angus.

"Scum like you—"

"Shut up!" said Angus. "Shut up or I'll kill her."

"Scum like you aren't seeking revenge. They're—"

"Shut up!" he hollered.

"They kill purely for selfish reasons. For the thrill of it. What'd you do with the horse, Angus?"

"Yo', lady cop, tell your boss here to shut his mouth up."

"Teener. That was her name. She too, was defenseless. Innocent. The perfect prey. How'd you kill her?"

Rage filled the teen.

"Poison? Starvation?"

"Lady, I'm talking to you. Do something. Or I swear, his sister's gonna die."

"That'd make you next," said Margaret.

"I'd say you slaughtered her," Driscoll continued. "What'd you use to carve her up?"

"Shut up!"

"A honing blade?"

"Shut up!"

"A chain saw?"

Angus looked to Margaret, disbelief in his eyes.

"Did you kill her first? Then cut her up? I'll bet that got you off."

Angus turned frustrated eyes on Driscoll.

"I'm betting you kept a piece of her? A trophy. You like trophies, don't you, boy?"

"Just shut up!"

"Did you bury it here? No, you wouldn't do that. You'd want to touch it. To—"

*   *   *

"Shut the fuck up!" he screamed, turning his weapon on his tormentor.

Driscoll fired first, then Margaret. Without getting off a round, Angus collapsed on the floor, blood gushing from a gaping hole above his left eye, and from another in his chest.

Cassie lunged for Angus's gun. Margaret tackled her. She and the girl nearly rolled down the stairs. As her back crashed against the banister, causing her to lose her weapon, Margaret felt the barrel of Angus's pistol against her stomach.

"Drop your gun!" Cassie shouted at Driscoll, as she untangled herself from Margaret. Raising the pistol, she pressed it hard against Margaret's temple. "Now!" she ordered.

As Cassie attempted to stand, Margaret shoved an elbow into the girl's ribcage, causing Cassie to fall into the lap of Mary Driscoll, who howled. But the gun had remained in Cassie's hand. She thrust it into Mary's mouth.

"Don't—"

"Don't what?" Cassie sneered at Driscoll. "You shot my brother." Her gaze drifted toward Angus, while the muzzle of the Beretta pressed against Mary's palate.

"Cassie, you can still walk out of here," said Margaret. "Why don't you put the gun down?"

"So you can shoot me, too?"

Driscoll was certain it was Angus who had fired the gun. Its safety was engaged. His gut told him Cassie wouldn't know anything about such things, so, he took a step forward. She did as he'd hoped. She squeezed the trigger. The gun didn't fire, and while Margaret moved in to cuff her, Driscoll retrieved the Beretta, pressing a forearm against Cassie's throat.

"Please, let me go to my brother," she pleaded.

The two officers released their hold. Though cuffed behind her back, she threw herself on top of Angus and sobbed uncontrollably.

Driscoll rushed to his sister, kissed the top of her head, and caressed her.

"How'd I do?" asked Mary.

"What?"

"Did I get the part? Boy, these actors are good, aren't they? Good-O! Will ya' listen to her? She sounds like she's really crying. Boy, oh boy! What a day!"

Driscoll didn't know what to think. "Mary, you just—"

"Ssshh. I don't think she's done."

Margaret smiled at the sight of Driscoll gently rocking his sister in his arms, fully in touch with both her detestation and her sympathy for the twins. Doing an about-face, she descended the stairs, leaving the pair of siblings to experience their own multiplicity of emotions.

Chapter 99

It had been two weeks since the apprehension of the killer twins. Most of New York's citizenry had turned their attention to a rash of fires that had spanned the last ten days. It was believed a serial arsonist was torching Catholic churches. In Queens, Saint Teresa of Avila and Saint Rita's had been targeted, as was Saint Margaret Mary's in Brooklyn. NYPD's Arson/Explosion Squad was on high alert and had joined forces with the Bureau of Fire Investigation. Their probe, or lack of it, according to the Brooklyn Archdiocese, filled the headlines of both the *Post* and the *Daily News*.

But Janet Huff didn't have the luxury of kicking back and reading either paper. She was too busy with her own. Hers was not like the *Post* in any way. Nor was it even remotely similar to the *News*. Although there would be a legion of people who would challenge her, every word, every sentence, every paragraph that went into any one of her articles was thoroughly researched and its validity substantiated.

When time allowed.

More often than one would imagine, an exclusive was handed to her gratuitously. Often anonymously. Although what she now held in her hand appeared to be gifted from such a person, her instincts told her the offering would end up in the trash. The flash memory card had arrived this morning by mail. There was no letter attached. No note. Not even a Post-it. The manufacturer's label had been partially removed. There was no return address on the small envelope, but the postmark said it'd been mailed from New York. The sender had managed to correctly spell the name of the paper, in red pencil no less, but that was not the case with her name. "Too Miss Jane Huffer" it read. Her donor was no rocket scientist.

Sensing either a grade-schooler or a prankster was involved, she declared it trash and had her arm cocked to toss it. But from the corner of her eye she spotted what she believed to be the manufacturer's logo on what remained of the label. If indeed it was, this had come from no elementary school digital. Whoever had purchased this one-inch square of blue plastic was into some very serious picture-taking.

Rummaging through her drawer, she produced a plug-and-play, set it up on her computer, inserted the memory card, and took a peek.

Chapter 100

Margaret Aligante was with Driscoll inside the Lieutenant's office. They were eagerly awaiting the results of a mission Thomlinson had taken on.

The Lieutenant was aggravated. He was certain Malcolm Shewster orchestrated the attempt to kill the twins, which, had Thomlinson not intervened, would have likely killed them along with his sister, several NYPD officers, and a host of innocent citizens. Perhaps, him and Margaret as well. He'd been informed a grenade could be lobbed from three hundred feet; the range of the launcher exceeded a mile.

His frustration involved the fact that Shewster would never be held accountable. Thankfully, because it had been interrupted, but exasperatingly because there was no irrefutable evidence to link the man to the crime. Crime Scene came up with nothing that placed the shooter, the utility transport vehicle, or Shewster on that rooftop or anywhere near it. Even if they had a tape of the probable phone conversation that set the assault in motion, Driscoll could produce no warrant to support the unauthorized tap.

He also knew that Shewster had Angus believe he and Cassie, the pair with a list of felony murder and kidnapping charges pending, would be airlifted out of the country. Probably with his own sister in tow. Their phone conversation surely pointed that way. But that surveillance was also unauthorized and the event never took place!

But the day wasn't over.

The only good news was that his sister thought she had been cast in a play throughout the entire ordeal. She was so intent on a good performance that she wet herself rather than asking Angus, the director, to take five. *Thank you, Lord!*

The eight-by-ten photos of the frolicking Angus and the young Shewster woman shared the front pages of the *Daily News,* the *Post,* and (in an edited version) the *New York Times* and were spread across Driscoll's desk.

His attention was diverted toward them.

"Angus's tattoos don't look so menacing in print," Margaret said.

"His eyes do. And they tell all. In contrast, look at the expression on Shewster. She looks to be having a hell of a time."

"It's a syndicated story. My money says Shewster's already hit every newsstand in a twenty-mile radius of his residence to purchase as many copies of the *Los Angeles Times* as the trunk of his Lincoln could hold."

"He's in for a challenge with the other eight hundred and fifty thousand subscribers hailing from Grand Forks, North Dakota, on down into San Diego," said Driscoll, eyeing six other graphic images that filled pages two and three of the *Post.*

"If he put the phone on mute, turned off the intercom at the front gate, and slept in, he may have missed it."

"He's in California, where anything's possible. Maybe CNN will send a beach plane with a roaring engine over his compound with Angus and Gwennypoo lagging behind, their vivid copulation boldly displayed on one of those tacky streamers."

"What do we really know about Malcolm Shewster?" asked

Margaret. "Who's to say he doesn't have a hidden chamber built under his house's foundation or a panic room even Jodie Foster couldn't break free from."

"What we do know is that he's got at least one big secret. That says he'll have a cluster of little ones. A man like Shewster doesn't give away much. He'd have surely found a way to hold back some of his daughter's inheritable traits. Believe me, he kept some of the deviant strain. Picture Malcolm Shewster, in his panic room, huddled like Saddam Hussein before they yanked his presidential ass out of his hole. Shewster's eyes are riveted to the widescreen of a WiFi laptop, voyeuristically stalking Anna Nicole Smith, Pamela Anderson, and Jenna Jameson, when he happens upon a blogger who's telling the world a mass communication missile, armed to disburse a payload of the tell-all photos, will soon make landfall on Shewster's lawn. And if he misses that one, he'll ultimately surf his way to YouTube, where he'll likely catch a slideshow of the complete set of his daughter's photos as the most downloaded."

"YouTube. Can you believe this generation? In a matter of seconds, the adventures of three buxom celebratantes, in Britney Spears, Paris Hilton, and Lindsay Lohan, get an uninvited avenue where their interpretation of the word *exposure* is redefined forever. We've come a long way from *Leave It to Beaver*. Did you know that the most hits on the Internet for the last three months were from people obsessed with the weeklong club-hopping escapades of three sip-and-flash amigas marking the 'Oops' girl's twenty-fifth birthday?"

"Hollywood will soon release a new film," said Driscoll. "They'll call it *Going Commando—The Twenty-first Century's Response to Twentieth-Century Streakers*."

"When I was in my twenties, skinny-dipping was the rage," said Margaret. "But always in a very discreet and secluded area. Today, the chance of catching me outside my apartment without underwear is between negative three and zero. Even if the place were on fire!"

Driscoll was grateful for the visuals. But since Margaret's face had suddenly reddened, he refrained from voicing his gratitude. Time to change the subject, he thought, putting aside the newspapers.

"I'm very proud of you, Margaret. I know this case wasn't easy for you. I tried to give you as much of the responsibility as I thought you could handle but I got to tell you, you surprised me. Maybe I should send Elizabeth some little goodie from the first floor at Tiffany's. I sense she helped you make it through what I suspect were some frightening tunnels."

"She's good at what she does. I'm thinking of writing my checks payable to 'Madam Therapist, Extraordinaire.' What she's managed to do in just four sessions is amazing. I'm beginning to realize the paths people take through life are diverse. And I'm also getting comfortable with the notion that it's my choice which path I take. I see that the twins had a choice as well. What kept them victims was their vengefulness. I didn't act out by taking an ax to my father, but they've made it clear that I could have. Realizing they let their past control their future, while I didn't, helps me shed my victim's cloak."

"That kind of progress in such a short amount of time is outstanding. Generally, people who haven't gone through therapy have difficulty understanding that it's a process, not a compass. It took me a long time to fully recognize that the key to changing how I felt was in my pocket. Elizabeth's role was to help me find it, then teach me how to use it."

"That's the cool part. It's like discovering a part of my brain I never knew existed. It sort of gives me an outsider's view. And I'm getting skilled at using it. Remember when I was first assigned to help track down these twin killers, and we were both in the dark about motive? When it was revealed they were seeking revenge for years of sexual and ego-flattening abuse, I felt like I'd been shot from a cannon. And all the demons of my past piled on to bite me when I landed. I'm happy to say that they're gradually shrinking in number."

"You're learning how to avoid inviting them into the present. That keeps them where they belong. In the past."

"I know I have you to thank big-time. Not just for encouraging me to see Elizabeth. You've been watching out for me throughout this entire investigation. I want you to know I could feel it. And one of these days I'm going to surprise the both of us by wrapping all of me around all of you and thank you like you've never been thanked before."

Wow, Driscoll thought, *she really is using a part of her brain she's never used before. And this kind of thank-you is sure to involve lots of other parts that have been neglected.*

"I'd like that, Margaret. Very much."

Silence settled as their eyes locked, slowing time.

Just as Driscoll was coming out from behind his desk, intent on shortening the distance between himself and Margaret, Thomlinson's face appeared at the door. The Groucho Marx bit he did with his eyebrows said he'd hit pay dirt.

Chapter 101

Malcolm Shewster had just finished breakfast. It was quiet and peaceful in his California mansion. The realization that the twins were no longer a threat thrilled him.

Pushing his plate forward, he reached for the paper and donned his glasses, intent on losing himself in world news. That's when his just-consumed Brie-and-onion omelet nearly came back up. He had to swallow hard to keep it from being propelled across the room. Anxious eyes scanned the syndicated story, avoiding contact with the eight-by-ten color photo emblazoned above the fold. His pulse raced as he noted there were more photos featured on page two. His knuckles whitened. Blood surged, giving his face a purplish hue. Slowly, he allowed his eyes to drift above the byline. What they saw caused them to widen.

He examined the unmistakable likeness of his daughter. The image was blurred over both breasts and what he could only assume was a generous mound of pubic hair. Her lips were puckered. One eye was closed, suggesting a wink. Her body, which resembled the letter *S*, was straddling someone. And Shewster knew who that someone was. It shocked him to discover that what he could see of Angus's body was completely covered with tattoos from below his neckline down. Some were hideous; others lascivious—all outlandish. What appeared on his daughter's executioner's face rattled him. Angus's glare at his smiling Abigail spelled contempt.

But what quickened his pulse and caused adrenaline to surge was the caption inscribed into the photo: "In twenty minutes, this female abnormality will be dead."

Rage filled him. He would not be held captive by a phantom photographer inside his own house. He was a resourceful man. He'd find a way out of this scandal. Warily, he turned the page, where he discovered a second, more demeaning, photograph. It featured his Abigail, clad only in a strap-on, feeding it to the mouth of a grotesquely disfigured, naked, and oddly shaped girl.

But it was the inscription etched inside this photo that cut to the marrow. It caused him to do something he hadn't done since childhood. He screamed. Then screamed again. And though both eyes were closed, these words helped themselves to his cornea: "That's it, you wild little thing. Deep throat the sucker! Just like I did for Father."

Chapter 102

Driscoll stood at the edge of the dock at Sullivan's. The tide had gone out and the sun was beginning its descent behind a cluster of clouds.

Aligante and Thomlinson had volunteered to stay behind and file the mountain of paperwork that the murder spree had generated.

His city had shed its armor. Driscoll knew it would be a short-lived hiatus, but he allowed himself to be comforted by the sense of safety and restoration of order.

Tomorrow, he'd return to his office early. He'd need extra time to prepare his formal request that Detective Second Grade Cedric Thomlinson be promoted to the rank of Detective First Grade. Cedric had found the fissure in Malcolm Shewster's grand scheme. The fact that Shewster would not be tried in New York no longer troubled him. Because of Thomlinson's discovery, Shewster would surely be tried in a California court. It had taken him and Leticia an enormous amount of time to unearth the evidence that proved Gweneth Shewster died in New York City at the hands of two maniacal twins, and was buried in a grave that bore the name of a sister, Abigail, who existed only on paper.

He had found a witness whom Shewster's intimidation had silenced years ago. The man knew then, and knows now, that Gweneth Shewster's California burial was staged.

Spurred by the results of a painstaking exploration of every aspect of Gweneth Shewster's death, Thomlinson sought to speak to one Giovanni Petrocelli. The detective wanted to know firsthand why Petrocelli had been dismissed from Richard J. Malone's Funeral Home immediately after the "burial" of Gweneth Shewster.

Giovanni Petrocelli was also a subscriber to the *Los Angeles Times*. After getting an eyeful, he was certain Shewster's influence would take a huge hit and when Thomlinson reached out to him, he was happy to speak with an NYPD detective who was investigating Gweneth's death. Petrocelli thought he'd carry what he knew to the grave. But the thing about vengeance was that it wasn't mired by any statute of limitations.

During Thomlinson's exchange, Petrocelli not only told him that the casket which purportedly held the remains of Gweneth Shewster was a weighted coffin, he informed the detective where it was buried. A disinterment in California would support that, while an exhumation of Abigail's body and an unaltered DNA analysis would further attest to it.

Driscoll headed for Sullivan's tavern to celebrate, albeit alone, making a mental note to buy Thomlinson a box of Cuban cigars. They'd say a louder thank-you than his duly earned promotion would.

As the Lieutenant placed a twenty on the bar, he wondered what Giovanni Petrocelli, an embalmer's assistant, considered a proper way to say thanks.

Turn the page for an exciting preview of
Thomas O'Callaghan's next shocking thriller starring
NYPD homicide commander John Driscoll . . .

No One Will Hear You

. . . coming from Pinnacle in 2008!

Chapter 1

"Hello? Is anybody there?"

The echo of her slurred query and the pounding of her heart were all she heard in reply.

Thoughts raced. *Where the hell am I? Why does my voice sound funny?* She tried to focus but couldn't. Frenetic thinking riddled her brain. "Hello? Hello?"

Attempting to move, she discovered her head was restrained, as were her wrists and ankles. *Something smooth. But strong. Cloth maybe?* "Rope!" she cried out, feeling a trickle of perspiration dabble her eye, compounding blurred vision. A glow emanated above her. It seemed to be in motion. She closed her eyes but reopened them as dizziness and the urge to vomit immediately set in.

It felt as though she were lying on moist sand. Cold moist sand. The limited mobility of her hands and the strained sighting of her nipples fueled her growing hysteria.

Why am I naked?

Adrenaline surged.

Jesus Christ! . . . What's happening to me?

Her sight was returning, but intermittently. The radiance above appeared to be still moving. Waves of nausea continued their assault, though less frequently and with decreased intensity. Closing her eyes, she found the dizziness had waned.

But worry plagued her. *Where the hell am I? How did I get here?*

Something slithered across her abdomen. It was followed by what felt like a tiny creature landing on her pelvis, before skittering between her legs. Trembling, she clamped her eyelids shut, willing her dilemma to evaporate like the remnants of a bad dream.

Am I alone?

The thought blindsided her. Her eyes sprung open and began a slow and anxious ascent against clay walls that formed an irregular rectangle, open at its top.

She was at its base.

Dear Lord!

She let loose a bestial scream. Blinked rapidly, and screamed again.

Willows, visible through the aperture above, swayed against a cloudless sky, deaf to her screaming and indifferent to her predicament.

Chapter 2

Inside the converted carriage house, Tilden put down the braided nylon cord he had been toying with and looked at his watch. One hour and thirty-seven minutes. He reached for a notebook and recorded the data: "Sodium thiopental, 100 mg.—ninety-seven minutes." *Hmm . . . allowing for the different doses, this filly recovered a little slower than the others.* He tapped on the pad with his pencil. *Fluke?* Cocking his head, he raised an eyebrow. *Nah! They all had the same physique. Maybe an interaction to the Isoflurane I used when I nabbed her? A clash of anesthetics? That could account for it.*

Pushing back his chair, he stood and faced the open door. "Aahh! Aahh!" he cried, mimicking his captive, before closing the door with his boot. Reaching for Tuesday's *New York Daily News*, he opened it again to page nine. Her abduction was featured in the lower right corner of the page. The diminutive headline read: PROSTITUTE REPORTED MISSING. He puckered his blistered lips, brought the paper to within inches of his beady eyes, and scrutinized the story for the third time. Satisfied there was nothing in it to cause alarm, he tossed the paper atop a pile of others, which included several copies of the *Newburgh Record,* The *Westchester Journal,* and the *Connecticut Post.* Only last week's rag from Connecticut mentioned the abduction in Bridgeport. But it looked as though his role in that caper had also gone undetected. He was pleased there were no references whatsoever in the other two dailies, going back to day one. He knew there were Web sites that listed information about missing persons, often providing details of where they were last seen. But with government eavesdropping being what it was, he wasn't about to arouse suspicion by visiting any of them. Hell, no one was about to miss the sort of lowlifes he made off with, but he'd monitor the *Daily News* to see if they did any follow-up on the Big Apple prostitute.

He did have one regret: snatching the homeless woman in Newburgh. He had to douse the van's interior with a gallon of germicidal bleach and use up a full can of Lysol spray to get rid of the stench. Lord knows how many creepy-crawlers he fried when he torched that turd's clothing. *What the hell was she carrying in those bags? It smelled like a freaking pig roast, for Chrissake!*

Narrowing his eyes, he put an ear to the door. Outside, he heard what he was hoping he'd hear. Nothing. Test subject number four had stopped screaming.

"'Bout time," he muttered, reaching for the shovel making his way to the grave.

Chapter 3

Silence filled the crowded New York courtroom as the jurors returned to their seats. A mix of emotions marked their faces. Fatigue and fear on some. Indifference on others. The defendant's eyes scoped each of the twelve, receiving not as much as a glance in return.

"I'm told you've reached a verdict," said State Supreme Court Justice Everett Hathaway. "Is that true, madam foreperson?"

She nodded, then caught herself, and quickly blurted, "Yes. Yes, your honor."

Judge Hathaway instructed his bailiff to retrieve the folded sheet of paper the woman held anxiously in hand. Upon receipt, he read what had been decided after two-and-a-half days of deliberation. "And you all agree on this?" he asked.

A slow but resolute response followed, with each of the jurors nodding or muttering yes.

Hushed murmuring intruded on the room's solemnity as the defendant was asked to stand.

The judge cautioned all present to stay in their seats and to maintain silence and decorum while the verdicts were delivered. He then turned his attention to the sallow-faced woman, who had regrettably agreed to act as the jury's voice.

"To the charge of unlawful imprisonment in the first degree, how do you, the jury, find?"

"Guilty, your honor," she answered, sounding as though she were whispering, prompting the court reporter to ask if she could speak up. "Guilty," she said, loudly.

"To the charge of predatory sexual assault against a child?"

"Also guilty, your honor."

"And to the charge of murder in the first degree? How do you find?"

The woman, feeling empowered, returned the twice-convicted man's glare. "Guilty," she said, looking as though she wanted to spit.

The defendant leaped across the defense table, bolted toward the jury box, and came within two feet of the foreperson before being tackled by a court officer, who slammed the defendant's face into the floorboards, pinned him with a knee, and cuffed him.

Pandemonium ensued. Judge Hathaway, pounding his gavel, quieted the crowd and ordered the aggressor be removed.

The lead juror's face looked like it had turned to alabaster. The same woman, who, only moments ago, had mustered the courage to stare down the coldhearted killer. The judge hadn't missed the transformation. He thanked the jury, particularly referencing the woman's resolve, and dismissed them. After setting a date for sentencing, he brought the session to a close.

From his seat near the back of the room, Lieutenant John Driscoll nodded, an unspoken gesture indicating he was pleased to see justice delivered. Reaching for his Burberry, he stood and was about to leave when he was approached by familiar faces.

"Mr. and Mrs. Keating, I thought I saw you leave."

The Keating woman smiled. "Not without saying good-bye."

"That's very nice of you. I hope the past few days haven't been a strain."

Mr. Keating took hold of his wife's hand. "We had each other to lean on, Lieutenant."

"We yearned for this day as much as we feared it," said his wife. "There aren't enough words to express our gratitude, Lieutenant. If it weren't for you . . ."

"No need to go there," said Driscoll.

The Keatings were the parents of twelve-year-old Lori Keating, a blue-eyed innocent who had been abducted, sexually assaulted, and callously murdered by the monster they had just seen convicted of his crimes. Driscoll, as commanding officer of the NYPD's Manhattan homicide squad, had led a task force of thirty dedicated professionals in the apprehension of the newly convicted felon Lyle Covens, bringing his heinous killing spree to an end.

"What my wife and I need to say, Lieutenant, is that because of you, many New York families have been given closure." He turned to face his wife. "Now would be a good time, Janice."

The woman opened her purse, withdrew a small envelope, and pressed it into Driscoll's palm. The pair smiled and ducked out the door.

Driscoll turned the envelope over. It was addressed to "Lt Driscol," etched in green crayon.

He opened it, retrieved a haphazardly folded sheet of loose-leaf paper and unraveled it.

Dear Lt Driscol—

Lori ment the world to me and now shes gone. I could tell her about anything that was bottering me. She would help me with homework and stuff. If I did somthin bad she would'nt tell on me. She was the bestest big sister to

*me. I know somthin bad happened. And I know she wont
be here anymore. But mom and dad told me you were a
magisian and would make sure she stays in heven. I
did'nt think you could get throne out but now Im not
sure. Anyways. Now Il'l always know shel'l be there
when I pray. It'l be like shes here again with me. Sorta.
Thanks for doing that for me. and my mom and dad. It
really really really meens a lot.*

your friend. tammy ☺

A small card fell from the envelope as Driscoll opened it
to replace the letter. He picked it up. It contained another
message. The handwriting was clearly not that of a little girl:

Dear Lieutenant,
    *We know you also lost a daughter to tragedy. We've
asked Lori to watch over her. For clearly, if you were her
dad, she, too, is in heaven.—J & R Keating*

A sheen of moisture coated Driscoll's eyes. He thought of
Nicole. No one's big sister, but his "bestest" friend. He
looked up. Smiled at the unseen heavens. Then disappeared
out the door.